Wild Thymes on the 22

Edited by Stewart Sheargold

WILDTHYMES ON THE 22
ISBN: 9781909031739

Published by Obverse Books, Edinburgh

Editor: Stewart Sheargold
Cover Design: Cody Schell
Cover Art: Paul Hanley

First edition: October 2018
10 9 8 7 6 5 4 3 2 1

A CIP catalogue record for this title is available from the British Library.

Printed and bound in Great Britain by TJ International Ltd.

Dedicated to the one, the only, "the original [Iris], you might say."
— Paul Magrs

Without whom...

AVAILABLE NOW FROM OBVERSE BOOKS

FROM THE DIARIES OF IRIS WILDTHYME

IRIS WILDTHYME AND THE CELESTIAL OMNIBUS

THE PANDA BOOK OF HORROR

MISS WILDTHYME INVESTIGATES

IRIS: ABROAD

15

WILDTHYME IN PURPLE

IRIS WILDTHYME OF MARS

THE PERENNIAL MISS WILDTHYME

A CLOCKWORK IRIS

LADY STARDUST

Contents

The Heart Pendulums

Steve Cole

It sounds like a children's story, but there's a world, you know, where Cupid reigns and every day is Valentine's Day. And living through those days on that world there was once a proud girl who didn't care to have love imposed upon her. She railed against her suitors, mocked and displeased Cupid to the point where, in the end, he fired a nasty little arrow right through the girl's heart.

The wound only tickled at first. But each day that followed, the girl's heart grew smaller, it shrank a little more, until in the end it was so small it could hardly pump more than a thimble of blood about her body.

At the end of the story the poor little sweetheart's left pasty and pale and too faint and feeble to write more than a word each day of the letter of apology she's told might save her. And the beat of her tiny heart sounds like Cupid's tiny fist tapping at her ribs, '*Knock-knock! Knock-knock! Let me in and perhaps your blood will flow again!*' And as for the ending of the story, well…

That's Spike Milligan for you, luvvies. He never was very good with endings.

I knew I'd find Spike alone at Number Nine. The towering townhouse in Orme Court where, by day, lovely Johnny Speight and Eric Sykes and Galton and Simpson and the rest conducted the hard-drinking business of comedy. It was quiet and dark; as well it might be in the middle of the night.

The September stars shone bright over Bayswater as Panda and I parked the bus outside and prepared for our big entrance. To Spike that was part of the magic of my visits—the way I'd simply appear, sometimes alone, sometimes in delightful company. He'd never given me the key, but I'd pocketed it years back during a bit of ruckus with Norma, his manager, who considered me a bad influence (as if!).

I only came to him when the black dog was on his shoulder, those dark and tender times when he would retreat into himself for days. The blinds would come down in room six. The electric fire would cast its drowsy blue spell. He wouldn't eat, wouldn't drink, wouldn't even use the bathroom. Spike was such a sensitive soul for one who seemed so rambunctious, and suffered so badly from the hurts the world provided. The tiniest thing could trigger his illness, and nothing on Earth could treat it save for time and solitude and popping Tryptizol.

On this occasion, in the autumn of 1968, he'd been set off by the Elfin Oak in Kensington Gardens: the stump of a 900-year-old oak tree carved and painted to look as though midnight folk and magical animals are peeping out of its gnarly bits. Spike had put a lot of effort into restoring and sprucing up that tree, and then vandals went and snapped off the wing of a fairy, and something snapped again in him and, well, here was the upshot: Milligan, the living dead of Bayswater, his vitality gone, his strength and spirit at low ebb.

I let Panda squeeze through the letterbox and open the door for me, then together we crept up the darkened stairs. There was a note on Spike's door, I read it in the flame from my lighter:

Go away. I'm ill. Jesus had it easy.

I tutted and pushed the key into the lock. Down at floor level, Panda pushed open the door so I could strike a pose as my charms were revealed, full length. The air was hot, smoky and stale.

Something grey stirred on the mattress with a hoarse cry: 'Iris!'

I preened. 'That's right, you old bugger.'

A tasselled lampshade rocked as a switch was thrown and a golden glow spilled cautiously into the room. It was a hunched, frail figure that rose to greet me. His hair was thin and in disarray. The strong, hangdog features played at doleful indifference but the eyes—even drugged and bagged to the cheekbones—gave the lie to that: bright with challenge and intelligence.

'Hello, Spike!' Panda waved regally from a tartan chaise longue.

'Who the hell are you?' Spike demanded with some amusement.

'I?' Panda blustered. 'Who am I?'

'You've met him before, luvvie,' I reminded him, though I thought he was probably just having some fun with my little pal. 'You know. Last time I popped by, back in '66.'

'He left an indelible blank on me.' Spike stared at Panda, wickedness in his smile, and I knew he'd never once forgotten. 'Is it a little bear or a big raccoon?'

'When I saw those dark pouches around your eyes I was going to ask the same,' Panda said sniffily. 'Particularly as bears and raccoons go into a torpor where they don't drink or eat or move about, just like you—a habit *not* adopted by any panda, I can tell you.'

Spike laughed warmly and turned to me. 'Are you working him or is he working you?'

'We *don't* work. We play,' I reminded him, as I turned the stiff catches on the bay window and slid it open. The night air was like a shot of adrenalin into the fug of the room. 'Operation Catflap?'

Spike giggled. 'I've had the operation,' he said in his best Eccles voice, 'right in the catflap.' He shuffled over to join me, his gait uncertain, and looked out over the double-decker below. Panda scurried over to join me and together we shoved Spike out through the window. He gave a comic cry and fell heavily onto the roof of the bus…

And disappeared right through it. I swept up Panda, hitched up my skirts and leaped after him, through the dinky little intradimensional portal I'd set up. We landed slap bang in a big squashy sofa in the middle of the top deck, all three of us, Spike laughing weakly from beneath my thighs.

The laughter stopped. I shifted myself. A grey, bearded face looked up appraisingly.

'I suppose it's either the mental home in Friern Barnet, or off to see *her* again?' he said quietly.

'It is, chuck,' I said. 'And let's hope things turn out better.'

The planet of Nang-Nong is a noisy old place, similar to Earth in some ways. There are cows and mice and monkeys and there are trees; forests of huge and mighty stumps like the Elfin Oak, and they all make unexpected sounds because they teem with little people. And as well as the little people, there are big people too, people who look quite like you and me, just as full of noise, and at their very noisiest when considering love.

You see, true and enduring love is the finest ideal, kindest law and noblest pursuit on Nang-Nong, and every day is given over to its celebration and purest expression in the arts. With love so prevalent there are no wars on Nang-Nong and precious little to do besides give your heart fully and freely to the one you've ended up with. Well, I say "freely"… but of course, sometimes lovers have to be assigned forcibly to one another if they've not found love themselves within an allotted period. And should one lover die, their surviving partner will be reassigned to another once a limited period of mourning has officially passed. Infidelity is not tolerated, and those guilty are banished from proper society and suffer exile in the remote and barbaric Louche Colonies on the Oojah-ka-Piv.

Hell of a place for a party!

The sky was a charcoal wash at all times in Oojah-ka-Piv, and the warm smoky air smelled like curry. The Louche Colonies had been built on swampland, much of which was constantly on fire for one reason or another. But the blazes never seemed to bother anyone; fire had little bite here—unlike the eel-like creatures that swam endlessly in the pink waters, they were always ready to nip.

Often we partied at the house of a matronly lady called Meeranda, who hosted, alternately, salons and orgies, though it wasn't always apparent which was which. Meeranda was buxom, long dark curls piled ornately on her head so it looked as if a cuttlefish had chucked up her ever-grinning face. It was a rude and happy place, her pad in the Louche Colonies, and Spike could enjoy himself there. On another world, unknown.

One time we were there, he told the story of our first trip to Nang-Nong to the appreciative wantons.

'There was this girl who, like you all, thought love was silly,' he said, sprawled on the floor. 'Her eyes were as blue as the seas where I'm from, and her hair was red and gold, and though she was tall it still came down almost to her ankles. She was surrounded by suitors but didn't like a single one of them. They gave her soppy poetry and she wrote back rude verses by return. They longed to take her away to far-flung shores of romance but she preferred to paddle in the stinky creek close to home. She did not need anyone else to complete her, though some important fools were quite sure that she did…'

'Sounds ghastly in its familiarity,' Meeranda clucked with sympathy.

'They tried to marry her off, of course,' Panda put in from the lap of a nymph, 'marry her off to someone very dull indeed.'

The nymph thought she understood. 'And so she strayed and ended up here?'

'Not quite,' I told her. 'When we heard of all this, we decided to do something about it. And so before the marriage ceremony could conclude, POW! Enter Spike Milligan, dressed as Batman. He rushes up to the vicar-equivalent and throws a pie in his face.'

Spike was giggling silently at the memory. 'And that was your cue, baby, to start hosing down the congregation with visual effects custard we stole from the BBC.'

'In all the hoo-hah, we got her away,' I concluded.

'The way she looked at me that day!' Spike beamed at the memory. 'Like after only moments I already meant the earth.'

Meeranda raised a glass and gazed about. 'So where is the lucky creature with the blue eyes and the hair down to her ankles? Why didn't you bring her along?'

Spike's gaze had grown soft and mournful. 'I wanted to.'

Fresh from outside Number Nine and Operation Catflap, the bus hissed and gyrated into rosy red reality in the Orchard of the Condemned. It was a peaceful place, though rather overgrown. Crimson grasses, the great stumps of black-leafed trees, strange fruit crowding the branches.

'Why did they have to lock her away?' Spike demanded.

'She was too particular to let just anyone love her,' I reminded him. 'And she refused to be a floozy so they couldn't exile her to the Louche Colonies.'

'She ran away with me, time and again!'

'You're out of this world, luvvie. Officially you don't exist.'

'Even unofficially, I barely exist anywhere.'

'She was a disruptive element,' said Panda ('I should fucking hope so!' said Spike). 'I am rather afraid they considered her a danger.'

'Like a tree is a danger to lightning,' Spike said bitterly. 'Best cut it down in case of thunderbolts.'

He'd seen her many times by now, of course. The girl refused to run away after we scotched her wedding because as far as she was concerned, she'd done nothing wrong. The authorities had to concur; hadn't the girl been kidnapped? Wasn't that why the nuptials had gone so terribly awry? The perpetrators of the pie-in-Love's-face had never been found so the truth of things was unclear.

The perpetrators were spotted again and again, though, whenever the wedding was rearranged. One time, an enormous bag of flour was dropped from above by Spike, who was dressed like a boy scout with two black eyes. It struck the groom and floored him, allowing a panda to burst out from beneath the vestments of the vicar and hurry the girl away.

On another occasion, a large, toothy saw, a tool unknown on Nang-Nong, emerged from the floor and carved a circle around the groom until he plunged down into the cellar before the ceremony was complete.

On yet another, a piano came crashing through the ceiling behind the congregation with Panda vamping "The Lady is a Tramp" for all he was worth. Then Spike led me on an elephant down the aisle and I leaped on the latest groom-to-be while he bundled the girl away.

Each time, we got away with it. The planning of each rescue seemed to bring Spike out of himself. The grey fog lifted. He answered to no authority on Nang-Nong, the ultimate outsider, and that made him bolder.

After one of those rescues we found our way to some ornate veranda somewhere far from the wedding-place, and the girl drank white Orvieto with us all, and Spike played his trumpet, and the girl watched him with such wonder in her gaze: this unlikely old wizard from a far-off world, this fragile crusader who appeared again and again in her hour of need.

'The bastards mustn't get away with it,' he told her. 'You are your own person. Not anyone else's.'

'No. No one else's.' The girl looked at him sadly. 'Not for long, at least.'

'How did you become this way?' Spike persisted, 'seeing things so differently, feeling them so differently?'

She only smiled and shrugged. 'How did you?'

'With him,' said Panda, 'it's a sickness.'

'It's not me who's ill,' Spike shot back. 'I'm suffering from contemporary society. I just want to write scripts and music and poetry and books that will make the world around me beautiful.'

'Beauty is in the eye of the beholder,' I mused.

'It is,' Spike agreed sourly. 'On my planet, the beholder usually gets it out with some Optrex.'

In the Orchard of the Condemned, he asked the inevitable: 'Why can't we go back in time to before they sent her away?'

'It doesn't work that way, pet,' I said. 'Trust me, cause and effect can get in a right old kerfuffle.'

'When were we last here?'

'For her, only yesterday.'

We'd come here a half-dozen times already, and hadn't managed to spring her yet. All those ingenious rescues from the wedding halls, they'd put us all on a bit of a high. I mean, I'd been flitting round having a hundred adventures for every one I let Spike share with me, but I knew how important it was for him that he made these flights of fancy. How important the girl had become.

'Think of her,' he said, 'think of this curse she has to suffer just because others don't see things the way she wants to. It's cruel.'

I nodded. He might have been talking about himself, of course. 'This was meant to be a bit of fun,' I reminded him. 'A little inspiration.'

'It's her we need to inspire now,' Spike said. 'Poor child. Each day, her heart shrivelling up a little smaller. I know we're going to get her out, but…'

'Shush!' Panda put a theatrical finger to his lips.

Ahead, there was a bed in the clearing, and the girl lay on it. Beside her was a table with a pen and a long scroll and a teapot. No cups, mind; only a teapot. The girl looked decidedly peaky, just as she had the last time we'd seen her: unmoving, her skin dull, only the faint rise and fall of her breast to prove she wasn't already dead.

The first time we'd come here in the bus, we knocked down the fences that guarded the Orchard of the Condemned. That did no good, though—those giant tree stumps were planted too close together to drive through. We tried getting in on foot, but these funny little things that looked like mice came pouring out, going '*CLANG! CLANG! CLANG! CLANG!*' at the tops of their tiny lungs, raising the alarm. What a terrible racket the little stinkers made! We had to take off in a hurry.

The second time we came, I fermented a rodent sedative in the bus's exhaust system and we backed up against the trees with the engine running. That took care of the mice. Hallelujah. Spike was killing himself as we began to steal into the trees on our rescue mission. We saw sheets of paper blowing about as if grazing the ground. Then these dirty great cow-animals came out, only they didn't moo they went 'BONG, BONG, BONG!' like bloody great alarm clocks and they looked ready to charge so again we had to beat a retreat. They chased us, but while they're good at sprinting, they don't have the stamina for anything more demanding (they live in the country, they can't do cross-country running; it's the bitter irony of the cow).

The third time, we made it through, using peashooters and ketamine-soaked peas, and we found her.

The girl was lying on the bed in a sunny glade. She couldn't run away with us, not that day.

Slowly, she told us of the ruler's punishments, her incarceration here, her body wasting from the drug that was wizening her heart day by day; it was as if by refusing to give it to somebody else she'd lost her right to use it at all. If she wrote a truly heartfelt apology—with what little heart she had left to feel—and an epic poem in praise of love, perhaps her pernicious fate could yet be undone.

But she'd written 'FUCK YOU' on one sheet of paper on a tray, and there was no sign of any others beyond those we'd seen fluttering about the trees.

'Wore myself out writing so much,' she said quietly.

'We're going to get you out,' Spike told her.

She shook her head, just once. But it exhausted her. She couldn't move another muscle.

'At least one of us is going to get older,' she whispered, as we left.

Now here we were again. The mice were gassed, the cows were tranquilised. Panda had his best shoes on, which I hoped would stop him stepping in a cowpat and trailing it all over the bus carpet. Spike and I had the stretcher.

Today was the day: Spike was adamant: We would get the Girl away.

We crept into the clearing that made her bedchamber. She seemed to be asleep. The 'Fuck You' note lay on the table beside the teapot.

'Seven letters,' Spike said sadly. 'She wore herself out writing seven letters.'

Her eyes flickered open. 'Not… those… letters,' she said at last. Her blue eyes were zigzagging between her heavy lids, as if gesturing to her right.

'Let's get her onto the stretcher,' I said. 'We'll find somewhere that will fix her heart again.'

She made protesting murmurs as Spike and I placed the stretcher on the ground beside her. As she did, I realised there was a split in the mattress. A dog-eared corner was peeping out from inside. Papers had been jammed inside the mattress—a fair few of them.

Every word was an effort: 'My epic poem in praise of love.' She looked up at Spike. 'For you.'

'Me?' You could see her words smack Spike about the face. 'That's no good, baby. I don't exist.'

'That's why I love you,' said the Girl.

I pulled out the little manuscript. She must've spent so much of her incarceration here writing to Spike as she wasted away: two words to the world that had tried to own her, and so many, many pages to the man who came and went.

She spoke like a clock winding down, penduluming a heavy rhythm, but a rhythm in which she found some peace, perhaps: 'You… made… me… this… way.'

I saw that the girl had drawn a picture on the first page. It was Spike, but not Spike as he was now. Spike as he would become, as the years dragged on and took away his cleaner lines: the sad, stiffened Spike of the 1990s.

'How did you become this way?' Spike had asked the girl, and the girl had answered, 'How did you?' And it struck me now, she'd been telling him that the same things had shaped them both.

Spike leaned over the Girl. 'I bet I can kiss you without touching you.' He pulled a one-pound note from his pocket. 'I bet you this pound.'

The Girl gave the barest nod, and he leaned in and his lips brushed her grey, cold cheek.

'You touched her,' said Panda.

He let go of the pound note and it blew gaily about the glade, though the wind had dropped. 'It was worth it,' Spike said.

The girl's smile settled gently like snow upon her face. Then the bastard teapot started to jibber and jabber as if by touching her we'd set off another alarm. The air turned cold, and the dark leaves shivered anxiously in the trees.

I tried to tip the girl off her bed onto the stretcher but there were *things* in the mattress, little folk reaching out their little hands and gripping hold of thick strands of her long hair, up and down her body. We couldn't get her off and out of here now.

'No!' Spike stamped his foot like a child, but Panda and I could hardly hear him over the teapot's jibber jabber. The crush and crunch of tree stumps and earth told us something loud and large was coming to patrol the clearing.

'Love, peace and light,' Spike whispered to the Girl.

Then we ran away again.

I put the bus into orbit around Nang-Nong, and we gazed out through the grimy windows at the red globe below us. Well, Panda and I did. Spike was reading all that the girl had written, the love poem to a man who stood outside the planet's laws.

'What are we gonna do now? What are we gonna do now?' He shook his head. 'At least one of us will grow old, that's what she said.'

'That's what she knows.' I nodded to the picture she'd drawn. 'She knew you all along. Only, for you, your first meeting hasn't happened yet.' I sighed. 'I've seen this sort of thing before. Ineffably tragic is what it is.'

'Fuck tragedy,' Spike said. 'If it was meeting me when I'm older but she's younger that helps to make her the way she is, that helps to put her… *there*, well then. I must never go to see her again.'

'But you do, love,' I told him, gentle as I could. 'You *will*. You saw the drawing, she wasn't imagining you old, was she?'

'Perhaps she was,' Spike looked at me, eyes watery, clinging to the words. 'I won't take the chance. You must promise you'll never take me back there.'

'But one day, you're going to find yourself—'

'For god's sake, woman,' Spike shouted. 'Just take me back to Number Nine and leave me alone.'

'You ungrateful sod!' I cuffed him around the shoulder. 'You're giving up on her.'

He put the papers away in his pocket. 'I'm saving her.'

'You think you can live with this decision now,' I said. 'But you'll weaken with the years as we all do and one day you'll find an opportunity of some kind, a way to go back and try to see her again, to try to save her from all that she's gone through. But all that will do is start the whole thing off. It's too late, love. The end is the only part you can affect now.'

'Affect? Me?' Spike's shoulders were stooping, it was as if he were shrinking back into his medicated self. 'Affect anything, when I don't exist…?'

I knew he'd always been lousy with endings. If you pretended they weren't there, things could go on forever. That could be a curse, to Spike's eyes. Or, perhaps, sometimes, a saving grace.

I took Spike back to Number Nine and let him crawl back inside the womb of room six, to the pills and the heat and the dark fug. I suppose he heard the engines of the bus pulling and plucking at reality's threads well enough. How did he feel, then? Did he really think I'd never come back?

There's no punchline, no resolution to this little sketch. It's not satisfying, but it's true to life at least. It's true to himself.

Rain and Regency
(or Prinny and Precipitation)
Neil Chester

From the journals of Iris Wildthyme, Transtemporal Adventuress Extraordinaire

Brighton, January 7th, 1817

I love visiting Brighton.

The combination of the glamourous and the tacky always appeals, and I love a quick blow along the front in the sunshine. The mingled smells of fast food, sea spray, suntan lotion and gently cooking bodies is such a tonic. Sadly, in the two days since we've arrived it hasn't stopped pissing down. Still, we're staying in the most glamorous and tacky place imaginable—The Brighton Pavilion. It's all gold dragons, and red silk screens and over-the-top opulence.

We're guests of my old friend Prinny—Prince George, the Prince Regent, and his unofficial wife, Maria Fitzherbert. Everyone's busy and bustling in preparation for tonight's party. Officially, it's for Prinny's daughter Charlotte's 21st, but she and her husband have buggered off home. (Poor kid!) Not that that's going to stop Prinny from having a party.

It's just Panda and I here at the moment—Tom's shacked up with some stable boy who caught his eye almost as soon as we arrived. Panda reckons he's a most unstable boy, but Tom's old enough to look after himself. Personally, I reckon that Tom's just put off by all the dressing up that the party would involve—the tight breeches and buckled shoes—and has ducked out for a tumble in the hay. Panda's taken to it though. I'm not sure that the shirt, embroidered waistcoat and bottle-green cravat really work without breeches, but I'm not going to spoil his fun. (Besides, he's only got little legs.) For myself I've opted for an understated, leopard-print gown, (it's the right style though—I was given it by a friend of Tom's—a drag queen called Morgan, who's gimmick is period costume. And a beard.) with a zebra-striped, velvet bodice and a violet pashmina, which brings out my eyes. Panda says that the combination of colours and patterns gives him a migraine, but I think he's just jealous.

'I swear that the Prince Regent's balls get bigger every year!'

Panda gave Iris a withering look. 'You've been dying to say that since we arrived, haven't you?'

Iris grinned, wolfishly. 'It was too good an opportunity to miss, chuck. Still, it is a hive of activity, isn't it?' The two of them watched as a battalion of manservants and maids bustled about the huge banqueting room, setting out candles, hanging decorations and laying tables. 'Makes me knackered just watching them. Should be a great party!'

'And all for someone who isn't even here.'

'Yeah, well...' Iris shrugged, 'Georgie doesn't need much of an excuse to hold a party—the fact that Lottie and Leo have gone home to Claremont isn't going to stop him from celebrating her 21st. Despite everything, he's a proud father. And he's always been a bit of a party animal. I remember his 21st—now that was a party! He hadn't met Maria then and I rather turned his head—he has always liked glamorous, sophisticated older women...' Panda snorted, but Iris was too caught up in reminiscence to notice. 'Anyway, there was this rather handsome Army Captain called Nicholas..., lovely, firm thighs..., who I was rather taken with, and... well, it's all a bit hazy... there was an awful lot of wine, and a fair bit of music and dancing, and I remember that on the third day of the party, I constructed a rudimentary Jacuzzi in one of the Carlton House fountains—it was a very hot August, I remember, and we all ended up...'

'La la la!' shouted Panda, clapping his paws over his little furry ears. 'I don't need to hear about your sordid, drunken peccadillos! Honestly woman—I've just eaten!'

'Ha! I don't recall you being so prudish when you were at that sauna party with Greta Garbo in 1929. Positively bacchanalian. And it took ages to dry you out. The bus stank of wet fur for days!'

Panda gave an embarrassed cough. 'That was entirely different,' he protested. 'We were discussing art. She was particularly interested in Renoir as I recall, and was enthralled by my opinions on his use of light and colour.'

'And your ability to pour champagne in a room full of steam...'

'Yes, well, it's a gentleman's responsibility to ensure that a lady wants for nothing. On the subject of which,' he continued, hurriedly, before Iris could make another ribald comment, 'maybe we ought to take stock of the liquid refreshment available for this little shindig? I'm sure that Georgie's taste in wine is excellent, but nineteenth century gin is as rough as turps.'

'And we're back to Renoir,' muttered Iris. Panda glowered at her. 'Alright luvvie,' she conceded, 'let's go and see Martin in the kitchens. I'm sure I can persuade him to allow us a little tasting of the available gin, purely for quality control purposes, of course.' She gave a wheezy giggle, 'Just between you and me, I think he fancies me.' Panda rolled his black, beady eyes, but refrained from comment. 'And if the gin's not up to snuff, then we've got a couple of bottles of Tanqueray back on the bus. Oh, and some of that Aldebaran stuff—it's not that nice on its own, but if we stick it with some fruit juice, some local gin, and a couple of other things we've got lying around, it'll form the basis of Auntie Iris's Patented Party Punch™. That should make things go with a swing.'

'Oh god.' Panda groaned, making a mental note to check the bus's stocks of Ibuprofen and Gaviscon. 'If you're making that we'll need something ceramic to mix it up in. It dissolved that metal punchbowl last time you made it.'

'That was your fault,' Iris objected, 'you would insist on adding that seawater from Marinus, "for flavour"...'

Bickering gently, the two friends left the room, still bustling with busy servants, and sauntered off down the corridor in the direction of the kitchens.

Harris, valet to the Prince Regent for some twenty years now, watched the mismatched pair leave the room with a nervous smile—he'd seen Mistress Wildthyme's behaviour at other parties and knew that he would have to keep a watchful eye on her this evening. He sighed; another duty on top of everything else. He turned his attention to the room, casting a critical eye over the preparations. At least this all seemed satisfactory—the staff were well trained and they all knew that Harris's gimlet gaze was upon them.

He glanced at the two young boys, Andrew and Matthew, perched precariously atop two tall wooden ladders, replenishing the slender white candles in the enormous, silver-chased chandeliers that hung from the ceiling, shaped like dragons in flight. Harris frowned—if the weather got any worse they'd need to light the candles soon just to be able to see what they were doing. He glanced at the golden clock on the mantle over the large fireplace—it was barely even three of the afternoon.

He crossed to the dining room's floor-length windows and his frown deepened at the sight of the heavy rain, pouring down from the dark grey clouds that loured over the palace. Fat raindrops, so close together as to look like one continuous sheet of water, battered at the lush foliage of the palace garden, creating an early twilight.

Another task to consider—he'd need to arrange for guests' cloaks and top coats to be dried; even the short walk from carriage to door would result in a soaking in this weather. Tutting, he turned to accost a nearby maid, when a movement from the garden flickered in the corner of his eye. He snapped his head back, his eyes scanning the gardens. He was sure he'd seen a figure moving through the bushes, slipping like a shadow towards the building. But now there was nothing. He stared for a moment more, and then shook his head in exasperation, turning from the window.

'Abigail!' he snapped, irritated at his own foolishness, 'put that tureen down and follow me—I have a job for you!'

In the garden, a tall, thin shape detached itself from the shadows at the base of a bedraggled tree, and slipped stealthily towards the windows. In the weak afternoon light, the surface of the shape shimmered with a glossy wetness. Further back in the garden, two more shapes, shorter and stockier than the first, but no less furtive, shadowed its movement.

Nell Cowley hated going down to the cellars and she strongly suspected that Mrs Knowles, the cook, knew it, and that was why she always sent her. The old bat took every opportunity to send Nell down into the damp darkness on the most trivial of errands. This time it was a fresh bottle of cooking sherry, and the second-best nutmeg grater.

Normally alcohol was the province of Mr Parsons, the bottler, but he was busy talking to that strange purple-haired, cackling woman and her odd bear, and so Mrs Knowles, the old trout, had sent Nell off instead.

'She's only jealous that Tommy Tanker asked me to walk out with him, and not her,' she muttered to herself, using her annoyance to mask her nerves. 'Ha!' she snorted, the noise echoing alarmingly in the stony quiet, 'As if he'd look at her! Old widow-woman that she is—all of eight and twenty if she's a day.' Secure in the confidence of youth, she pictured the young man, Tiger to the Prince, resplendent in his livery, his lithe, slight frame perched on the back of the Prince's cabriolet...

A scuffing noise jolted her out of her reverie, her smile fading. The sound had come from up ahead. She strained her ears, listening for any further sound, beyond the ever-present drip of water, and the now slightly ragged sound of her own breathing. There was nothing.

'Don't be silly,' she muttered to herself, 'it's just a rat.' But her heart was pounding as the stories that the other girls told—of ghosts in the cellars, of the phantom white lady—filled her head.

The light shed by the stump of candle that she carried seemed pitiful. The shadows crowded in, flickering and dancing, as the candle shook in her grasp, its glow occasionally glinting off bottles and polished utensils.

Alert now for the slightest sound, she tiptoed forward to the racks of bottles along the left-hand wall. As her hand closed around the neck of a bottle of sherry, she gave a small gasp, her feet splashing, unexpectedly, in cold water.

Glancing down, she saw a large puddle, about an inch deep, had collected in the corner of the room. Lifting the candle, she could see the water glittering in the light, not only in the corner by the wine racks, but also stretching back into the far corridor that led off the wine cellar, under the palace. She'd have to tell Mr Parsons about this—there must be a leak somewhere, and the near constant rain of the past few weeks had found a way in. She frowned momentarily—it had been raining, seemingly non-stop, for weeks but this puddle could only have formed today, otherwise Mr Parsons would have seen it. The water seemed to ripple and shift as she looked at it. Unnerved, she tore her glance away and scanned the shelves hurriedly, looking for the gleam of the nutmeg grater.

Another scuffling sound. This one louder. And nearer. Another.

Nell Cowley turned. And screamed...

'Now, Mistress Wildthyme, I know that you're partial to a quick nip of the old Lightning Strike,' said Martin with a grin, unstoppering a bottle of gin. 'Try this. My brother-in-law makes it for Sam Shergold at the Castle Inn.'

He poured her a generous measure of the clear liquid, and Iris's nose was immediately tickled by the familiar, welcome smell of juniper. She took a tentative swig. Her eyes bulged as she swallowed the mouthful and she gave a gasping wheeze.

'That's. Huh. Um, that's... not too bad actually.' She took another, slightly smaller, swig. 'Bit vigorous, but I expect the second one will go down easier. Yeah, not a bad bit of Old Tom. Now if you can find me a ceramic punch bowl—'

Iris was cut off as a sudden scream rent the air.

She and Panda exchanged a swift glance and dashed off in the direction of the scream, Iris still clutching her glass of gin.

The steps down to the cellar were steep and so Iris was obliged to carry Panda, tucked somewhat unceremoniously under her arm, whilst she juggled the glass of gin in one hand, and a slim, and entirely anachronistic, pen torch in the other.

'At least try and hold me upright, woman!' snapped Panda crossly. 'I can't see a bloody thing.'

'There's nowt to see yet chuck,' said Iris. 'Besides, I've only got two hands. And it's not my fault you've got short legs.'

'I'll have you know that there's nothing wrong with the length of my legs. It's these steps that are stupidly deep. Besides, if you held me upright, I could carry the gin.'

'Ha! Nice try. I'm saving it for the poor girl who screamed. I reckon she'll need it. See?'

As Iris stepped off the bottom stair and into the cellar proper they could both hear the sound of a frightened crying from up ahead.

'Hello?' called Iris, 'Are you there, love? It's only yer Auntie Iris...'

The duo rounded the corner of a short corridor that led them into the bottle room, and there, huddled against the racks, was the sobbing figure of Nell.

'Hey luvvie,' said Iris, squatting beside the girl, her knees cracking like pistol shots in protest, 'drink this, and tell Panda and me what's wrong.'

Nell looked up, her expression blank with shock and fear, her eyes red-rimmed and puffy. 'It was the w-w-white lady! I saw her!'

'The white lady?' queried Panda.

'A ghost that's said to haunt the Pavilion,' said Iris, pushing the remains of the gin into the girl's shaking hand. 'Never seen her myself. Here, drink up love.' Nell gulped the gin, barely registering the burn as it went down. It seemed to do the trick, as her hands stopped shaking. She gave a heavy sniff.

'Now, are you sure you saw her?'

Nell nodded. 'She were tall, and slim, an' she wore a long black cloak with a hood, but I could see her face in the light of me candle. She were so pale. Pale and beautiful, like a statue. And then she moved...' Nell tailed off, fear flickering in her eyes.

'Did she hurt you?' asked Panda.

'No. She never got near me. I screamed. I must've closed me eyes, an' when I opened 'em she were gone. But you don't understand,' said Nell. 'She were walking on top of the water!'

'Water?' In reply, Nell gestured to the large puddle on the other side of the room. Iris turned the torch on it and watched the light shimmer on the surface.

'A sinister puddle,' said Iris, gleefully, 'this party's getting better and better!' She crossed to the puddle and after regarding it critically for a few seconds, stuck her finger in. She then popped her finger into her mouth. 'Mmm, just water,' she pronounced, 'a bit bricky and plastery, but other than that, pretty normal.'

'I'm surprised you recognise the taste,' said Panda. Iris ignored him and addressed Nell instead.

'Did she appear from this direction?' She gestured to the short corridor leading off from the room. Nell nodded.

'Fine. You get yerself back upstairs to the kitchen, chuck. Panda, you and me are going ghost hunting...'

In the gloom of the garden, two more dark shapes slipped through the undergrowth, taking up sentry points in sight of the grand main doors. The rain continued to hammer down.

'Only you,' grumbled Panda, 'could promise me a fabulous royal party in an elegant palace and then take me on a trek through some damp, smelly cellars looking for a ghost. I mean—a ghost!'

'Ooh stop moaning—you love a mystery as much as I do. Besides, ghosts don't leave wet footprints,' said Iris, gesturing with the torch to a line of neat, wet splodges leading down the flagstone corridor.

Panda peered at them. 'So, our "ghost" was barefoot then? And...' he looked a bit closer, 'it might be my imagination, but are those footprints webbed?' The two friends exchanged a glance.

'Maybe it's the ghost of Martha Gunn?' suggested Iris.

'Or some sort of mermaid?'

'Ooh,' Iris grinned.

'You're picturing Patrick Duffy in *Man from Atlantis*, aren't you?'

'You say that like it's a bad thing. Those little yellow trunks!'

'We're looking for a woman, remember?'

'Oh yeah.' Her face fell. 'Ah well. Come on, the sooner we get this sorted out, the sooner we can get ourselves around some gin.'

They moved off down the corridor, following the footprints. After a short distance, and a sharp right turn, the corridor opened out into another cellar. This one was full of old furniture—piles of unwanted chairs and abandoned occasional tables reached up to the vaulted ceiling. Iris swung the torch around the room, making the shadows dance. 'Nowt here.'

'And it seems to be a dead end.'

'Not quite luvvie—look!' Iris gestured with the torch to a wooden door, partly obscured behind a stack of chairs. They crept across to the door, which was slightly ajar, and peered through.

'Stairs. And leading up.'

'Good. Let's get out of this cellar. The dust's playing havoc with my fur.'

'Have you given any thought to what we're going to do when we find this ghost?' said Panda as Iris scooped him up and mounted the stone steps.

'What I usually do Panda—improvise. And give them a good talking to for frightening poor Nell.'

'Oh good,' muttered Panda, unenthusiastically.

At the top of the steps was a short passage, with a door at either end.

'Which way now?'

'Fifty-fifty,' Iris replied thoughtfully, putting Panda on the floor. 'The footprints have dried up. I reckon that,' she gestured to the door on the left, 'is the back door. So, did our "ghost" go outside...'

'... or further in to the palace?' finished Panda.

Iris shrugged and crept forward. She grasped the door handle and flung open the outer door to be greeted by nothing but rain.

'Well, if they've gone out that way there's no hope of finding them in that,' grumbled Panda, looking at the sheets of water pouring into the garden.

'I guess you're right,' agreed Iris, peering intently into the gloom. Had she caught a glimpse of a shape? Of something moving in the undergrowth? She was about to turn away when she caught another flash of movement.

'Hey!' she bellowed. 'Hey! Come back here!' And with that she darted out into the rain.

'S'wounds Iris! What on Earth is going on?' thundered the Prince, his enormous stomach and jowls quivering as he paced the room. 'Terrified maids! Ghosts in the cellars! Mysterious figures in the garden!' He snorted; a little, Panda thought, like a bull about to charge. 'Why is it that trouble always follows you?'

'Just lucky, chuck,' said Iris, from where she sat, wrapped in a blanket in front of the huge open fire, gently steaming.

'If I may make so bold sir,' Harris cut in, 'I believe that I saw a figure in the garden little more than an hour since. It was just a flash, and so I thought it a trick of the light. However, in light of Mistress Wildthyme's testimony...' He tailed off, discreetly. 'Also, sire, Nell Cowley is not, by nature, an impressionable girl.'

'So, you think that my palace is haunted?'

'Well sir, there has always been the story of The White Lady...'

'I don't know about "haunted" Georgie-boy,' Harris winced at Iris's informality, 'but I definitely reckon that you've got some uninvited guests. There were at least two fellers in the garden. I lost 'em in the shrubbery, but they were definitely there. We've just got to work out why they're here and what they want.'

'Hopefully just a drink,' Panda muttered.

'Do you think that there might be any danger?' the Prince asked, a touch of anxiety in his voice.

'I dunno yet,' Iris replied thoughtfully. 'Just you carry on as normal, and Panda and I will have a nose around and see if we can't find some more clues.'

The Prince glanced at the ornate clock on the mantle above the fireplace. 'The guests will be arriving in just over an hour, Iris.'

'Then we'd best get cracking.' Iris launched herself out of the chair, shucking off the blanket. 'Come on, Panda.' She stopped on the threshold and glanced at the Prince, 'Just in case, I'd have a pair of your more strapping lads meet the guests' coaches.'

Panda rubbed a paw over the rather grimy glass of the window and peered out into the garden. The long gallery ran along the west side of the top floor of the Pavilion and so afforded a good view of the grounds. Or would do if it weren't nearly pitch black. Panda could just make out the two lighted braziers acting as torches by the main entrance. The flames flickered crazily in the wind. Suddenly a flash of lightning illuminated Panda's view in stark white light. 'Oh bugger!' he exclaimed, leaping off the broad windowsill, and hurrying from the room.

In the gardens, briefly revealed by the lightning, were four muscular figures in dark cloaks, each with a sword strapped across their back.

'It's the same out front, luvvie,' said Iris, when Panda broke the news to her, 'Looks like it's a party-under-siege.'

'The first guests will be here any minute. Have you found anything?'

'Only a couple of wet footprints here and there, nothing conclusive.' Iris admitted, 'There's at least one person in here who shouldn't be, but I don't know where. Let's get down to the front door, maybe our mystery guest will make their presence felt once there are a few more people around.'

In the Saloon, the Prince, resplendent in a coat and breeches of mauve silk and a brocade waistcoat, its golden threads glittering in the candlelight, stood with Maria Fitzherbert, and awaited the arrival of the first guests. The Prince, Maria noticed, was oddly nervous and kept glancing at the windows, as if expecting to see something in the rainy darkness beyond.

'Is anything wrong, my love?'

'What?! Ah. Nothing old girl, nothing,' he blustered. 'Just thinking how wet everyone's going to be with all this dashed rain. It's deuced bad, you know, deuced bad...' He tailed off and glanced at the window again.

Well, thought Maria, that was as big a bag of moonshine as she'd heard in a long while, but whatever was bothering him would soon fade once the guests arrived and he got half-sprung. She squeezed his hand, and then they both started as the sound of thunderous knocking came from the main doors, followed by the booming voice of Sam Shergold complaining about the terrible weather.

The Prince seemed to relax and grinned at Maria, 'Sam's here—the party's started! Time to look corky!'

An hour later Iris was drinking her sixth glass of gin and surveying the banqueting room from her vantage point near the buffet table. Next to her, Panda perched on top of a tall cabinet, gnawing idly on a chicken wing. The party was in full swing and the room was bursting with noise and life. There were over thirty guests, all dressed in their fashionable finery. Iris had already complimented one young buck on his rather tight britches. Like noisy, brightly coloured birds, they twittered and chattered and laughed. In the centre of the room, several young couples were dancing to the music of eight members of The Royal Band, the full orchestra not being appropriate for an intimate party.

In the middle of the group was the Prince's enormous bulk, as, panting and red in the face, he tried to keep up with both Maria's nimbler step, and the rhythm, which was gradually getting away from him.

As the current piece ended, George extricated himself from the throng, leaving Maria to be partnered by a slimmer, and more able, dancer, and made a beeline for Iris.

''Pon my soul, I'm hot!' he exclaimed as he reached her. He scooped up a pastry topped with quail eggs from the table and shovelled it into his mouth. 'And hungry! Builds up an appetite all this jigging about.'

'That's your problem Georgie-boy,' said Iris, unsympathetically, 'too many quails, not enough quadrilles. You're not in shape anymore.' She chuckled. 'Not like the old days, eh?' She elbowed him in the ribs.

'I'll have you know that my figure is the height of fashion,' he retorted, grandly. 'I'm stepping into the Music Room to cool down.' He left, with a large glass of wine and as much dignity as he could muster.

As he did so, Panda hissed in Iris's ear, 'Look—up there!' Iris followed the line of his paw and, sure enough, up above the press of brightly-coloured bodies, a figure in a black hooded cloak was lurking on the gallery overlooking the banqueting hall, like a raven watching over a host of peacocks. As they watched, the hood moved, following George's path, and the figure turned.

'That's our ghost!' exclaimed Iris, 'and she's heading for George!' Scooping Panda off his cupboard, she charged across the banqueting room, scattering dancers and spilling drinks as she went.

As they careened out through the ornate double doors of the banqueting room, they saw the Prince moving down the Long Gallery in the direction of the Music Room. 'Georgie!' bellowed Iris, causing a footman, mid-way through bowing at his master's passing form, to start so violently he almost upset the Chinese vase beside him.

The Prince turned, letting out a gasp of surprise as he spotted the slender, hooded figure descending the stairs from the gallery above. At the sight of the Prince, the figure paused on the stairs, one slim hand grasping the bamboo-effect balustrade. The figure pulled back its hood, revealing a beautiful face, pale as porcelain, with large, dark eyes. Eyes that locked with the Prince's.

'I have come for you.' The voice that issued from the shapely lips was light, musical, with a trace of an exotic, unidentifiable accent. She gracefully descended another stair.

George, his eyes wide with a mixture of fear and fascination, took an involuntary step forward.

Then he staggered as Iris barrelled into him.

'Time to go Georgie-boy.' She swiftly linked her arm with his, using the momentum of his stagger to pull him around, and dragged him away from the Long Gallery, towards the entrance hall.

Panda, following as quickly as his considerably shorter legs would carry him, glanced back towards the Banqueting Hall in time to see Maria exiting behind them, drawn, no doubt, by their hasty flight. Maria's glance moved swiftly from the retreating figures of Iris and the Prince, incriminatingly arm in arm, to the beautiful figure on the stairs, and an expression of annoyance settled on her face. Oh dear, thought Panda, as he hastily followed Iris and George, that does not bode well...

Panda, George and Iris burst into the Music Room, which was just off the Long Gallery, and slammed the door behind them. The Prince was panting fit to explode. Panda winced at the rather bilious yellow of the patterned wallpaper, as he helped the wheezing Prince to a chair. Iris opened the door a crack and peered through.

'I think we've lost her. Right, Panda, you stay here with Georgie, I'm going to go and have a scout round for our uninvited guest.'

'I will not be a prisoner at my own party!'

Iris sighed. 'It's for your own good, luvvie. We don't know who she is or what she wants. Or whether she's dangerous. But she's clearly after you, so we have to keep you away from her, until I can find out what's going on.'

'I must be seen by my guests! I cannot simply skulk in here like a hedge priest at a funeral.'

'Fine. Panda, you'll have to look after him. Keep a sharp eye out for her. And Prinny, try and keep a low profile, eh?' With that, Iris slipped out of the room.

George sat in the Music Room, idly, and rather petulantly, picking at the golden brocade of the stool he was sitting on. This party was not going as expected. He was supposed to be dancing with Maria, flirting with his friend's wives, drinking and eating and generally enjoying himself. He was not supposed to be pussyfooting around his own palace, hiding from a sinister but beautiful woman, and generally having no fun at all. Moreover, where was that damned Iris Wildthyme? She had left him a good ten minutes since, promising to sort it all out. It really was all too bad. At least he had persuaded Panda to slip off and get him a drink. That was something. All this running about left a man parched.

He looked up expectantly, as he heard a footstep 'Ah, there you Panda. Stout fellow—' His voice died in his throat.

There she was. Drifting towards him from across the room, her hood thrown back, the candlelight flickering across her pale, beautiful face, her dark eyes shining.

He scrambled to his feet as fast as his bulk would allow, overturning the stool as he did so. 'Wh-who are you?' he managed to stutter, backing hurriedly towards the door. 'What do you want?'

'I am Kristina, Queen of Subtamba. And I have come for you, George.'

He gulped, the colour draining from his normally florid face, as his hand scrabbled for the door handle. He pulled the door open and almost fell backwards through it.

Straight into Maria.

'George!' Maria exclaimed, a mixture of surprise and annoyance in her tone, 'What is going on?' She tried to peer around his considerable bulk into the Music Room, half expecting to catch a glimpse of a disarranged maid, but there was nothing to be seen.

'What?! Oh, err, nothing my love.' George blustered, his face flushing. 'Nothing at all. I was, um, just cooling off after our dance.' He hurriedly pulled the Music Room door shut behind him and slid a nervous arm around Maria's waist.

'Oh yes? I suppose running off with Iris Wildthyme was meant to cool you down, was it? And who was that other woman?'

'Other woman?' he replied, with studied bewilderment. 'What other woman my angel...' He tailed off—he could tell from Maria's stony expression that she wasn't buying it. 'Oh, you mean the woman on the stairs? Dash it all—I've no idea. Never seen her before in my life. Some piece belonging to one of our guests, no doubt. Pretty though, what? Someone's a lucky feller...'

Strategically positioned behind a nearby parlour palm, Iris watched as Maria angrily broke free of Georgie's encircling arm and stormed off in the direction of the Banqueting Room. The Prince hurried after her, calling in a beseeching tone.

'Right,' Iris muttered to herself, 'I've had enough of this. Time to bring things to a head, I think. Panda should be ready by now.'

In the Library, Panda quickly opened the French windows, and peered out into the rainy gloom. He wasn't entirely convinced by the wisdom of Iris's plan to bring all of the mysterious intruders into the same room at the same time; it would leave the two of them rather outnumbered, but Iris had been insistent.

He took a generous swig of the drink that had originally been intended for the Prince, and then, with a not inconsiderable effort, struggled to move one of the heavy, ornate armchairs into place by the fire.

''ere, Sam...' Much to his annoyance, Sam Shergold was jerked roughly from his study of the charming décolletage of Lady Pelham and brought face to face with Iris Wildthyme. 'See that woman approaching? The one in the black cloak.' She pointed down the Long Gallery.

'What?!' said Sam, testily. 'Yes. I see her. My, yes,' he perked up, 'a rare beauty.'

'Yeah, well, she's looking for Prinny. I need you to intercept her and tell her that he's in the Library.'

Sam frowned. 'But I've just seen him go into the Banqueting Room.'

'Which is precisely why I need you to tell her that he's in the Library. Panda and I want to have a little word with her.'

'I might want a little word with her myself,' retorted Sam with a lascivious grin.

'Maybe later. For now, just deliver the message!' Iris gave him a shove in the direction of the woman. Iris was already moving in the direction of the Library. 'And don't shilly-shally!'

Sam turned his head to protest, but the damnable woman had gone.

Kristina sailed in to the Library, her cloak billowing, like a shark sighting prey. Nothing now could stop her meeting with the Prince. She crossed noiselessly to the high-backed chair near the fireplace and swept around it... to find herself confronted, not by the man that she had pursued all evening, the man that she had travelled from her far distant kingdom to find, but by a small, and rather overdressed, furry black-and-white creature. As her words of greeting died in her throat, and the barely perceptible gill slits in her neck rippled in surprise, she heard the door to the Library shut with a determined click.

'I think it's time you and me had a little chat missy,' came a firm but not unfriendly voice. Kristina looked up to see a woman detaching herself from the shadows behind the door. It was the same purple-haired woman that she had seen with the Prince earlier. She assumed a haughty expression.

'Who are you to talk to me in such a fashion?' Her light, musical voice was sharp. 'I am a Queen, not some common maid.'

'Yeah, well, I'm Iris Wildthyme, Transtemporal Adventuress Extraordinaire, and I've met my fair share of old queens in my time. It takes more than a title to impress me, luvvie. Isn't that right, Panda?'

'Too right!' said Panda, 'Once you've had tea with the Mad God Queen of Kwaaaloon, you become a bit blasé.'

'Anyway, yer Queenship, I reckon it's about time you told Panda and me what you're doing here, and why you've been chasing my mate Prinny around all evening.'

'And why you've got some hulking great, heavily armed blokes lurking around in the shrubbery,' added Panda.

Iris gave a discreet cough and gestured towards the open French windows. Panda craned his neck around the wing of the armchair and stared.

'And why you've got some hulking great, heavily armed blokes, standing right over there,' he amended, nervously.

Kristina looked bewildered. 'They are my bodyguard,' she replied. 'Surely you do not expect a Queen to travel so far without an escort?' She gave a slight gesture with her hand, and the men relaxed slightly, but remained watchful.

'Fair point.' Iris conceded with a nod. 'And where have you come from? Because unless I miss my guess, you're not entirely human, are you?'

Kristina nodded. 'It is true, I am not a surface dweller like you. My people are the people of Subtamba, an undersea kingdom, in the depths of the ocean.'

Iris shot Panda a glance. 'See—mermaids! You were right.'

Kristina laughed—a pleasant, trilling sound. 'I am aware of the legends of your people, but, as you can see, I have no scales, or fish tail.'

'Well, they're not my people love, I'm as much a visitor here as you are, but I see your point. You do have gills though, I notice.'

'My people are at home in the water or on the land. My kingdom consists of a vast undersea area, some of which is in huge, dry, airy caves. Our cities are ancient and my people lead carefree lives, at peace with each other and with the creatures and plants of the deep. There are even some surface dwellers amongst us. Those who have been lost at sea and rescued by my people. That is how we learn of the surface world. We live on the ocean's bounty.'

'It sounds idyllic,' said Panda.

Kristina frowned, a shadow passing over her fine, pale features. 'It was idyllic. Natural formations of rock shielded us from above and kept us safe from prying eyes as well as from the most dangerous ocean predators. Until the day, nearly two years ago, when the world around us was rent asunder.'

'An explosion?' queried Panda

'I do not understand the term,' said Kristina. 'The world was rent asunder. There is no other way to describe it. The earth beneath us shook as if one hundred Krakens had crashed into it. Our buildings were destroyed. The rock formations that protected us cracked and splintered and rained down upon us. The oceans boiled as terrible heat seeped from the cracks and the light that filtered down from the surface of the water was blotted out, as if a cloth had been thrown over the whole ocean. Many, many of my people were killed.' Her beautiful features were creased with sorrow at the memories. 'My own father, the old King, and two of my younger brothers were killed.'

'Oh course!' exclaimed Iris. 'Tambora!'

'Bless you,' replied Panda facetiously.

'No, it's a volcano. A ruddy big one. It erupted in 1815. Huge clouds of dust were thrown up into the atmosphere—that's why the weather's been so bloody awful for the last year. Lava everywhere, massive seismic disturbance. Thousands on the island and its neighbours were killed. It must've also caused some structural damage to the cave system where Madam's kingdom is situated.'

'Alright, so that explains where you're from, but it doesn't explain why you're here. What do you want with George?'

'Why, to marry him of course!' Kristina's tone was surprised, as if her reasons should have been obvious.

Panda accidentally inhaled his mouthful of gin and coughed his surprise.

'Marry?!' shouted Iris.

'Of course.' Kristina explained, calmly, 'When my father died I became Queen. I must have a consort; it is my duty to my people. Moreover, that consort must be someone of rank and status. Sadly, most of the males of suitable status amongst my own people were killed in the cataclysm. However, I have heard much of this Prince George, the Prince of England, who rules in his father's stead, and I have determined that he must be my Prince Consort. So, I swam here, over many leagues, to get him.'

'As simple as that?' said Panda sardonically.

'As simple as that,' replied Kristina. 'I am a Queen, he is only a Prince. He cannot refuse me.'

'Weeeell, there are one or two potential problems,' said Iris, thoughtfully.

'Namely his existing wives,' muttered Panda.

'I will brook no refusal,' Kristina asserted, 'I must have a consort. I will not return empty-handed.'

'Look, I understand your position,' said Iris, sympathetically. 'I really do.' She spoke slowly now, an idea forming in her mind, 'But Georgie isn't really the man for you. Between you and me, he's not suited to be King. I mean, he's a lovely feller and all, but he's feckless, frivolous and a bit of a wastrel. He's only really interested in leisure and pleasure—drinking, eating, gambling and gaming. And women. He's not the sort of man you need at all. He'd be no good at rebuilding a shattered undersea kingdom. Too lazy, too indolent...'

'Too buoyant,' muttered Panda.

Kristina's face fell.

'However,' said Iris, with a crafty grin, 'I can suggest an alternative. Handsome, charismatic, energetic, and with a lovely singing voice. And a King in his own right. Yes, the man I've got in mind would make you a perfect consort.' She clicked her fingers at her friend, "ere, Panda love, pass me my handbag.'

'What are you up to?' he hissed, handing her the gold lamé bag dumped by his chair.

'You'll see luvvie.' She grinned. She looked at Kristina as she opened the bag, 'I've got a photo here...'

'Elvis!!' exclaimed Panda. 'Are you serious?'

Kristina was standing by the fireplace, gazing at the glossy 8x10 of the King of Rock 'n' Roll that Iris had fished out of her voluminous handbag, whilst the two friends had a hushed conference on the other side of the room.

'Why not?' said Iris. 'He is a King after all—that's what she wants. I reckon he'd be good for her. Better than Prinny at any rate. He's lost a fair bit of weight since his "death", and he's getting bored of life on Jal'how Sirroc. He's homesick—he told me so the last time we visited. We'll slip out of here, get on the bus, jaunt off to Jal'how in 1982, introduce them, and let nature take its course.' She grinned. 'Or do you want to explain to Maria that a mermaid queen wants to steal George away from her and take him to her undersea kingdom to raise lots of baby tuna?'

Panda shook his head in exasperation, 'Fine, you win. It's the best plan we've got. You're incorrigible.'

'I try my best.' She turned back to Kristina. 'Come on Your Majesty. My transport is outside. Let's get out of here and go find your King.'

Iris's hand was on the handle of the main doors when she heard a voice behind her. 'Hullo! What's this? Iris, are you stealing this beautiful creature away? That's deuced bad form old girl, deuced bad.' Iris turned, as the enormous form of the Prince emerged from the Red Drawing Room. Iris gave him a once-over—it was clear that a heady combination of lust and gin had overcome his earlier apprehension. He swayed slightly as he approached.

'Sorry Georgie, but I think it's better for all concerned if we slip away.' The Prince pulled a face, like a child whose favourite toy was being taken away.

'Surely not without a kiss from those sweet lips?'

'Oh, alright,' said Iris, puckering up.

'Not you! I mean this bewitching lady.'

Kristina smiled, 'You are right, my Prince, after the dance that I have led you this night, I owe you that much.' She stepped forward and the two kissed. And kissed. The moment seemed to stretch on for quite some time.

'Well, that's the benefit of gills,' Iris said.

'Iris!' Panda hissed in a stage whisper, 'Aria-may is oming-cay!'

'Eh?' She frowned at him. 'Are you pissed, luvvie?'

He glanced nervously down the corridor, jerking a paw to indicate an approaching problem. 'Mistress on the starboard bow!'

'Oops! Time to get Her Majesty away!' Iris nipped out of the double doors, past the pair of kissing royals, and grabbed Kristina's arm, pulling her from the Prince. 'Sorry to break up the happy moment, but it's time we were off.'

George opened his mouth to protest at Kristina's sudden removal.

'Maria!' Iris hissed at him, waggling her eyebrows in the direction of the corridor. 'Panda,' Iris whispered, in a tone that she clearly thought was sotto voce, 'get her on the bus!'

'Right-ho!' Panda darted through the Prince's legs, grabbed Kristina's skirt and pulled her rapidly in the direction of the bus. Once in the courtyard, Panda gave a sharp whistle. At his summons two of the muscular bodyguards emerged from the shadows and helped him to hustle their queen on to the bus.

'George!' Maria Fitzherbert called, a note of suspicion in her voice. 'What is going on?!'

The Prince Regent turned with a grin that was, in Iris's estimation, just the right combination of innocent and smug.

‘Oh, there you are my angel. I was just bidding Iris farewell. She’s been called away unexpectedly.’ George gestured towards Iris, who had assumed her most guileless expression seconds before Maria hove into view.

‘Yeah,’ said Iris, ‘It’s a shame I’ve got to go. Panda and I were having a lovely time but I’ve got a message from a friend of mine. He’s having a spot of bother in the diamond mines of Marlion, and so we have to go charging off to the rescue.’ She gave a men-what-can-you-do shrug. She couldn’t really blame Maria for being suspicious—Georgie had led her a right merry dance over the years.

Maria felt a faint tug of suspicion. All evening she’d had a feeling there was some havey-cavey business going on she was unaware of. Every time she entered a room, Georgie had “just left”, and when she’d caught up with him his expression had been so innocent that she became immediately suspicious. And there was that mysterious woman in the black cloak that she had seen earlier.

Looking past Iris she could see her impossible horseless carriage, gleaming vermillion in the torchlight. Light poured from the windows and in the cabin at the front Panda, looking relaxed in shirtsleeves and waistcoat, his green cravat rakishly loosened, was working at the controls. He looked over, catching her eye, and waved a stubby paw in farewell. Maria waved and turned to Iris. As she did so, she was half convinced she saw a flicker of movement further down the bus, but when she looked back, she could see nothing.

Suddenly Iris’s face was in hers, her eyes sparkling, her mouth puckering up, ‘Bye luvvie!’ she said, kissing Maria on both cheeks. ‘Keep an eye on this one—don’t let him run you around.’ She gave Maria a conspiratorial wink. ‘And as for you, Georgie Boy,’ Iris cackled, jabbing him in the ribs with a finger that disappeared up to the knuckle in brocaded waistcoat, ‘try to behave yourself! Thanks for a marvellous party! See ya!’ With that she turned, her preposterous leopard print gown billowing behind her, and hopped aboard her bus.

With a throaty roar, the bus chugged into life, and with Iris giving a final wave, pulled out of the courtyard.

Maria and George waved at the departing vehicle and then turned to go back into the pavilion. Unseen by Maria, George, the Prince Regent, gave one last, wistful glance at the 22 to Putney Common.

'Woof, woof!' he muttered, under his breath.

Iris Wildthyme & the Bush Offensive

Stewart Sheargold

From the sensational, scandalous, and possibly untrue journals of Iris Wildthyme

'It's in the trees! It's coming!' cries Tom in a register you'd never have thought possible from such a deep-voiced boy.

'Oh, for goodness sake, you lummox…'

It's only me, luvvies, pushing through the undergrowth, gettin' all twiggy and unkempt. Hair unravelling like candy floss.

Tom's never been one to face down a monster. He's a quiverer, good at the kind of facial expression that makes the monster laugh. So when I emerge from the trees, bedraggled and breathless, I can't help but guffaw at the frightened height of his eyebrows.

'Iris!' he snaps. 'Stop beating about the bush. This is serious.'

He has a point.

This is when I notice that he is struggling to hold Kate, who is pulling away from his grip. She is smothered in a sickly green glow™, her pre-Raphaelite hair on end. There, on the clifftop, she strains for the sea. Her eyes: dark as pitch.

And the sea throbs with mossy light (ooh, that's a nice bit o' poetry).

Fortunately, I have the Winklegruber™, cadged together from bits of the bus, stubby silver nose pointed at the singer.

'Do something!' yells Tom. 'I can't... hold her... much... longer.'

I raise the device, humming with intent. The device, that is, not me. I don't hum, dearies.

The ivy on the cliff thrashes and grasps at us. Over the past days, it's pulled the house closer to the edge. The stone crumbles in rivulets.

Kate whips round, dark eyes glistening with alien, arms out as though to dance.

'Sorry, dearie. This might pinch a bit.'

She screeches like a banshee.

I press the big red button. The Winklegruber™ powers on, gives a satisfying belch, then gives out a puff of smoke. Does nothing.

Tom's eyebrows go so far up they disappear.

Kate takes the moment. Bites down. Tom yells. She pulls free from his grip, throws herself backward—is suspended atop the cliff, writhing with green light—then smiles.

And falls.

Tom yells the requisite negative.

I shake the Winklegruber™ with some annoyance. A dislodged part rattles. Stupid thing. Never trust a device powered by an erotic frisson.

Tom and I gather ourselves, walk slowly to the cliff top.

'Well, here's another for the history books, Iris.' He gives a sheepish frown. 'We've just killed Kate Bush.'

Which makes me swear. In several alien languages.

From the collected writings of Thomas Daley — "Big Red Bus & the Bag Lady from Time", sometime companion of Iris Wildthyme. Fourth edition.

Devon, near East Portlemouth, 2027

We'd been here a few days, and still the strange wailings continued. Iris moaned about the lack of proper soundproofing, but I rather liked hearing Kate's vocal ramblings. She hummed and keened and willowed in any room of the house, and the sound crept into the day like a ghostly presence. It was her final album, and, being Kate Bush, she wasn't going to compromise. Across her oeuvre she'd used the natural, but this time she was inhabited by it. She thought she'd found ghosts in her walls (and, in a way, she had), and she cried out in strange ululations. Iris called it her "screech work". The album, *Nine Stones*, went on to win every music award on the planet. Later, we wondered whether the aliens in the songs contributed to the success.

Kate was always in the kitchen, making bread and scones and cakes. When I walked in, she was there, wide-eyed and childlike, holding out a tray. Watching as I took a muffin, then a mouthful, smiling at me, eyes brimming with mischievousness.

'I should be in the studio,' she said, in that Earth-mother tone, 'but the kitchen just keeps calling me back.'

'A woman's work is never done,' I said, and she shook her head at me good-naturedly.

Around the crumb I asked, 'How's it going?'

'There's a few good songs, perhaps.' She shrugged and smiled, almost uncaring of the work. 'Where's your friend?'

Iris had gone tramping over the moors beyond the house.

'Gone to find trouble,' I replied.

But Kate wasn't worried. She looked at the tray of muffins she'd released, frowned and gave a short laugh, 'When she's back, she should come to the studio.' She considered me. 'I think she could be musical.'

'Most people call it noise.'

Kate smiled knowingly. 'It's what you do with the noise that's interesting…'

The smell of fresh-baked dough and rosemary and apricot; the sunlight streaming in the windows. Nothing could go bad here. Kate winked and left the room with the muffin tray, back to the studio. I picked up my book, *The Day of the Triffids*, with its evocative line drawing of the alien plant, and, finishing my muffin, I opened the French doors off the kitchen and went out into the garden.

Kate's house was atop a cliff that was slowly crumbling into the sea. It was a spacious home with a wide glass frontage, and, upstairs, light-filled bedrooms with modern, square bay windows. The front lawn was only metres from a private bay and the grasping sea below. Years had eaten away the clifftop path, and every month the wind and the rain took more into the sea. Worrying heights, you might say, if you were witless.

But the view was good. Straight out to a glittering sea, no one around, and I mean no one. Kate was a recluse. There were security fences and bright spotlights to discourage anyone who got in. I was still surprised Iris hadn't set off alarms when she landed the bus, and was accepted so easily in Kate's routine. But perhaps that was just the special Iris *thing* she had. Ingratiating herself in people's lives before they knew how troublesome she was.

Iris could spend all day on the moors if she wanted. I was going to read my book about the end of the world and be happy not to be participating in one. But that was before Kate's dense muffin put me to sleep, and I woke, an hour later, shivering in the cold wind blowing off the sea. Waking to the sound of blackbirds, crying in weird circles over the house.

And a creaking, sinister slithering.

Finding my feet roped in ivy.

Iris was happy because she knew something was wrong. They were out on the wild, windy moors behind the house, looking for ghosts. There was a scent of heather and sea salt. Her time senses were tingling, a light shiver over her body, not unlike her pores rising under a cold shower. Brisk but not unpleasant.

She loved a good jaunt, though there was a mite too much nature about, what with the straggly heather that snagged at her Westwood boots, and the threat of the quicksand bog that Kate mentioned with a gleeful smile at Iris's displeasure.

'Oughtn't you have a map, dearie?' she asked the singer. 'I don't want to get my shoes mucky. Vivienne'll drop me as her ambassador quicker than a hot potato.'

She saw Tom roll his eyes and glared.

But an hour later they'd traversed the featureless hillocks, always going up, until they reached the circle of nine stones. The Bridlyn Stones, Kate called them, and gestured for Paddy to set up the audio recording equipment.

They were here to conjure ghosts, who were known to appear within the stones. Nine stones of dolomite; three short, toppled or eroded by rain and wind and time. Kate had read in a local history book that they acted as aerials. She wanted to hear what they transmitted.

Iris put Tom in charge of erecting the tents. While he tripped and cursed about the poles and the flapping fabric in the rising wind, she took an interest in the stones. She stood in front of each in turn. Apart from their menhir shape, there was nothing remarkable about them, only the imagination's fantasy giving them features and faces, thighs and crooked backs. Yet, what was that noticeable hum gathering in her ear? Was she standing in a circuit of some sort? A thrill went through her. She wanted to hear the stones. Ignoring Tom's pleas for help, Iris went straight for Paddy and with knowledgeable gestures began to unpack, connect and power on the audio equipment.

'Ooh, I love a good séance,' she said, earning a disapproving frown from Kate. But Paddy grinned and revealed more power cords, more screens, more technology.

'D'ya know, last time I tried this I was with my pal, Poirot, debunking a famous clairvoyant, Madame Sosostris. Everyone went to her. Even the Prime Minister. But it was all fishing line under tables and guttural voices.'

With a practised gesture, Tom flicked the canvas and the tent popped into shape.

Iris coughed.

With a practised gesture, Paddy plugged the last port, and with an electric hum every monitor flickered into life.

Kate clapped once.

Immediately Iris was serious. 'I hope we haven't come all this way without any food.'

'Of course not,' said Kate, revealing a large container of stew.

'Excellent,' Iris replied. 'Cause I've brought a bottle or two. Just to be sociable.' She reached into a cardigan pocket and pulled out one, two, three, four, then five bottles of gin.

Everyone looked aghast.

She clocked their alarm. Said, 'Ooh, I hope I brought enough.'

A banshee screech in the night had Iris awake and scrambling from the tent. Stepping on Tom's hand, who cried out, making her scramble back in.

'Was that you before, luvvie?'

'Yes,' he said, rubbing his palm.

'Do it again.'

'What? No.'

She reached out and slapped him. He cried out. Put a hand to his reddening cheek. 'Have you gone entirely ins—?'

Outside, a banshee shriek in the dark.

'Thought not,' she said, and grinned. Fairly leapt out into danger.

Tom wriggled from his sleeping bag, wrapped himself in a parka, and, with hangover in tow, begrudgingly followed.

The night was filled with fog. It twisted sinuously around them. Ropey fingers gathering them up. Iris was a squat shape across the circle, speaking urgently with Paddy, who, with his wiry hair, telegraphed alarm. Tom heard his worry: 'Where's Kate? Have you seen her.'

Iris's response was considered. 'I think we may have 'eard her.'

Everyone was quiet, listening for things in the fog. A rustle of clothing; a sigh of wind; a stertorous breath.

'There!' said Iris, peering fiercely across the circle. They walked slowly forward, the white parting around them. To see: a figure, leg up, arms out, wrapped around the largest of the stones. It was Kate. Her mouth was open wide, her eyes rolled, and it was horrible to see. She appeared possessed, drooling down her chin.

Paddy went to help but Iris stopped him. 'Turn on the machine,' she said, calmly. He hesitated but her tone commanded.

The click was loud in the night.

Iris walked slowly toward Kate. As she closed the distance Kate's head whipped round, her teeth snapped open and shut. She let out a raven cry.

'Now, now dearie, there's no need to be frightened. I'm your Auntie Iris, not some squeaky girl with a Ouija board.' She sniffed. 'I've been about, you know. I know an alien possession when I see one.' She stepped closer. 'So, what do you want to talk about? Shoes? Rock 'n' Roll? Conquest of the Earth? It's not as easy as you think, chuck.'

Kate's lips curled into an unkind smile. She spoke an ancient word.

The smell of ozone.

The stones crackled with green electric light.

Surrounding them in the fog, eight black-skinned, painted figures stood in front of each stone. Their eyes glistened like jet.

Ghosts in the circle.

Kate barked.

The figures moved inward. The fog shrouded them, gave menace to their slow, deliberate intent.

Tom squirmed. 'Erm… Iris…'

Iris thrust out her chest, let the ghosts come near. Their eyes did not waver, focused solely on the three humans now back-to-back in the circle. Within touching distance, they all suddenly reached out, arms up. Tom gave a squeal. Paddy frowned, eyes on Kate.

The ghosts paused. There was no escape.

Iris pulled a microphone from her pocket and said, 'How about you sing a song for us, chuck?'

Switched it on.

The night screamed with white noise.

The ghosts shuddered and bucked and disappeared.

The fog retreated beyond the stone circle, lurking like a spell.

Kate gave a cry and dropped to the grass. Paddy ran to check her vitals, stroked her hair. She was breathing hard, but she was breathing.

Iris took in the scene, measured the apparent safety of the stones, then calmly went and pressed stop on the recorder.

The screeching signal cut out.

Only the wind and the bleat of a sheep and a clatter of stones.

'Well,' she said, satisfied, 'I, for one, would very much like to hear that take. Sounded like a master to me.'

From the collected writings of Thomas Daley — "Big Red Bus & the Bag Lady from Time", sometime companion of Iris Wildthyme. Sixth edition.

Devon, near East Portlemouth, 2027

It's been a tense day, what with Kate confined to bed, after her turn, and Iris in argumentative mode, demanding to listen to the "fog tapes" as she's calling them. But Paddy's hidden them away, concerned, not for the strange noises, but for their hideous effect on Kate. Iris was left to mutter and stomp and finally slam a door on her way out onto the moors. I wondered why she was so irritable—we knew the sounds ended up on Kate's final album, looped through loops and distorted, but still, unarguably, *there.* We played the album many times on the bus. I recognised the harsh, unfiltered sounds even on the hilltop. Was Iris tinkering? Was she putting her mark on things? Her influence scattered in legacies across the universes. I wouldn't put it past her. Behind that wild (thyme) smile was a wicked subversive.

I insisted on sitting by Kate, letting a worried Paddy sleep. Before he left, he brought us scones and jam and a pot of tea. With the singer awake, though with dark circles under her eyes, we refreshed ourselves with the lukewarm sweet tea and lashings of homemade raspberry jam and cream. Kate's eyes brightened with the sustenance, and I thought I should talk to her, part of me trained to find out what was happening.

'Nothing a good cup of tea won't cure,' I said.

A soft frown from her. 'But I haven't caught anything.'

I blinked. 'But that… sound… coming from you.'

She was instantly alert, eyes big as an owl's. 'Did you record it?'

'I, um, I think so.'

She was quiet, thinking. Took a sip of her tea. 'I hope I didn't frighten you. I didn't feel frightened. I felt…' Her face flowed like water into a smile. 'Excited.' She regarded me and I was enveloped in her calm, vital intellect. 'Connected to something, something large and important. Something…' Her eyes flickered as the cogs moved in her mind. 'Noisy.'

She gave a girlish laugh. 'Funny, isn't it? All this while I've sent myself away, out here, in the middle of nowhere, for silence and calm. Now I want noise.' Her children's-book-voice cracked. 'It is quieter without Bertie.'

'Iris said it was the cry of the banshee.'

Her teeth clenched at Iris's name. She breathed in—those gusty lungs—and centred herself. Held out her cup for more tea. I dutifully poured. The aroma of bergamot and wood and lemon.

'Tom,' she said, and a thrill spilled down my spine at her dusky tone, 'this is a land of ancient things—curses and fogs and pirates and witches. There's at least two witches in my family tree.' Again that light, mischievous smile.

I recalled the sleeve to *Never for Ever*: Kate, arms out, bat-like, or skirt raised to let out all manner of night creatures.

'I don't read reviews, but my agent tells me the word banshee was used early on in my career.' She looked at me. 'Do you think I weep and wail, Tom?'

I admit I was bewitched, sitting there beside Kate Bush, who amid gathering alarm, remained serene.

'I think you're more a siren,' I said. 'Luring us into your strange but phenomenal world.'

She gave a breathy laugh. Then, suddenly serious, said, 'Oh, Tom, if only you knew how hard it is to make and keep that world. To know that everything you do is watched, discussed, dissected, analysed, reported on. And that doesn't matter. Because I'm not the music, or the song.' She shrugged. 'I spent two years baking, not writing a note, to prove I can be Kate, the mother, the teacher; the lover.' She slurped back the last of her tea, lathered a scone with jam. 'But always, always I wonder: what will I leave? Is it good enough?'

I assured her that she would live on well after her death, her albums notable, cherished works of art. I may have gushed like a fanboy. She gave that tender smile. I wondered if there would ever be a time when no one listened, when she was a footnote in history. Perhaps, sometime, at the end of the world; when many days accumulated, and many new garish, distracting *things* existed. But not now, not anytime soon, would she become irrelevant.

'Which is why the new album's important,' she replied. 'It must be made of sounds nobody has experienced. It must be strange and unknown. It must make people listen.'

Making people listen to Kate Bush was never a problem. Stopping people bend to the will of an alien power in her music… that was another issue.

From the largely embellished, if not outright ridiculous, but very satisfying, journals of Iris Wildthyme

Hello, dears. How have you been? I hope I've not been neglecting you. Planets to drink, loves to be had, huge balls to be hurried away from. And, if I'm being honest, journals to be written and serialised for Playboy, or is it Playmonster now? I've been round so many times I'm dizzy with the loop.

But that is not what concerns me today, chuck. No. Today I want to know about the tape of hill sounds, made in the fog. Because it makes me wonder, dearies, oh yes, makes me wonder… what dark, painted aliens want with a singer of abstract pop songs.

So, naturally, going about this the subtle way, I asked to be included in the recordings.

'Get out of my studio!' Kate cried.

I spread my hands, acting all innocent. 'Kate, me old mucker, I only want to watch a geni…' I couldn't force myself to say it.

Kate gave me a level look. 'Yes?'

'… genuine star. In her natural orbit.'

She pressed her lips together.

'Oh heck, just let me hear you sing and press a few buttons.' I flashed my eyes encouragingly. 'You know, Bowie said I was his muse on *Never Let Me Down*. And I didn't.'

Kate considered.

I could tell what she was thinking: this glamourous woman appeared to know wise, worldly things. She left the studio and went into the live room, closing the door with a crisp *click*.

'You know how to operate a sound desk?' she asked through the monitor.

The very insinuation I couldn't, dearies! Alan Parsons himself was my mentor. Course I nodded and settled down and pressed a few buttons and twiddled a dial and pushed a lever. Then depressed a few buttons and un-twiddled a dial and pulled down a lever to get rid of that terrible noise the desk was making.

Kate gave me a stern look beyond the glass. Despite her elfin features she could be quite fearsome with that leonine hair and those wild eyes. Happily, dear Paddy had, through osmosis, heard my call from the sound desk, and popped in. I explained the situation and made him reveal where he'd hidden the fog tapes. He was reluctant to reveal their whereabouts until your Auntie Iris sidled up close and gave him a squeeze and a lascivious grin, and then he was most helpful. Men can't resist me, luvvies!

Paddy had them stashed under the desk in a hidden drawer. He brought them out with a distinct whiff of the old herb, if you know what I mean. Kate warmed up in the live room, making childish sounds that came to us through the monitor. Paddy, giving me a guarded look, slipped one of the tapes into a player. Hesitated.

'Go on, chuck.'

He looked at Kate, tossing her hair about.

Pressed play.

A low hum started. Nothing remarkable. Paddy fiddled with knobs.

'That ain't what I got,' I said.

'Shh.' Paddy held up a finger. 'This was ambient sound I recorded, before we went to sleep.' We listened for a while, then ran the tape on. There was a light hiss now, and a bubble to the hum, as though it ballooned then went quiet again. Paddy did some clever tricks and pulled it out of shape and back in again, and all at once, me luvvies, there was a kind of railroading skip.

Then Kate started improvising.

'Ah-rumby-hey-rah, ah-rumby-hey-a-nah…

'Ooh-we-ah-whoo, ooh ah-we-ooh-NA!

'Tiddick shum na tiddick shum na shumty shumty eh

'Crrrrrip hey Crrrrip bah… rush-a-rum-a-hey.'

It was mesmerising watching her sway in time to her vocal haunting. As I watched, she came to a halt and stood there.

The tape clicked over into an odd ululating wail. 'Turn that up.'

Paddy did as he was told.

I listened hard, and though I hadn't heard the sounds before, there was something familiar about them. Beneath the wail were guttural grunts and glottal stops.

'They're words! Alien words. They're trying to communicate.' I beamed. I always like the bit of the story where I get to bring out me credentials.

Paddy's smile faded when the tape ran static and screeches.

He looked to Kate. Her hair was on end and her eyes were wild. Wilder than usual, that is, positively bugging.

And behind her, in the isolation booth, was a solid black figure, the blackest black you could ever imagine. A green edge of electricity sparked around him. A second figure pushed out of the wall. One moment—nothing, then: there, substantial. Black as pitch. As a raven. As the bottom of the sea.

The tape kept up its shrieking.

Paddy raced for the studio door, but it was stuck.

Kate tremored with fear. Then arched as electricity spat around her. I watched, fascinated. Would they say something?

The black figure reached out and touched the singer.

Instantly he filled with white lines, criss-crossing his face, his arms, his chest.

Kate opened her mouth wide.

Yes, they were going to say something! Probably been trying to get through for years to someone as intelligent as your Auntie Iris.

But then the tape shut off, there was a bright green glow, and, when it cleared, the figures had gone, and Kate was hunched over on the floor.

Tom chose that moment to fall into the control room, tripping over his pyjama bottoms. Rather cutely covered in pandas.

'Bloody Hell, Iris! What have you gone and done, now?'

I blinked and frowned. 'Settle down, pet.' I motioned to the calm around me. 'It's all under control.'

Then I noticed he was covered in ivy.

He ripped a length of vine from his shoulder. 'Iris, it may have escaped your attention, but while you've been sounding off here, the house is under attack. I went for a pee and was rudely propositioned by the ivy.'

Spiralling slightly, just slightly, out of control, then.

It was unusually silent in the usually noisy house. Everyone had gone to bed after a wild scene of action, Iris and Tom and Paddy beating at the thrashing ivy with brooms and spoons and rolling pins and anything that came readily to hand. Until Tom had the idea of raiding the garden shed, finding secateurs and saws they used indiscriminately on the flailing plant. Snipping it into thin lengths seemed to cut its angry lashing. They sighed with relief, had a hot toddy of brandy each, and said goodnight.

Hours passed.

Night breathed deeply on them.

The sea rolled in and crashed whitely on the sand.

Iris, in the attic bedroom, in bed with Tom, stealing the sheet, murmured in her sleep. 'Mmmmno, not with… leather chaps…'

No-one was about when, in the studio, a switch clicked, and the desk powered on.

A dense, heart-pressing hum.

Stillness, for moments. Then, levers on the desk operated themselves. No sound, but a green glow pickled the studio.

The live room: empty, still.

Then—after a brief second of displacement—inhabited by silhouettes. Jostling against one another. White-painted faces, and dark eyes.

Fog poured into the room.

Tom woke when the house shuddered. Realised that the shaking that woke him was advancing into the room, like ripples in a pond. Watched with alarm as the window frame creaked and, with a dramatic movement, shifted sharply upward. Glass splintered, showering the carpet.

Then silence—the night and the dark. And there at the bottom of it, the sea. Crashing ashore.

As he pulled himself together he noticed the green glow lighting up the garden.

This can't be good.

He went to the smashed window and felt moisture on his face. A wind was up. There was something wrong with the scene. Then his mind righted itself and he realised that ivy thrashed about the house, vines whipping and writhing, and, *there*, beyond the cliff, was a sinister green glow emanating from the sea.

He ran down the attic stairs, crashing into Iris at the bottom.

'Kate's gone,' she said. Her eyes darted. 'Out on the cliff top.' He realised what was coming. 'Go!' She shoved him.

He stumbled into the garden, fighting against the strength of the possessed ivy.

A song started up, away, toward the cliff edge.

Kate, singing. *Mmmm, yes…*

Tom raced onward, seeing the figure teetering, thinking of nothing but saving the singer. Throwing himself about her, clamping arms to her waist.

Kate struggled in his grip. The ivy thrashed. The sandstone crumbled underfoot.

He thought: Just… have… to hold on…a little… longer.

His nose tickled with the aroma of night-scented stock.

Then Iris arrived, like a dreadful hound, coming out of the bushes.

And he lost his grip.

From the reverential, highly sought-after music journals of Iris Wildthyme

And that, dearies, is where we came in. You remember, don't you? Ivy whipping about like angry snakes. Green glow from the sea. Kate falling off the cliff. That last point wasn't the best of things to happen, I'll admit.

Though you needn't worry. She didn't come a cropper on the rocks. Tom and I were a mite surprised when the green glow from the sea rose and light turned on her, stopping her fall, holding her. As we watched, mouths agape (well, Tom's anyway, and he really should be more experienced at this game), the beam swooped Kate out to sea and then, in a sudden movement, snatched her under the dark waves. Tom went on about us killing Kate Bush, and I rolled my eyes. Because she's not due to die for years yet. Tom accusing me of mucking up history again. I let him have his rant and then I shoved the suddenly bleeping and entirely functional (though not, I might add, because of a working erotic frisson between Tom and I, no, no at all) Winklegruber™ at him.

'Look at that,' I said.

'Look at what?' he replied, nonplussed. (Isn't nonplussed a lovely word, dearies? And so very Tom.)

'What?' I said. 'That!' I pointed to a flashing screen.

'What's that?' he asked.

'That,' I said, calmly, 'is what the Winklegruber™ does.'

'What,' he said, with an expression of annoyance, 'does it do?' I opened my mouth. 'When it isn't broken?'

Ooh, sometimes that boy needs a good slap. Slowly, so the nonplussed could understand, I explained how the Winklegruber™ wasn't a weapon of destruction or even a little bit unkind (despite its fearsome appearance and the red nozzle with a painted shark at its muzzle). It simply winkles out hidden things, whether that's bus keys or hobnobs down the back of the couch or lost moons (additional battery power required for this). Or the whereabouts of singers abducted by sinister green light.

'So, it's an impractically large homing device that won't fit in anyone's handbag,' he said.

I had to concede his point. 'It's an impractically large homing device that won't fit in the handbag of most species (let me tell you someday of the Verushka Bangalangs, whose entire material life is kept in ever-expanding handbags as they grow). But it *will* tell us the location of the aliens under the sea who've kidnapped our Kate.'

Finally giving me his serious face (though his white staring eyes need some work to perfect that), Tom handed me the Winklegruber™ and said, 'So, it's you and me looking for Bush again.'

Fifteen minutes later I'd piloted the bus (most skilfully I might add, with only a few teacups breaking) into the control room of the alien spacecraft on the seabed. We stepped out into a green-lit fish tank. These aliens really need interior decorators. If the first impression I gave was a bit, well, green, I think anyone who was in my presence would feel unwell. And the coral embellishments on the walls and the surfaces… Really, what were they thinking? Give me some rococo flourish, a Corinthian column or two, a few Turkish rugs, and a bookshelf; a lovely mishmash of styles. That says experienced traveller, worlds of wonder; *here be adventures.*

That said, the modernist art piece in the centre of the control room was impressive. Like someone had taken a warehouse of pipes and twisted it together, then shoved an enormous tuba in the centre, and pointed it at the ceiling. With a dainty, rickety seat attached. An alien telescope, that's what it looked like, made all of silver piping. Either that, or their company logo. Bathed in that sickly green glow™. Someone ought to patent that saying, dearies. (Reminder: pop back and patent "sickly green glow")

'It's all a bit too… green for me,' said Tom.

'Is it?' I replied, nonchalant. 'Hadn't noticed, chuck. Seen one spaceship, seen 'em all.'

What I had noticed was a frosted cabinet in the wall. I read the vitals and, for once, liking the bars in the green, I popped the lid. To find our Kate inside, hair frazzled, skin pale as milk, but backlit rather well. There were tubes filling her with liquid. Tom and me got her out of there quick smart, I can tell you. She was limp as a rag doll. We propped her up against the tuba machine. I lightly slapped her face to bring her round. But when those eyes opened, oh dearie me, dearies… they were filled with pure evil green.

Tom gasped and stepped back. Then gasped again when he bumped against one of the shadows coming from the walls. The shadows with white painted faces, ancient masks of corroboree. Five of them surrounded us, closed in.

The green gloom pulsed horridly.

But then the shadows, arms out to grab, stopped.

Kate was standing, straight as a dart, arms akimbo, her green eyes glowing. The shadows watched her. She paused momentously, then threw up her arms and began to dance. A strange balletic motion, bird-like—dipping, rearing, stabbing—like a puppet gone wild. Then she began to sing:

'Ah-rumby-hey-rah, ah-rumby-hey-a-nah…

'Ooh-we-ah-whoo, ooh ah-we-ooh-NA!

'Tiddick shum na tiddick shum na shumty shumty eh

'Crrrrrip hey Crrrrip bah… rush-a-rum-a-hey.'

The natural run of her voice filled the chamber. Her Mother-Earth sonorous tones. And the shadows began to sway… and tip… and then one after the other stamped a foot in mimicry of her, until they were moving as one. Even Tom nodded his head to the strange beat.

This went on for some time. When the dance wound down, like a toy using all its batteries, I gave Tom the eye and we snatched Kate away, giving her the upstairs bed in the bus.

I watched over her for a while with a necessary G&T, using the time to update my diary. I'd just finished and was putting it back in the bedside drawer, when Kate reached out and took my wrist.

'You're wrong, Iris,' she said, a bit feverish if you ask me. 'They don't mean any harm. They just want to leave.' Her grip hardened. 'They need me… to write them a song.'

Kate explained (with convenient exposition) that the alien lash-up, the tuba machine as Iris called it, was, for them, a sort of sound studio. They'd been on the seafloor for a year, having crashed in a storm, but were called out by noise. Not any noise but tones that touched the higher registers. When Kate began to tinker with the idea of a new album they tried to reach out, thinking they could communicate their despair. Make someone listen. They realised they could use their tuba machine to send out electrical current across leylines, into stone circles, onto audio tape. They just wanted someone to listen. But nobody heard. So they took Kate, plugged her in, and gave her their crude alien sounds. And, being a musical genius, she understood them.

'We have to make them a song to power their ship.'

Iris thought the idea a bit iffy, but Kate was adamant. She went straight into the studio to start noodling with key changes and progressive chords.

Iris shook her head. 'Course she hasn't thought this through, poor thing. 'ead still addled by aliens poking about inside.'

'What do you mean?' asked Tom.

'Oh chuck, use *your* 'ead. Once she's made this song, is she just going to rock up to the spaceship and slot a cassette into their tuba machine?'

'Ahhh.'

'Yes. Ahhh. Like my good friend whatsisname Baker says.'

So, for once, Iris was the practical one. The aliens harnessed electricity. Kate's song would need to be turned into electrical impulses and sent to the alien spacecraft. Fortunately, Iris had the Winklegruber™. Tom thought she should rename it the McGuffin. But Iris said someone already had the patent on McGuffin. Einstein, or Galileo; "someone sciencey." In any case, she could turn it into an aerial and boost it using the bus.

Kate spent a day in the studio, stopping only to drag in Tom and Iris for backup support. The resultant tapes are some of the strangest, most perturbing, exciting music recorded. (Though the perturbing parts have been explained away by music journos as the atonal style of the female backing singer, with her wilfully strident Na Na Hey Heys).

The next morning, after a hefty full English breakfast, Kate handed Iris a hard drive. 'This is the master, Iris. Do *not* lose it. It's some of my best work.' Her eyes flared. 'I'm *trusting* you.'

Tom followed Iris to the bus, parked over a hill beyond the house. She was unusually solemn as she fiddled with the cables and connections to the cassette radio, finding one that matched the age, clicking the drive into the clear case. She paused a moment.

'What's wrong?' asked Tom. He knew that hangdog expression.

Iris glanced up, her eyes moist. 'This'll be her final album. And no-one'll know the lead single saved an alien.'

Tom coughed. 'No-one'll know it was the first number one for an alien species, either.'

'Pfft!' Iris frowned crossly. 'Isn't it time you got up top and attached the Winklegruber™ to the aerial?'

And, with much grumbling, Tom attached the Winklegruber™, and Iris pressed the chunky play button on her Casio radio, and Kate's willowing voice swelled into the bus and out into the improved aerial, and the song was captured by the tuba machine and turned into electrical impulses, and the ivy began to thrash around Kate's home, and with a shudder and a green pulsing light the spacecraft lifted out of the sea, dripping water, and rose into the grey sky, and stopped, and hung there, and with a crackle of static, Kate's voice burst into song and shimmered and vibrated the very fabric, and a rent tore in the sky, a rent to another universe, and the spacecraft seemed to dip in a nod of gratitude... then shot away into the dark.

And the sky closed.

And the song shut off.

And the ivy stilled and lay its soft carpet down.

And Tom wiped a tear.

And the house crumbled a little more.

And Iris said, 'Not her catchiest tune, that one.'

From the collected writings of Thomas Daley — 'Big Red Bus & the Bag Lady from Time", sometime companion of Iris Wildthyme. Ninth edition.

Sometime in the future…

Back on the bus. Strange how a giddy, unreliable time machine has become my fixed abode of late. Iris is upstairs, trying on outfits for the event. She's pleased; everything sorted out. 'Never know how during the adventure, but it always does,' she said, after we put Kate to bed and stole away to the bus for a gin and tonic. Course that's not all we stole. I had words with her when I found the hard drive in her carpet bag.

'Iris! You've smuggled away Kate's new album.'

'How'd that get in there?' She pleaded innocence. But I saw the gleam in her eye, and she saw me see it. 'Oh, hush it, Tom. I couldn't let aliens influence the airwaves.'

I was confused, thinking they only spoke to Kate in the strange sounds. And Kate was their conduit. But Iris was suspicious, music being a special medium, a single note or chord could create a deep emotional response. She'd take it to her good friend, Mr Eno, who knew all about experimental sound. When he declared it safe, they'd make a quick trip to return it to Kate.

But when the bus touched down, many mad adventures after but only months later, we found that Kate had gone, taken mercifully quick by a brain aneurysm while walking along the beach. Paddy found her, waves washing her thick dark hair. When I looked at Iris I was shocked: her mouth hard, her eyes angry. I knew what she was thinking: Had Kate's death been a result of the alien influence?

Not staying a second longer, she marched back to the bus, and, cursing and straining at the brass controls, she tried to wrangle the bus back in time. 'Stupid fixed points,' she snapped. But no matter what she did the bus refused her attentions, and she had to concede to history.

And so, solemnly, we spent a night playing Kate's strange, beautiful, wistful, nutty albums, getting a bit teary, exhausting the gin supply. Waking the next day hungover but with purpose, sealing the hard drive in a padded envelope, mailing it to Paddy.

Now, Iris stumps down the spiral staircase and stands arms akimbo. Her grin splits her face. She's wearing an exact replica of the costume: a red chiffon dress with billowing sleeves, pleated skirt, a choker of peonies, red tights and soft black slippers. She spins twice. Reaches out a hand to stop herself tipping. I bite back a laugh.

'You went with the red, then.'

'Course, chuck. White's all yours. Sets off your skin, and those frightened eyes.'

I huff and glare at her. She looks me up and down in my white dress with brocade front and nods approvingly at my own touch—silver-painted toenails.

'Something's missing.' She frowns and appraises me. 'A-ha!'

Plucks the rose from her hair and slips it behind my ear. Then picks the red bolero hat from the chaise behind her, pops it on her head and angles it rakishly.

'Rightyo, ducky. We're seriously ready to win this.'

The bus, with wise mechanics, chooses a clear patch of grass, and materialises. Startling the hundreds of people who've come to pay respects. The doors wheeze open and out we come, like Goddesses, to oohs and ahhs of wonder.

The clifftop is covered in a sea of red and white. Dresses billow in the wind. I kick at the sandy ground and wonder how much of it is her house.

I look at the faces turned toward me. Thoughts spin in my head. Before I can say anything, the squeal of a megaphone scratches the day. An official statement from the organisers, welcoming all and praising the genius of Kate. And my heart swells to know that I'd been here before; I had spoken to Kate and she'd listened to me; and, perhaps, a tiny part of me was made better by knowing her.

The megaphone cuts out and the crowd moves as one to stand stiff and ready. A crackle from the speakers, then the first strains of piano.

Iris takes my hand. 'You remember the moves?'

I smile. Course I do. We'd been practising for weeks.

Kate speaks the words, and, as one, we dance:

"Heathcliff, it's me, I'm Cathy
I've come home..."

Drowned in Moonlight

Kenneth James McGowan

SCENE IV. INT. SPACESHIP—CORRIDOR

Open on a bright white corridor, receding from the viewer. A klaxon blares and smoke hangs floor to ceiling, diffused into a bright haze by the overhead lights. Red symbols flash on the bulkheads. Battle stations!

A volley of scarlet blaster bolts rip towards the camera from an unseen source as two figures burst through the smoke, running forwards.

The first is tall and elegant in a stylish leopard print swing coat, paired with a chic golden cloche, set off by a trio of peacock feathers in the hatband. More blaster bolts whizz past her, but she is unfazed. Her companion is older in appearance, shorter and puffing to keep up, plainly but stylishly dressed all in black with a big wraparound cardigan. She's dragging around a dumpy little French Bulldog she keeps tucked into a tote under her arm. She'd be able run all the faster if she ditched the mutt but there's no telling her that.

Enter IRIS WILDTHYME and CARRIE FISHER.

CARRIE
Iris, do something. They're gonna kill us!

CUT TO:

Three huge gunmetal hunter-killer robots stalking along the corridor carrying enormous blaster rifles, beady red eyes glowing as they zoom in on their quarry. The unlikely pair they are pursuing nip nimbly around the corner of a T-junction and out of view, dodging another volley of blaster fire.

'Iris?'

Typewriter keys continue to clack, click, clack arhythmically.

'Shush, I'm just about to do something clever.'

CARRIE
They're getting closer!

IRIS
Shush. I'm just about to do something clever.
Now, where's my astrospanner?

IRIS reaches into her gold lamé knee-length boots and fishes out an eight-inch long silver socket wrench circled with neatly flashing little lights and the odd button stuck on it here and there. She peeks around the corner and another blaster bolt zings past.

IRIS
Almost there, almost there.

Just as the robots round the corner, IRIS lobs the astrospanner right past them where it hits a small control panel on the wall at the other end of the T-junction, smashing it into smithereens. Immediately, an airlock begins to open right behind the robots and they are sucked backwards through the hatch into space.

CARRIE gasps and clutches the bulkhead as the decompressive gusts pull at them. She links arms with IRIS who clamps her free hand on top of her head to secure her hat. IRIS shoots a wink at CARRIE.

IRIS
Y'know, luvvie. Sometimes I amaze even myself.

'Iris. Stop it.'
'Iris!' The inexpert typing halts. 'That's not even what happened.'
'Oh, what would you know about a good story anyway?' replied Iris peevishly.
'Story?' snapped Carrie. 'Goddamn it Iris, this isn't a story. It's my life. And if we don't find whoever kidnapped Princess Leia then my story is going to be over for good.'

Extract from Carrie Fisher's private diary (unpublished)

There was a time when it wasn't unusual for me to wake up and not remember how I ended up on the floor. It's been a long time since the last time, and only a handful of times in the last two decades. But it's familiar.

There's an old woman peering at me, a bright pink hat halos her face. She's fuzzy and out of focus. She looks about my age. Hell, am I old, I wonder?

'Dorothy was right, after three you *are* under the table.' She swirls a dirty martini under my nose and a waft of strong booze and salty brine demands my attention. I bat it away.

'No. No, I don't want that.' Not today.

She downs the drink with a flourish. 'If you don't want your nerves settling, I certainly do. You didn't half give me a start.'

Things swim back from a comforting blur to firmer focus as I retrieve my eyeglasses from where they are laying in the flatware and green leafy wreckage of my lunch. Gary, my trusty companion, pads over to me and pants rapid little French Bulldog breaths. He gives me that look of his, half "you okay, girl?" and half "hey, you got this," and the world immediately feels like a better place.

A waiter hovers nervously and some of the other customers in the West Hollywood bistro are beginning to break their cool to rubberneck. Will I have to worry about my photo splashing across the Internet later and salacious stories about the drunk crazy lady that used to be a Space Princess? One of the weirder things about my life is that I haven't been a drunk for twenty years but I'm always going to be a Space Princess. I knew intoxication and this wasn't it. Drunkenness is the magical release from the shackles of sobriety. This was like the worst hangover and the worst come down all at once, that moment on the bathroom floor where you feel like you're being turned inside out. The last thing I could remember before the carpet and the salad was a shock of cold and then, as everything went black, the strange sensation that unseen parts of me were being ripped away into the darkness.

'Here,' she helps me up. 'You took a giddy turn there, right in the middle of our entrée.'

There's something familiar about the voice. Comforting and ruddy and just a bit grating about the edges. Someone who knows more than she should about strange and weird.

'Iris? What's happening to me?'

'We weren't even in outer space, Iris,' said Carrie as the other woman huffed and got up from the little typewriter perched on a messy fold-down bureau. Papers and journals cluttered the surface and teemed from the cubby holes and little drawers alongside nick-knacks and souvenirs from across time and space.

'It was the sound stage at Elstree. That spaceship was just a set. And we weren't being chased, we were the ones running after the robots kidnapping Princess Leia.'

'You talk about her like she's somebody else,' said Iris, pointedly.

'Iris, none of this feels real,' sighed Carrie. 'My younger self has been abducted from the past and I still can't believe it even after I watched it happen with my own eyes.'

After her turn in the restaurant, Iris had taken Carrie back to her wondrous transdimensional omnibus, parked incongruously just off Melrose Avenue, a shining red beacon in the Californian sunshine. She'd sat her down in the cool of the dimly lit chintzy interior while Gary sat close by, eyeing Iris implacably and panting slowly. Iris poked and prodded Carrie and hooked her up to all manner of odd devices before proclaiming that her timeline was unravelling like a badly knitted jumper. Something had gone so strangely wrong in the past that it was affecting her in the present, the only thing to do was to travel back in time to find out where and when in Carrie's personal history things had gone awry.

'We can fix it then?' asked Carrie. 'Just by going back? It doesn't sound like it should be that easy. I mean, there's plenty of stuff in my past that some people might say needs fixing. Where the hell would you even start?'

'Tricky stuff, temporal mechanics. You don't know whether pulling a thread on the warp and weft of reality is going to mend the tear or rip a right ruddy big hole through the entire nature of reality itself.'

Iris headed to the driver's cab and began happily throwing switches and turning dials and readying the miraculous engines of her beloved bus. 'Still, probably best not to worry about it.'

Extract from Carrie Fisher's private diary (unpublished)

You're probably wondering how I come to know Iris Wildthyme, Transtemporal Adventuress Extraordinaire and legend in her own mind.

I remember Iris, just not quite how we met. She tells it differently. Claims we met when I was filming *Star Wars*. She was George's muse and convinced him it needed more robots and bigger spaceships: after all, she'd seen long ago, far away and days still to come and knew exactly what it was all supposed to be like. She told him about a planet full of pandas that once overthrew a tyrannical Empire; that the faster you flew, the fewer parsecs it took to arrive; that there was no underwear in space. At least, that's how Iris tells it. That's not how I remember it.

Here's the thing about my memories, I've lost some I never knew I had. Part of a pact I made with science to save myself from those crippling feelings of defeat and hopelessness. They hooked me up to the mains and turned Princess Leia into the Bride of Frankenstein. Except that's not really true either, because real life is nothing like the movies and whatever you think you know about electroconvulsive therapy is probably wrong. They gently let me sleep and when I woke up the electricity had soothed my savage black dog and I was a different person. A not unusual side effect of this is that my mind feels whole but my memory is full of holes. I guess that's why I get along with Iris. She sometimes looks different but is always the same underneath, I'm the same on the outside but who knows who you're going to get running the show.

I remember Iris being cast in the third film. Yeah, that's right, the one with the damn gold bikini. She had five lines and was the only other woman in that great big boys' club of a movie who got to speak. She was a blast to be around when the cameras stopped rolling but on set she was awful. Truly awful. Kept demanding that she use her own wardrobe and makeup and couldn't remember her lines. Said the lines didn't matter, she could do it all with a look. In the end they had to recast. Iris was livid.

They set down in the back lot of Elstree, swapping the blue skies of LA for the off-white blur of a British summertime. The doors of the bus swished open and Iris swanned out in a new outfit and an entirely unnecessary pair of Jackie O sunglasses. Carrie couldn't remember seeing her change, perhaps it was while she gazed out of the front windshield, mesmerised by the swirling colours of the mysterious interstitial highways and byways that Iris's celestial omnibus traversed. Did Iris really skip so blithely from one end of creation to the other that she didn't even need to keep one hand on the wheel?

'I thought it was going to look smaller,' mused Carrie, stepping from the bus with Gary on a little leash. 'Like when you go visit your old high school.'

'Come on, let's go find you.'

Iris strode off into the bustling ranks of chippies and sparks and gaffers, ingratiating herself and greeting them by name like old friends. Carrie couldn't be sure if Iris actually knew their names or it was all part of how she went through the world.

'It's all an act, y'know,' Iris had confided to her once. 'The whole "been there, done that" thing. I mean, in my case I usually have, but it's still all an act.'

Carrie approved of Iris. She was brazen, unapologetic and completely shameless. She showed up everywhere in a big red bus and nobody ever seemed to notice, almost like her entire personality broadcast that she was absolutely not going to explain herself so don't even bother asking.

Carrie found herself moving instinctively towards the main sound stage, guided by some cartography of memory. Iris appeared at her elbow.

'You're not in your trailer, I just checked.'

'I'm doing a scene, I mean she's doing a scene. Don't ask me how but I know exactly which one. This way.'

From the star-studded and startlingly sophisticated journals of Iris Wildthyme

I've got a highly refined sense for all sorts of transtemporal shenanigans. I can catch a whiff of them from miles off. So as soon as I set foot off the bus I knew we were close to the action.

Carrie was on edge, probably the first time I'd seen her do anything other than take the world by the scruff of the neck. Moving through the place like she was in a dream, drawn by a fearful magnetism towards her younger self. I took her hand as she led me and that funny little bulldog of hers through the mansions of her memory and the crowded chaos of a working soundstage. We crept through a warren of walls that were spaceships on one side and wooden flats on the other, until she finally saw herself. Hiding in the half light, gracefully hooded in her robe, beautiful and pristine as menacing figures in white armour crept towards her. Oh, but she's no ivory-towered wallflower our girl—quick as a flash she guns one down with her blaster and turns on her heel to run.

'And Cut! Print, check the gate,' shouted a beardy little fellow in a baseball cap and then the set was suddenly filled with people and activity, the trooper helped off his backside, effects reset, makeup checked, and a dozen other jobs done in the orbit of the younger Carrie Fisher—smiling and relaxed and the centre of their little shared galaxy.

'There I am,' breathed Carrie, disbelievingly. 'Princess Leia in the flesh.'

Before our eyes the scene began to falter: everyone, star, director, crew, began to slow down, slower and slower until they were standing as still as a game of statues.

'Iris, what's happening?' gasped Carrie as she instinctively tried to run towards her younger self, only to find her limbs suddenly heavy and slow.

'Look!'

Three bright silver robots faded into view around the Princess. I've seen a few robots in my time and these are something smart. Sleek, aerodynamic, Art Deco automata, they moved swiftly towards her immobile form. One lightly touched her on the temple and she crumpled out of her frozen state, caught on the way down by the second robot and cradled carefully in its metal arms.

'Something's affecting time,' I cried. 'It's like moving through treacle.'

That's when I noticed that the crew only looked frozen in place. My keen eyes and extradimensional senses spotted that they were actually still moving, almost imperceptibly, like a film advancing frame by frame.

Whatever grace we were afforded by being transdimensional travellers meant we could still move, but at a snail's pace. Try as we might we couldn't cross the few metres separating the two Carries.

'Iris, do something!'

But it was too late. The third robot carefully picked Princess Leia's blaster pistol from the unresisting hands of a props master. The three turned, looking each other in the blank circles on their smooth faces where eyes would likely be. Then, quick as they arrived, they faded from view.

Standing where Princess Leia, the young Carrie Fisher, had been moments before, I swore. Carrie swore louder and longer. It's part anger and frustration, but then she clutched her belly and doubled over and it became a vocalisation of visceral pain.

'They've stolen you from between two moments in time,' I say as it dawned on me what's going on. 'It's the same thing you felt before, rippling up and down like turbulence through your timeline. We'll get you back to the bus, you'll feel better there.' Gary panted in agreement.

'If you're going to be sick, use that dustbin thing over there.'

Back on the Celestial Omnibus, Gary gave Carrie a comforting stare while her waves of nausea subsided and Iris pecked away at a noisy old typewriter, getting her thoughts in order and planning their next move.

'Feeling better, luvvie?' asked Iris. It had taken an age to get back to the bus, but as soon as they stepped aboard they snapped back to normal speed. Iris immediately flung herself into the cab and, with a lurch, the uncanny vehicle left Elstree and England and 1976 behind and plunged into the inexplicable space between there and here.

'Did you notice, Iris? The robots?'

'Couldn't miss them. All deadly and impassive. I never like the ones that don't even care if you're there or not. Strikes me as dismissive.'

'Did you see, when they took me?' Carrie paused, trying to make sense of what they'd both seen. 'They were careful with me. Almost gentle.'

'Yes, that's good news. Looks like whatever they're up to they need you in one piece. For now anyway. There was another odd thing too.'

'It gets weirder? For real?'

'One of them took your blaster. Just as carefully as the other was carrying you.'

'But it's just a prop. Doesn't even fire squibs. Why would they ever want that?'

'Can't say I've got a clue right now. But I do know how we can find where they've taken you.'

'Iris, that's fantastic.'

'Well, I am a marvel. It goes without saying. Well, perhaps it doesn't, so it is nice to hear it now and again. It's something of a stroke of genius even if I do say so myself.'

'Iris, darling,' said Carrie, carefully not rolling her eyes. 'I'm waiting with bated breath to hear about your genius.'

'It's going to be just as much you as me,' clucked Iris, happily. 'You see, my old bus runs on more than engines and etheric beams, it's powered by affinity, the ineffable attraction that binds the multiverse together. That's how I steer my way through infinity, not just with gears and levers, but by finding the path between where I think I should be going and where I actually need to get to.'

Carrie and Gary both stared at Iris, nonplussed.

'The answer's been right in front of me all along, ever since your first funny turn. You and your other self are connected. All we have to do is find that shining thread that connects you and give it a good old pull.'

There was a long pause while Carrie stared at Iris, mouth slightly agape while Gary looked gnomically between the two women.

Oh, that's done it, thought Iris. It's all gotten a bit much for her.

A moment later Carrie broke into a bright smile, her eyes shone and she let out a long breath.

'I can do that. I know her so well, that me. Nineteen years old and just a little bit too old to be precocious but still smart as paint. I've had a long time to think about being her and being the Princess and how we're all just one and the same. Sure, it was hard sometimes and I screwed up in ways I'm glad I can't remember anymore. But if I could go back and do it again I'd still be her, still be me and still love being Leia. I should probably want to change a whole bunch of stuff but I don't. Like you said, Iris, all those twists and tangles: I wouldn't know which thread to pull that wouldn't unravel the whole damn lot. I don't even need to look for that special thread, I've been hanging onto it my whole life.'

She smiled, triumphantly. 'Wanna go rescue a Princess?'

Extract from Carrie Fisher's private diary (unpublished)

So even after all that bickering, Iris came through for me. Sat me right up there in the driver's cab with Gary on my lap, placed my hands on the wheel and a crown of lights on my head. It tingled and made me feel warm all over, invigorated, every tiny hair on my body standing to attention.

But the real deal was going on inside. In the gut and in the head I could feel myself being pulled backwards, my whole life unspooling before me as I raced giddily back through each scene. Oh, there were some I wanted to hide from, the hardest and darkest of days, but there was so much sweetness too. Everyone I had loved, my daughter, my mom, lovers and friends, whirling past me like the most frenetic of surprise parties.

All those memories were mine again, if only for an instant.

Until I find the end of the thread I have been following and steal a glance at our destination. A shining fortress among the stars, remote and forbidding. There I'm imprisoned, illuminated by moonlight, yet standing proud and strong. How did I never realise how beautiful I was? I feel a surge of love for her and it pulls me onwards towards that shining white figure until the moonlight is so bright it is all I can see.

'You did it, girl!' crowed Iris. 'We made it!'

Carrie blinked and opened her eyes. She was back in the cab of Iris's bus, where she had been all along, despite feeling like she'd been on an incredible journey.

'We made it?' murmured Carrie, as if awakening from a deep sleep. 'We're here?'

'You did great. Sat there like some bold seer in a trance, guiding us through our own mischance,' Iris continued, waxing lyrical. 'A few clever tweaks from me, here and there, just to keep us on track, but you got us where we need to be right in the nick of time.'

Iris fussed about her, adjusting controls and disconnecting her from the apparatus. Carrie noted that she'd found time to change again—a wafting kaftan of midnight blues and silvers set off with a turban that would have made Norma Desmond envious.

'Where are we?'

'Far, far out in deep space. Some kind of big old space station. Let's go have a nosey around.'

Iris, Carrie and Gary stepped gingerly out into the gloom. The bus was parked, incongruous as ever, at the edge of a large room that looked like a huge, domed Victorian glasshouse. Grey cast-iron columns and frames supported huge panels of clear glass that revealed a sparse starscape with wisps of purple nebulae. Encircling the dark room were large, regularly spaced cylinders on plinths: each a bell jar containing a single humanoid figure.

They crept forward, hardly daring to breathe. A bright moon emerged from the penumbra of an unseen planet and the room was bathed in ethereal white light.

'Iris, look… in the jars.'

Carrie recognised every single figure, each frozen in place: the swooning, satin-draped frame of Fay Wray in *King Kong*; Ursula Andress wet from the sea and holding a conch from *Dr No*; Raquel Welch in skins from *One Million Years BC*; Jane Fonda, bouffant and lamé-clad as Barbarella; on and on past the immobile icons of the silver screen they crept.

'Carrie,' Iris touched her arm lightly and pointed. Ahead of them was Carrie's younger self, encased in glass and locked in a defiant contrapposto with one hand on her hip and the other with blaster raised—Princess Leia in all her glory.

'Ladies,' boomed a voice. 'Welcome to my collection.'

The room filled with light as each cylinder became spotlight bright. Carrie gasped in shock and dropped Gary. With a hiss of steam, a circular hatch spiralled open and a platform rotated upwards from the centre of the floor. On it was a large throne-like chair flanked by screens and control panels. Slumped in the chair was a man in a formless grey jumpsuit, sallow faced with avaricious, dangerous eyes.

'I call that flashy,' said Iris. 'Coming up like an organ player at the Ritz. Have you been under there this whole time, you ridiculous man?'

'What? I…' he spluttered. Then rallied angrily, 'Guards, seize them!'

The same sleek robotic forms they had encountered at the studios glided from between the cylinders and in moments had caught Iris and Carrie in their strong metallic grasps. They dragged them struggling and cursing towards the central plinth.

'So, let me see what we have here.' The robots pushed Carrie and Iris forward, holding them from behind in an immovable grip. 'Two battered old baggages?'

'We'll see who's battered when I get my hands on you,' retorted Iris, angrily trying to raise her hands like a pugilist.

'Let these women go, you creep,' demanded Carrie. 'You're not keeping me or anyone else in a glass case.' She nodded towards the cylinders.

'Ugh.' He crumpled his face in disgust. 'I don't want *you* in my collection.'

Carrie glared at him, realising not for the first time that powerful men weren't always smart.

'Look around you. The finest, most pristine and iconic beauties ever seen. Unique and perfect, each and every one.' His voice took on a lascivious note. 'And all mine.'

'You're disgusting,' said Carrie, her voice hardening. 'I've known people like you all my life. My hometown is full of men like you. You want to control everything about us, have us look how you want, do whatever you want. You don't want real people, you want life-sized action figures.'

'Listen here, mister Collector,' said Iris. 'All this grabbing famous women out of time and space, as well as being creepy, it's incredibly dangerous to the nature of reality itself!'

'They're iconic!' he crowed. 'Nobody else will ever have a collection like this.'

Iris and Carrie exchanged worried glances.

'How did you even get them here?' asked Iris. 'This stuff is all way too advanced for you.'

'My guards bring them to me,' he murmured. 'They bring me whatever I need.'

'Guards,' mused Iris. 'I thought this setup looked familiar. A circle of cells and a central guard station. This is a Panopticon Prison. That means you're in the wrong seat, chum.'

'He's a prisoner?' asked Carrie.

'This is a very advanced prison ship. He's an inmate turned gaoler,' cried Iris triumphantly.

'Oh, aren't you the clever one.' His face curled in disgust. 'You've found me out. I'd better dispose of the evidence then: Guards, throw them into deep space!'

Before the guards had a chance to move, a bang echoed through the chamber as smoke and sparks exploded from the plinth. Lights flashed erratically across the controls and the robots jerked and flailed, releasing both women before falling still and silent.

In one bound Iris was on the platform and there was a *crack* as she delivered her best right hook.

Carrie stared in astonishment to where Gary stood, still panting, leg cocked over the soaking and short-circuited control relays.

Extract from Carrie Fisher's private diary (unpublished)

So, that was that. I hugged Gary and gave him every dog treat I had. Iris treated her bruised knuckles with ice from the bar aboard the bus and her nerves with a stiff G&T. According to Iris, who looked at the prison data banks, this mysterious Collector was just a grubby little man from mid-C21st Earth with a sense of entitlement and a taste for unobtainable women. He didn't know that the latest movie star he was stalking was a genuine Outer Space Princess, though I gotta say I feel like I got my thunder stolen on that one. (Iris won't tell me who, she's being discreet for once, but apparently if you know what to look for it's a dead giveaway.)

Now, this kid's mother didn't take kindly to her daughter having to put up with the same misogynist shit that every other woman on Earth has to on a daily basis. This Empress set the law on him: in this case the kind of interplanetary law that locks you in a deep space prison for the rest of your days. Score one for the Matriarchy, finally. But, something went wrong like it invariably does and somehow he's the only one who survives. Now, you or I would probably have gotten the super powerful time-travelling robots to take us home. Oh no. He takes his sick little obsession up to the next level.

'So, what are we going to do with him?' I ask Iris. She's elbow deep in control circuits and halfway through her second drink. There's a pop and a fizz and the robots hum back to life. They look at her in a "your wish is my command" sort of way. Difficult, given they've not really got features.

'Give him a taste of his own medicine,' she says. 'Throw him in one of the empty cells.'

The three robot guards immediately glide into action and carry the unconscious lump effortlessly away.

'We can't just leave him here, can we?' I wonder, aloud.

'It's not up to us, really. He's still under sentence according to intergalactic law. I'll let the Empress know as soon as we've finished using the robot guards to send everyone back where they belong. I'd take them all back by bus but waking them up would mean a lot of difficult questions and, frankly, it's a hell of a lot of work.' Iris set down her empty glass and sat heavily in the big chair. 'I'm knackered.'

'Will they remember?' I sit down wearily next to her, Gary on my lap.

'Do you remember? You're one of them, don't forget,' asked Iris, kindly.

I'd had time to have a good look at my younger self. Frozen in place, she didn't look real. I've been looking at her, at that version of me, most of my life.

'Iris, my memories... For a second there I had them all back and I'm so, so glad. Thank you. Some of it's fading like a dream now and I'm not even sure which bits are gone. But I know I didn't remember any of this at all.'

'There you are then, lovely. The robots can pop everyone back from in between the moments they were stolen from. Time will be restored and you'll all be none the worse for wear.'

'And then what?' I ask. How do you follow a day like this?

'And then I'll take you home.' Iris patted my hand. 'We could both do with a rest. Though there's always time for a quick holiday on the way.' She smiles and there's a wicked glint in her eye. 'Next stop, planet of the pandas!'

The Most Faithful Panda in the World

Richard Wright

Edinburgh, Jan 18th, 1872

Dear Diary,

This is ridiculous. I need a better numbering system. Curse of the time traveller you see. Chronological diary entries don't work at all. Three pages back it's September 2327. I've got five different entries in three different journals for 31st December 1999. Someday there's going to be a biographer, probably, and she's going to have a nervous breakdown trying to piece all this together.

Note to self. Better numbering system.

Second note to self. Concentrate.

It's amazing what goes through your head when the world's ending.

It's 1872, and I don't think we've done enough. I'm sitting in a graveyard in Edinburgh, waiting for a god to be born. Panda's with me. You'd think his exposure to the Scottish elements over the last decade would have toughened him up, but he's shivering to bits beneath the tatty remains of the disguise we cobbled together when all this started.

It's been hardest on Panda. I know that. He soldiered through it though, faithful as ever, to sit with me at this moment.

Our backs are to a mighty headstone, the engraving long faded so that it would be impossible to tell who it once honoured even if the sun weren't down. Somebody with delusions of grandeur, given its size. Now it's a bit of shelter from the wind while we stare at the overgrown patch of ground opposite, with its tiny marker, and wait. The ground there is glowing like it's about to burst into flame, and to be honest that might be what comes next. Some kind of explosion? I'm not sure. Don't really know what to expect. I should have asked when I took the Godseed in the first place, half a lifetime ago, but I'd had a few swift ones and you know how it goes, diary. Wasn't thinking.

At some point a dramatic *thing* will happen, and a god will emerge from that little grave, and then?

Well, that's the question. That's what we've been waiting to find out. If we haven't done enough then it will dance through the city's squalor, embark on slaughter, and I've no idea how we'll get in the way of any of that. Panda and me are pretty handy in a pinch, but we're *not* gods and it *is*. Seems a bit uneven.

If we haven't done enough.

Panda reported at our lunchtime meeting that the grave had finally started to warm up, and now there can't be more than an hour left until emergence. Everything we've done, all the little changes just under the radar, to try and make this city better than its urges. Is it going to be enough?

I need to distract myself. Same thoughts going round me head. I found Panda's journal earlier. Had a quick shufty through, but there's less in it that you'd think given how much time he's had on his paws. Poor mite's exhausted, sitting there half asleep even though he's freezing his socks off in what might be the last hour of his life. Sure he won't notice if I pass the time with some of his observations. Might be something in there that helps. He's been watching this place for a long time.

A very long time.

Let's see what he has to say.

I probably won't have time to fill anything else in here, diary. When the god comes, it's going to be fast. If this is the last you hear from me, it's been nice writing in you.

See you on t'other side.

18th November, 1870

Her greatest triumph, she said. The act that would single-handedly transform the Old Town of Edinburgh from regressive slum to progressive beacon. 'Why don't you come along love,' she said. 'Take a break from the graveyard shift. That's no way for a healthy stuffed Panda to be spending all his days.'

I have spent several years now pretending to be a grieving terrier camped next to the grave of a man who once had the cheek to imprison me. Waiting to see whether the god that would be born of his corpse was a nice deity or a naughty deity, while Iris has buzzed around the city trying to make it in some indefinable way a "better place". My grim undertaking is not the result of some poetical whim, but rather the product of Iris's own inebriated clumsiness. I point that out to her whenever an opportune moment arises, but she still makes it sound as though I am some heartbroken emo teenager writing mopey poetry among the tombstones.

Still, the end is surely in sight, and Iris's latest project cannot be faulted for its ambition.

Three years ago, in 1867 she immersed herself in the local women's suffrage movement, attending meetings, planting ideas, probably making sure everybody drank too much and fell over. Last year, 1869, through a campaign of blackmail and bribery targeting the medical fraternity, she helped seven women led by one Sophia Jex-Blake to become the first to matriculate at a British university. Today they will sit their anatomy exams.

A triumph for humanity! A social breakthrough that will echo right the way to the halls of legislature! A modernist revolution that will bring humanity one step closer to true enlightenment! Edinburgh will rejoice!

So I thought.

I scampered through the streets from Greyfriars church to Surgeons' Hall, the now somewhat bedraggled grey fur coat I make use of as a disguise wrapped tight around me. Away from my usual stomping grounds I caused the raising of many curious eyebrows, handsome beast that I am, but the closer I got to the university the less attention I drew.

At first I assumed that the excitement among the many male students I dodged was due to some universal sense of occasion. We were, after all, present for a triumphant moment in history. I knew the seven women had been given a rough time over the course of their studies, but that's par for the course when revolution is in the air. Influenced perhaps too heavily by my extensive library of movies, in which the outsider is accepted by his or her peers at the triumphant end of their travails, with many a tear shed in the moment of acknowledgement, I assumed that they would have won over the hearts and minds of their male peers by now.

This clearly was not the case. The crowd of chanting, placard-waving students waiting outside Surgeons' Hall in the rain was not filled with a sense of purpose or occasion as befitted the emancipating endeavour that they attended. Instead there was anger in the air, even hatred. These women, it was now clear to me, were not welcome. The crowd was there to block them from the very institute where they would sit their exams.

I hopped up on to a wall as the women approached, led of course by Iris herself. They paused when they saw the crowd, now a hundred strong at least, and Iris turned her head to whisper words that were probably as offensive as they were encouraging. Whatever she offered put steel into the girls, and they resumed their march forwards.

One young man began to shout the slogan on the placards, and the rest joined in. *"Midwives not doctors! Midwives not doctors!"* Very disappointing. These were students after all, and would it have been too much to expect a little wit or wordplay?

The women would not slow, and the first projectiles were thrown. I wanted to drop down and start biffing hooters, because while they were entitled to their Neanderthal opinions I did not concur that this allowed them to proceed to a full lynching.

They surged forward before I could act.

I realised my mistake then. Iris had understated the hostility the women had engendered through their assault on patriarchal traditions. This was not a protest. This was a mob, and the boys would do whatever they could to prevent the girls from sitting the exam. Surely somebody from the faculty, a stern professor, would emerge from the open doors and calm the situation?

No. The doors slammed, leaving the Edinburgh Seven and Iris to their fate. I caught one glimpse of her as the spitting throng—allegedly the most intelligent and best educated young men of their generation—descended on them, and then all was chaos.

Just last night I had been whiling away the long hours of my watch squinting at the pages of one of Iris's diaries outlining the facts of a previous attempt to improve Edinburgh's nature. She has dozens of diaries, leaves them all over the place. Some have only got a single entry. I slipped this one from her bag when we met for the usual lunchtime stew, and hell mend her if she's upset. Having all but abandoned me for the last decade, I refuse to feel guilty at taking a small piece of her with me for company while I sat about my task.

I will leave space here to copy out its contents, then return to the matter of the Surgeons' Hall riot.

Jun 23rd, 1864

Sometimes it only takes a single person willing to do the right thing, and just a nudge to make it so. Henry Littlejohn is one such. Cheated a bit and looked him up—doctor, trailblazing early forensic scientist, might have been an inspiration for Sherlock Holmes. Nice chap. Turns out he's going to be writing up a report on city sanitation next year. Bit of prodding, bit of needling, and I've already got him looking askance at the miasma of disease in the Old Town and wondering what the solution might be. When he's asked to put that report together, it could be the beginning of something... well... fresher.

Iris Wildthyme. Saving the world one privy at a time.

Still, it all adds up. Little tweaks. Nothing flashy. Haven't drawn the wrong sort of attention yet, and have to keep it that way.

I thought Thomas Askern would be another easy nudge. Public executioner, up from York to hang the Ratho Murderer. Bad business all round, some bloke called George Bryce slit the throat of a young cook in one of the big houses outside Ratho. Loads of witnesses, straightforward verdict, and the times are what they are. Can't change the death sentence, but what's as ugly is the show of it, all in public for the world to ogle. Every time there's an execution it feels like the city takes to the streets to watch. Whole families. They bring picnics, shout and cheer while the deed gets done. I can't be having that. A god being born in a city where death is a spectator sport? Doesn't bear thinking how that might influence things.

So I met the executioner the night before. Tracked him down to *The White Hart* where he was tucking into a pie and a pint. Not much of a looker, Thomas Askern, but he seemed glad of a bit of company, and it went right to his head when I said I recognised him.

'Ah miss, warm's the old heart to meet a fan, miss. It's a thankless job I do, miss. So few what appreciate the art of it.'

'Oooo, a craftsman,' I says. 'Tell 'em all, I do. Anybody can string 'em up, but that Askern, he knows how to make it quick and clean.'

He looked a bit dubious at that, as though "quick" and "clean" were not terms he had often given thought to. 'It's all in the measuring miss. Get the rope measured out right and everything follows.'

‘Must be hard, with all the noise.’

‘What’s that miss?’

‘The crowds. All that hollering. Bet it would be easier done in private, eh?’

‘Oh I don’t know about that miss.’

I felt a little of my ambition leak away at his certainty. ‘Really, Mr Askern? You wouldn’t rather be conducting the business away from prying eyes? Bit of dignity for the condemned?’ A tankard shattered somewhere behind me as a fight broke out, but Askern barely noticed. His eyes had got a bit misty.

‘Dignity, miss? Oh, they don’t deserve dignity. Not them as dangle. They’ve got debts to pay, and people needs to see them make their accounting. Crowd’s got to see. Crowd’s got to cheer. You can’t have silent justice, see? That’s how I know I done a good job. The small snap and the big cheer.’ He drew his knife through the pie and pink juice dribbled out, pooling on his plate. I decided I’d best be drinking on an empty stomach. Askern though? He saw it, and he licked his lips. I swear he was a heartbeat from shedding a happy tear.

I could kiss goodbye to tapping into some deep buried thread of existential dread running through this man. No noble speeches on the gallows for this one. No downing tools and leading the crowds to understand the error of their ways by example. Thomas Askern was a believer, and a man who liked his work a lot more than I had assumed possible. George Bryce was going to swing for the amusement of the masses.

My spirits tumbled as I resigned myself to the worst possible course.

‘Wait right there,’ I told him. ‘Auntie Iris is getting the drinks in.’

I will bloody well improve this city, whether it wants improving or not. I have to remind myself sometimes why I’m doing all this. Making changes. Altering paths. Not my usual style at all. When it gets muddled up like this, there’s one particular diary entry I reread, from a couple of years ago. It’s well-thumbed already, barely legible in places. I’ll reproduce it below, give myself time to put my thoughts together about the hanging.

Here it is, with Panda’s bits too.

Sept 18th, 1861

It's harder than I thought, trying to improve a city without the Universe noticing, but I've got to find a way to do it. Go too slow and the little goods you do don't stack up fast enough to turn the place around. Go too fast and you'll be noticed. Heck, it might even be somebody like me doing the noticing, and I'd definitely want to poke around and put things back how they were. Interfering with the course of historical events? Can't be having that.

Three long years we've been on the slow track. Hard to imagine how Panda must be feeling, poor mite. Listening to the rain lash down from inside this coffee shop where I've eaten lunch every day for three years, with the thunder loud enough that the owner Mr Traill jumps at every crack, makes me shudder. Panda though, he's out in it doing the hard graft. Horrible.

I'm not saying I'd swap places with him, of course. Bloody hell, no. Wouldn't catch me out there on a day like this, and it's not like being inside drinking the tar they pass off as coffee is a marvellous adventure he's missing out on. Doesn't know how lucky he is, actually. I'm doing him a favour.

Besides it's not as though I could pass myself off as a Skye Terrier, is it? Not even in dim light with me shabbiest fake furs on. Had to be him.

Simple enough plan at the time. John Gray died with the Godseed on him. Don't know if he lifted it from me stuff on purpose or by accident, but it doesn't matter now. His death wasn't enough to bring the thing to term, so now it's sucking in the character of Edinburgh to finish the job. Problem is, Edinburgh's foul—especially the Old Town where he's buried. The god that's born from such a place? Wouldn't want to meet it in a dark alley. Or a brightly lit one. Wouldn't want to meet it full stop. It'll be all pestilence and misery and resentment.

That's why we have to stay. When it's born, we have to be here to meet it. Only problem is we don't know when that's going to happen. No skipping to the good bits this time. We've got to take the long road, same as everybody else. Can't risk missing a single day.

Finding the corpse of his dog was a stroke of luck. It had tried to stay by its master's grave—can you even imagine the devotion? It couldn't stay that close to the budding seed without paying the price though. Now it's buried with its master, and that was where I got me plan. Greyfriars Bobby is a legend, see. He wasn't supposed to die in the weeks following his master. He hung about for longer. Much longer.

Good thing Panda doesn't know the story. Not sure he would have agreed to take the dog's place if so. Seems to have got it in his head that little Bobby might have stayed by his master's side for a couple of years, no more. Can't imagine where he got that notion. I mean, maybe I should have put him straight, but...

Well.

Somebody has to watch the grave. On the day the god emerges we need to be there.

Every day I meet him at the coffee shop and buy him stew. He has to eat it from a bowl on the ground, because he's supposed to be a dog and History's watching. It used to be that he was always late. No pockets for a watch in the fake fur disguise I rustled up from a throw I found over a seat at the back of the bus. I'd wait for hours before he slumped in, depressed and moaning. All that time wasted where I could have been finding little wrongs to put right.

There. A cannon blast from the castle. The Time Gun, they call it. My idea of course. Needed a reliable signal, something to stir him from the doldrums and get him over here. Massive cannon blasting out every day, one o'clock on the dot. Useful for ships on the Forth to set maritime clocks to help with navigation on the open seas. Also useful for summoning Pandas. Just took a word in the right ear, and Auntie Iris is your uncle.

He'll be coming now. I dread this bit. He's half the Panda he was, in stature and temperament. We're not made for the long road, but that's what's ahead of us. A long, weary, grubby road, and nary a sign in place that we're accomplishing a bloody thing. Come the end, the god could still rip us to pieces and take the world for pudding.

I wish I'd been more careful. Panda tries to hide his irritation at me, but I know what's in his heart. Well, his journal at any rate, because I stole it. Here's his exact words on the subject, verbatim.

17th March, 1858
Of course she lost the Godseed.

There are inevitabilities written into the clockwork of the Universe, certainties around which reality winds itself. On worlds where suns rise, they will also set. If a child is born, then one day it will necessarily die. If you step on the wrong butterfly then at some point in the following centuries you will have caused a genocidal fascist dictatorship, and that's on your head, and who on earth decided that butterflies should be Time's punctuation marks in the first place, that's what I want to know? We'd all be a lot better off without the butterflies is all I'm saying.

Sorry. Shouldn't drink and diarise. Irresponsible.

I was talking about irresponsibility. Bloody irresponsible, giving Iris a Godseed. Never saw it myself. Apparently sucks up the energies of a powerful death and blooms a ruddy, actual god that's imprinted with the persona of that energy. Joyless way to go about procreating if you ask me, but different strokes and all that.

It's very important that the wrong person doesn't die with a Godseed on them. Lots of bad gods came about that way, and demanded blood sacrifices, and dark rituals, and cheese before bedtime, and everything bad in the world.

Iris has got deaths to spare of course, like all of her kind, so she was entrusted with one to keep until the critical moment. Not sure a god with Iris's inclinations would be a totally good thing, but I suppose she's got a good soul in her. And apparently you can only be a Godseed surrogate once, and all the better candidates had already had a go.

So they gave her one. Probably held their breath while they did it. No idea how long she'd been carrying it around, but my word, her face when she realised it was gone. Right after we'd done Christmas in Edinburgh.

On the bus we climbed, our hangovers weighing us down, our pride still in that grotty little cell, Iris convinced that she'd proven some stupid point or other about how slumming it in dismal taverns was every bit as fine as cocktails at the Ritz. Into the vortex we roared, too ill even to contemplate the hair of the dog. As is often our custom, we each retired to separate corners and opened our journals. I was reaching for my thesaurus, stuck on a particularly trying turn of phrase, when she dropped her pen.

I've fished out the very journal entry she was composing at that moment, hoping it might make clearer how it is I've come to live in the graveyard I find myself in today. All she offers is this.

No Time, The Vortex, Everywhere & Nowhere, Sort Of...
The night of December 24th 1857 was as messy as it gets.

We weren't intending to do anything but make merry, me and Panda, and by heaven we managed that. Edinburgh's a magnificent city for merry. Always has been, which is what I took him there to prove.

'No Iris,' he pomped at me. 'It might *become* a party city, but it hasn't always been the case. Edinburgh was as rotten as everywhere else, back in the day.'

Poor mite. All the stuff I've shown him and he still doesn't understand how good times work. They're better where it's bleak. If you want the best time, you go to the grimmest dive. The further you get from that, the more wines you can choose from or fancy burgers they serve, the more detached and forgettable the revelry gets.

So I took him to Christmas 1857, right in the heart of the Old Town, and it were grim all right. Tenements crowded to the rafters, generations of families sharing single rooms. Effluent slopping about the cobbles and down the closes, freezing in runnels as the dissolute huddled in doorways. Acrid smoke on the air weren't near strong enough to mask the stench. Fighting in alleys, blood in the shadows, the rich long since evacuated to the shiny New City far above. The Old Town were filth and shame rounded up and compressed into just a couple of square miles, a concentration camp of squalor.

And yet.

And yet.

From the first slug of whisky at *The Last Drop* in the Grassmarket, looking out at the gallows where the city wreaked ugly vengeance on those who had wronged it, surrounded by raucous Irish workmen letting the season wash over them with song and hard spirits, to the epic pub crawl up to the university and back down Cockburn street (pronounced Coburn, like somebody worked out afterwards what they'd done there and tried to pretend they hadn't meant it), to the boozy smear of Fleshmarket Close, and the scrum to get to the bar at the tiny *Halfway House* sitting halfway up the cliff of steps between Cockburn on high and Market Street down low, I showed him that Edinburgh was one of the greatest party cities there ever was and that it always had been.

Even waking up in a grimy cell the next morning didn't properly change that I won the argument, though as the exhausted watchman swung open the door to send us on our way, his irritating, yappy little dog barking at our heels, Panda harrumphed as though it had. The watchman coughed wetly as he watched me stuff me belongings back in me bag and pockets—I wish I could remember emptying them for him the night before, if only for the look on his face when it kept on coming.

'Merry Christmas, pet,' I told him as we climbed the stairs to be on our way. 'Get yourself to bed, eh? Sounds nasty, that. Be the death of you if you're not careful.'

17th March, 1858

That's when she dropped her pen and turned a peculiar white.

'Blooming hell,' she spluttered, and began rummaging in her bra.

I averted my eyes. 'Dear god woman, some decorum please. My nerves are quite jangled enough!'

She threw the bus into a handbrake turn that repositioned my stomach in truly unfortunate ways. Not a bally word of explanation, just a hard landing back in Edinburgh, a rush to the watch house where we'd spent the night, and the calamitous realisation that more haste does not make more speed.

'What do you mean he's dead? We just saw him! Right as a trivet he was!'

'Well,' I tried to interject, 'he did have a bit of a cough...'

The watchman behind the desk leaned back, rightfully nervous. 'Tuberculosis ma'am, as your little... ah... friend observes. Are you sure it's Christmas Eve you're talking about? John Gray was the only man stationed here that night, drew the short straw, but he's definitely... well...'

'Impossible. When did he die?'

'Just last month. February fifteenth. Small funeral up at Greyfriars. Me and the lads had a whip round for the stone.'

'February?' Iris fumbled a pocket watch from beneath her shawl. 'February 1858? Bloody hell, we overshot!'

'I've told you before about emergency stops you know. The old bus isn't as grippy as it used to be. We skidded a month or two, that's all.' I didn't understand what the fuss was then, but she filled me in as we climbed up the street to the kirkyard. By the time we got there I was livid.

'Oh you've done it now. A god. A great big bloody god! Hang on though, he can't have had the seed on him when he kicked the bucket, can he? Maladjusted newborn gods are conspicuous. We'd have noticed one hanging about.'

Iris strode through the kirkyard gates, the great square box of the church facing her down in the frosty morning light, then darted off the path to march up and down the tombstones, looking for the right name. 'He's just a fella, Panda. Just an ordinary human. Full of life right enough, but he's a shot glass of the stuff. I'm a tankard.'

What were tombstones to Iris were oppressive, clammy towers to me, and soon she was out of my sight. I tried very hard not to scamper, for as a being of diminutive stature I work tirelessly to retain some shred of dignity, but strutted as fast as I possibly could. 'Your point?'

'Not enough in him, love. He'll have got the ball rolling, but it needs to draw in more. Background noise. Ambient personality. It's imprinting from the city itself, and all hell's going to follow.'

'Oh come now, don't be dramatic. Edinburgh's not that bad. I'm sure it will make a lovely little god.'

At which point I tripped over the damp, abandoned corpse of John Gray's annoying little dog, and whacked face first into the grave dirt covering the man over.

That was how we met Greyfriar's Bobby for the second time.

Sept 18th, 1861

Twice was all we got. Greyfriars Bobby was unexpectedly, unremarkably dead, just weeks after his master.

That left an opening. I'd already been turning over how to keep an eye on the place when people were regularly chased off the property as potential grave robbers. We buried the doggy in with its master, popped back to the bus for some material, and whipped Panda up a little outfit.

And so his watch began.

At least with the Time Gun in place he gets down here in time for one good meal a day, and it keeps me on track to meet him too. This afternoon the oddest thing happened. A little spark, that made the journey seem a little shorter.

Five minutes after the gun went off, I went to the door of the coffee house and opened it to let him in. The stew was already on the floor by the table, and he crouched over it with his back to the room so nobody could see the little spoon he used to scoop it up. As he ate, I filled him in on what I'd been up to, and he murmured replies under his breath.

As he finished his meal he seemed to shrink at the thought of wandering back into the storm. After some early attempts to shoe him away, the groundskeeper had erected a little shelter for Greyfriars Bobby, but it was still cold and wet out there. 'It must be soon, mustn't it Iris?' His voice was heavy, as though he already knew I was going to lie but wanted me to do it anyway. 'The little dog can't have lasted more than a couple of years, could it? In the story?'

'I'm sure it didn't. Is there anything from the grave?'

'Dead as a... poor choice of simile, sorry. Nothing to report.'

'Right you are then. Same time tomorrow, I suppose.'

He nodded and stood, and two tables along an old lady also rose. She drew her shawl around herself as she approached, a little nervous.

'Pardon dearie, but is that your dog?'

'No. It comes across from the church for a bowl of stew every day. Some stray, I suppose.'

Panda slumped, inhabiting the role more than I liked.

'Oh no, dearie. Not a stray. That has to be Greyfriars Bobby. Most faithful dog in the world. Still watches over his poor dead master, so he does. All weather, rain or snow or shine, he sits by the grave to be near the man who loved him best on this world. Beautiful, so it is. This dog's a hero. Can I pet him, do you think?'

I was going to advise against it, but the oddest thing had happened. Panda seemed to have grown as she spoke. I nodded cautiously, and to my amazement he failed to offer a retort when she rubbed his head. 'Going to tell the girls about this. Every day, you say? Always here?'

I nodded, and she chuckled with delight. As she shuffled towards the door, Panda followed her out, all but strutting now.

Give him a poor dead dog to impersonate, and he is crushed. Give him a legend to inhabit, and that Panda rises up like a phoenix from the ashes.

And his legend grows. Now I can hardly get near him at the coffee house for fans wanting to see him, or touch his fur. He's careful with it, but he draws from their energy to get him through.

They draw from him too. A little hope. A little comfort that there are good and honest things in the world.

That's what he's doing now. Greyfriars Bobby, my Panda, is spreading a smear of goodness over these streets through his presence and his legend.

All right, he's using outright deception to do it, and it's gone to his head a bit, but right now we'll take what we can get.

Edinburgh is a smidgeon nicer because of one small dog who isn't, and every little bit helps.

June 24th, 1864

The hanging of the Ratho Murderer took place on the Royal Mile leading up to the castle, near the corner of the High Street and George IV Bridge. All I could see was the backs of heads, a bobbing, lice-ridden sea of them between me and the gallows. The morning was cold and grey, and the smell of unwashed bodies cloyed in the still air.

My hangover was of cosmic scale, so vast that it dulled my senses. I'd had breakfasts aplenty to soak things up, but if the business had taken any longer then I'd have risked jettisoning a kettle load of oats and sausage in properly explosive fashion.

Fortunately Askern was in worse shape than me. Man could hold his liquor to a point, but in the end he was only human. I watched him stagger as he climbed the steps up to the platform, and when the crowd roared its approval he swayed on the spot like he was being battered by a tide. I wasn't close enough to see his face in any detail, but his pallor was snow white. From a distance he looked like death, which was appropriate given the occasion.

A roar of hatred went up as George Bryce was led onto the Mile and walked towards the gallows. I didn't get a glimpse of him until he climbed the steps, but could follow his course by the trajectories of the stones and rotten veg arcing through the air to find him. The city was a unified lynch-mob, incensed by the exaggerated stories that had been circling through the taverns in the months since Bryce was arrested. Just the previous night, while drinking Askern under the table, I'd overheard one man swear on his life that the Ratho Murderer was eight feet tall and had bitten the heads off three women.

Against such tales, the frightened, confused man who mounted the gallows that morning, chaperoned by two disgruntled guards who had each taken their share of the projectiles intended for the condemned, was so disappointing that the crowd's roar reduced momentarily to a murmur on seeing him. I hoped for a moment that it was conscience that had stilled them, but it was only surprise. There was blood on the air, and the crowd had a craving.

'Always give the people what they want,' Askern slurred at me as I helped him to his lodgings the previous night. I felt a pang of guilt, remembering that. I don't think the executioner was a good man, and I can't approve of the satisfaction he found in his work, but it was 1864, and he was no more or less a product of his time. I might have wished him to be better than he was, but wishes don't make fishes in this world.

Somehow Askern had tied off the noose and set Bryce up on the trapdoor. All was ready. I wanted to look away, but if all played out as I thought it might then I was more responsible than anybody there. I had to watch.

The attending minister stepped back, having given final prayers that nobody could hear.

A signal was given.

The crowd hushed.

The trapdoor opened, and Bryce began to drop out of sight, behind the black drapes that ran from the edge of the platform to the ground.

Then he stopped, barely through the trapdoor to his thighs.

Askern hadn't measured the rope against the condemned at all when he tied the noose. He'd barely been capable of tying the knot at all.

Bryce's neck didn't break, and he began to kick and twitch as he rotated gently on the rope, his face purpling further with each turn. Askern stumbled forward, mouth open in horror, perhaps to cut Bryce down and start again, but one of the guards held him back. Dead was dead, and this would get it done.

The crowd jeered for the first minute, but it was increasingly awkward, and soon turned to moans of sympathy and horror. It took the man five minutes to die, an inelegant horror of a thing that wrote vivid descriptions of messy mortality upon the memories of all those watching. His tongue and eyes bulged, his face turned colours no person should be, his bowels and bladder loosed.

After the first two minutes the crowd began to jeer again, but their anger was not at the murderer. It was the guards and Askern himself who found themselves the victims. It was the sound of a tide turning, of a city waking up to itself. It was shame turned to rage, and the beginning of the end for public executions in Edinburgh.

18th November, 1870

What on earth is it with Edinburgh and mobs? Baying crowds at a hanging, and a bleating mob at what should usually have been the least remarkable thing on earth—university exams. Is rioting some sort of sport here?

I craned forwards from where I perched on the wall enclosing Surgeons' Hall, straining for some glimpse of Iris. Every now and again I got one, a blaze of colour amidst the wintry browns and blacks of the students.

No punches had been thrown yet, though other unsavoury things had found their targets and some of the girls were dripping with filth. Some violent shoving was being undertaken though, and to my surprise and delight the women had the upper hand. Iris's bag was whirling, and the Edinburgh Seven were making progress.

To what end though? This was not improving the city's character, not in the least. The doors were closed, and bolted too if I were any judge. The women could drive hard toward their goal, towards the examinations against which they so sorely wished to test themselves, but they would find themselves pinned outside, the mob at their back and the stout oak of the doors denying them still. Their peers did not wish them to succeed. The university had elected to keep them in their place. There was violence on the streets. All was shame and ugliness.

There was a shriek of metal from the doors, and as I turned they opened. I did not see clearly who had cleared the way, but the silhouette that shrank away was not that of a stern master. I would swear I saw the outline of skirts. A cleaner? Some secretarial personage who had perhaps been inspired by those fierce, intelligent women fighting for rights that should never have been denied them? I like to think so.

The boys saw it too of course, and redoubled their efforts. The women fell back, one pace, then two, and now there were bloodied fists and noses.

I caught Iris's eye, and her face spasmed with what I usually consider desperation, but which she would no doubt claim as inspiration. Her arm shot out to point at me.

'Look!' She bellowed over the mania. 'Look up there! LOOK AT THE CUTE LITTLE DOGGY!'

My cheeks flushed. I wanted to run away and hide. Instead I puffed out my chest, trying hard to look both noble and endearing.

One of the protestors cried out: 'Is that Greyfriars Bobby?'

They all turned. Performance anxiety struck. So many eyes looking my way! I dared a little dance, and jaws dropped.

The girls, seeing their chance, bolted for the door. Before the mob could regather themselves, they were inside. The doors slammed closed, and it was over.

What awaited the girls inside, I do not know. More disruption perhaps, but we did all we could. Iris will tell me the rest, I'm sure.

We got them in there, and we had help. Somebody opened that door, not because we tricked them or forced them. They did it because they thought it was the right thing to do.

A little difference, but it might be enough.

We'll find out, soon enough.

Jan 19th, 1872

There aren't going to be any more public hangings in Edinburgh. Public sanitation improvements are underway in the Old Town, and less children die of disease than before. The Edinburgh Seven sat their exams, despite somebody setting a panicked sheep loose in the exam hall, and when they were done a group of boys who were appalled at what their mates had done saw them safely through the gathered protestors to their homes. Some of them continued to act as unofficial bodyguards to the women as they went to and from classes in the following weeks.

The legend of Greyfriars Bobby grows by the day. Some people weep with a sad sort of joy to hear it.

Today we finally let the little dog die, fourteen years after he died the first time around. We had to find a suitable corpse, but the streets aren't lacking for dead dogs. Can't say it looked much like Panda, but hardly anybody really knows one mutt from another. It's the legend that counts.

There's talk of a plaque and a statue. A collection is being held to give the dog a grave near its master. He won't admit it, but now that it's all over Panda's pleased as punch.

In the end, it was all enough. The god burst free last night, and it was kind. I don't know whether it understood that we had watched over it through its gestation, but if it did then it did not spare us a thank you. It took one look at us and sailed heavenwards. Nobody died.

Edinburgh might not have created a generous god of love and plenty, but neither did it birth a monster. Not a bad motto to live by, that. Don't birth monsters.

And don't go out on the lash with a Godseed in your bra. That's a good motto too.

Probably sounds better in Latin. I'll get Panda to look it up.

Hillbilly Heavens

Brad Wolfe

'These darned June bugs are in the way of the screen,' the young blonde girl said with a Southern drawl. 'I can't see the movie.'

'I'll flick 'em off,' said Austin.

The athletic young man leaned over the young girl in the passenger seat to scrape the bugs off the windscreen. His other hand flailed for purchase and conveniently landed on the young girl's chest.

'Austin!' The girl said shrilly, wriggling uncomfortably. 'Don't think I don't know what you're playing at.' She pushed at the much larger teen and he fell back in his seat, knocking a soda from the dashboard and spilling it all over himself.

'Oh, Dolly, look what you made me do!'

Angry hissing and shushing erupted from cars around the drive-in cinema.

'Don't blame me for your wanderin' hands!' Dolly said. 'I think you oughta drive me on home right now if you think I'm that sort of girl.'

Austin opened the door and stood, a small pool of cola drizzling down the front of his jeans. More shushing came from a neighbouring car. Looming over them, a scaly-costumed lizard-man advanced on a damsel in distress on the flickering screen.

The young girl opened the door and stood next to the car. 'I mean it, Austin, you can drive me home or my brothers will give you such a whippin'!'

Austin's face softened. 'But the movie was just getting good!'

'Would ya knock it off?' a voice called from a neighbouring pick-up truck.

Suddenly the picture on the screen vanished, the light from the projector disappearing and the lot plunging into darkness. There were murmurs of surprise, followed by louder exclamations. 'Hey, what's going on?' one male voice called out. 'I want a refund!' complained another.

As Dolly's eyes adjusted to the sudden gloom, the stars began to twinkle brighter in the night sky above. Her blonde hair, already piled high in a bouffant on her head, frayed at the edges as the air brimmed with static electricity. Car doors creaked open and slammed as moviegoers emerged indignant, buttoning shirts and straightening crooked dresses.

'Dolly, it was an accident, I swear,' Austin spluttered.

But Dolly's eye was caught by a glimmer in the distant sky. Was it a shooting star? It seemed to be getting bigger. Ignoring Austin's protestations, she sat on the car bonnet and swung her legs up, stiff with denim, and stood on the bonnet.

'Dolly, you'll dent it!'

Dolly shushed him. 'Be quiet. Look up—what is that?'

The twinkling star was becoming larger and brighter. A couple of other drive-in patrons had seen Dolly stand on the bonnet and followed her gaze to the sky above.

'Look!' one girl cried.

The crowd's attention began to follow Dolly's gaze. In his booth the hapless technician struggled with the powerless projector. Frustrated boys sighed as their canoodling was interrupted.

The twinkling tumbling star was now close, scintillating celestially. 'It's gonna crash!' one of the girls shrieked, and several others shrieked in turn. So did Austin. He swept Dolly from the bonnet, his arm around her petite waist and lowered her to the ground. 'Get in, Dolly! We gotta go!' He opened the passenger door and bundled her in, her high hair cushioning her head from an otherwise painful knock.

Around them engines started and horns blared as cars lurched from their spots and towards the exit. Austin dashed around to the driver's side and got in, twisting the ignition key and revving the engine.

Dolly quickly opened the passenger door and hopped out.

'Dolly, what are you doing?' Austin yelled.

'I want to see the shooting star!'

'You're a fool, Dolly!'

'Don't you say that, Austin!' She slammed the door behind her.

'You're crazy! I'm outta here,' he called through the open window. He revved the engine and the car pulled away.

Dolly leaped back, waving the dust away from her face.

As the dust cleared, she looked up, just in time to see the tumbling star shoot overhead with a whoosh of air, warmer than the summer night around her. The star was so bright, it was impossible to tell much about it, but through the glare Dolly thought she could see a glint of metal. Was it a NASA satellite?

As it roared overhead she spun around to follow it, oblivious to the cars driving and swerving around her, teenage boys and girls shrieking alike.

The star crashed through the white drive-in screen like a bullet, which sent it on a careening trajectory, wobbling left and right as it continued spinning into the distant trees, vanishing into the dark.

By now Dolly was alone but for the lanky cinema attendant, who stood knock-kneed and slack-jawed with a torch limp in one hand, the other on top of his head as if to scratch it, staring incredulously at the smoking hole. If Dolly hadn't been so excited she would have laughed.

She ran up to the young man and fluttered her eyelashes. 'Would you be ever so kind as to lend me your torch?' His jaw flapped like a catfish dragged out of the Tennessee. Dolly took the torch from his hand. He didn't resist. 'I've got to go find that fallen star!'

As Dolly turned to run, she heard another noise in the distance, and coming in fast—a spluttering engine. *Why, if that's Austin back to get me, he can sit on a tack*, she thought. The engine got louder, and Dolly looked toward the entrance gate, expecting to see headlights.

However, with a *whoosh* that flattened her bouffant, something flew overhead. Dolly spun around and shone the torch up, its weak light barely illuminating what appeared to be a flying red double-decker bus, the type she had seen in magazines from far off England, light blaring from its windows.

'What on God's green Earth...' she breathed as the bus leaped and dived through the air, narrowly missing the white, perforated screen of the drive-in cinema. Over the din of the spluttering engine, Dolly could have sworn she could hear an argument, a man and a woman bickering, much like mama and papa every second day.

The bus flew off towards the trees, banking left towards Sevierville, and disappeared into the night, light and sound fading.

There was a thud behind Dolly. She looked down to see the cinema attendant prostrate on the ground. She giggled this time, then turned and hotfooted it towards the woods.

'How dare you say that about Bonnie Langford!' Tom shrieked, as the bus lurched, as if the time-travelling vehicle were drunk itself. *Which wouldn't be impossible*, thought Iris giddily, given they had just taken an unexpected plunge through one of the Magellanic alcohol clouds near the Horsehead Nebula, dipping out of the time and space vortex to avoid another space-travelling bus barrelling towards the 1950s. The very air itself now smelt like booze.

'Oh, chuck, I didn't mean that,' Iris placated over her shoulder, one bejewelled hand on the steering wheel, the other frantically attempting to kick-start the long-dead air-conditioning unit she had been sold by a dodgy hawker on Manussa. 'The '80s were a difficult time for all humanity. I mean, just look at some of dear David's musical missteps.'

'David?' Tom cried. 'If you're about to start criticising Bowie…' He lost his grip on a tatty leather strap hanging from the ceiling and fell backwards, knocking an old chest from its precarious perch and disappearing in an explosion of sequinned bustiers and feather boas.

'Would you be careful, you great oaf,' Iris bellowed. The bus dipped and weaved. Brass wind chimes clanked alarmingly and a drinking vessel somewhere aboard met its demise. The stars and nebulae spun through the window—or was it her own vision?

'You've been drunker than this before and driven better!' came a muffled response from the pile of costumes.

'I've got more important things to worry about than your revisionist takes on terrible 1980s British pop music,' Iris yelled. She squinted ahead. 'That dastardly blob is getting away. Do you know what will happen if it reaches a civilised planet in this era?'

Tom emerged from the pile of costumes, a bra around his neck.

'Terrible pop music?!' he squawked incredulously. 'That's it, Iris! I'm packing my goodies and next time we're on Earth, I'm marrying the first man I see.'

'Well, you're in luck, chuck, because that's where we're heading! Hold on!'

The bus took a sickening dive.

From the diary of Iris Wildthyme, Transtemporal Adventuress Extraordinaire

Dear Diary,

I'm quite prepared to concede that taking a detour through the Magellanic alcohol clouds and their many floating asteroid bars was not the fun sidestep I had hoped. And it's very rare that I, Iris Wildthyme, would be drunk under the table by anyone, let alone a quivering silver jelly, but I'm prepared to possibly concede that defeat too.

Truth be told, that shiny little glob probably wasn't even there to drink at all. I don't think it can. Unbeknownst to me, it had just stopped to recharge on its journey—rest in peace Ms. Rosemary Beads, the drag act that night, who I thought had just called in sick—and it had rummaged through my purse while I was at the bar. I hadn't even noticed till I went to show Tom the crystal later, on the bus.

The Vainglorious Cluster, the origin of the nasty little blob I'm talking about, was a rare mystery even to my own people. Nobody was ever sure if it and its composite parts had evolved or were the by-product of some long-forgotten wayward artificial intelligence. The Cluster was comprised of little seeds of shimmery matter, known as Vainglories. Driven mad by an inability to see their own reflection because of their own reflectivity, they emitted a kind of narcissistic psychokinesis, driving everyone to give in to their deepest desires, draining them, freezing them in a state of excess.

The whole Cluster had been time-locked millennia before, but not before some of its spore had escaped—goodness knows how many seeds. Many a civilisation had collapsed overnight from a Vainglory taking seed, sucking the life out of a place and then shooting off for another destination seemingly at random.

I'd walked through many a wasteland left behind by Vainglories, citizens of the cosmos frozen like so many shining works of art. In fact, I had even sneakily taken a few of those statues for my summer house in the Blue Mountains in New South Wales. Panda had thought it obscene at the time, but I thought it was a way to honour their memory. After a while there is no way to reverse the process.

Truthfully, I could think of a few places I'd like to lob a Vainglory, but pre-Galactic Empire Earth was not one. Unfortunately, one of my recent shopping jaunts there had drawn Earth to its attention, and now all of the grand old US of A was at stake.

Nobody had believed Dolly when she had gone home later that night with a wild tale of a shooting star and a flying bus. They put it down to her usual wild imagination, and Dolly was threatened with a spanking for coming home late and alone. Dolly knew secretly her Papa had just been glad she came home with her homemade pokeberry make-up not smeared from kissing.

'Dolly's been wearing make-up again!' her brother Denver cried. 'I saw her trying to rub it off before she came in.'

Her father seethed and glared at Dolly. 'Where did you get make-up from?'

'I made a little money singing at the County Fair,' she protested. 'But I gave it to Mama for food!'

'That's true, she did,' her mother said.

Her father strode over to Dolly and lifted her chin.

'Well, you still had enough to get some make-up by the looks,' he said. 'I didn't raise no Jezebel!' He turned to his wife. 'I told you that fancy cinema was no good, all them high-falutin' Hollywood ideas.'

'It's not real make-up, it's only burnt matchsticks and pokeberries,' Willadeene sniggered. Dolly turned and glared at her younger sister. The other children giggled.

Their mother sighed. 'All right, you children, that's enough, it's time y'all turned in. Dolly, go and scrub that mess off your face, you've got church tomorrow.'

Dolly sighed, and with a further glare at her sister, she opened the front door to head to the spare water bucket on the porch. As she knelt to splash water on her face, she paused, seeing the reflection of the stars in the water. A star had fallen in Tennessee that night, and this town wasn't big enough for the both of them.

Dolly left for school the next day, kicking a stone down the dirt path as she made her way towards the town and the small schoolhouse. She was not prepared for what she saw when she got there.

Gathered outside the schoolhouse were the other students. Dolly's friend Judy was standing at the back, and they were all staring up at the little building.

'What's going on, Judy?'

'Hi, Dolly. You'll never believe it,' Judy giggled. 'Ms Hutton...'

'What about Ms Hutton?' Dolly said worriedly. She hoped nothing had happened. Ms Hutton was one of the dullest ladies in town, but she was sweet. She loved her books, and while modest, Dolly shared that love, even if Dolly preferred to sing than stay as quiet as Ms Hutton.

'Out, damn spot!' came a shriek from the school. Dolly looked up. She couldn't believe her eyes. The boys in her class laughed. Ms Hutton—her hair normally in a tidy bun and usually wearing boring brown tweed—stood in the doorway, hair long and wild, wearing a puffy dress from what looked like a circus or theatre costume chest.

Dolly would never have imagined Ms Hutton to own such a dress.

'Come along, children, it's time for Shakespeare! We're all going to read aloud and in costume today.' Her face had a peculiar silvery sheen to it. 'All the world is a stage...'

With a cackle, Ms Hutton disappeared inside the building.

Dolly looked askance at Judy. 'What on Earth...?'

Judy shook her head disbelievingly.

The laughing students began to file towards the schoolhouse and inside. As Dolly moved to follow, she was drawn to the sound of an engine. She turned and couldn't believe her eyes. A red double-decker bus was chugging down the road towards the middle of town.

'Would you look at that,' Judy smiled. 'What a strange day.'

Dolly turned excitedly to her friend. 'Judy, it's the bus!'

'What bus?'

'The bus I saw last night, flying through the air.' The bus she had searched high and low for last night in the woods.

'Has everyone gone crazy round here?' Judy shook her head. She kept moving toward the schoolhouse.

Dolly bit her lip. She would get an awful telling off if she skipped class, but with Ms Hutton acting so deranged, she might not even notice. She looked back at the bus, which was turning a corner and almost out of sight. She had to follow. It might lead straight to that fallen star.

Dolly turned and ran after the strange vehicle.

From the diary of Iris Wildthyme, Transtemporal Adventuress Extraordinaire

I squinted at a sign as we entered what looked like a main street. Sevierville TN. I'd heard that name before, a distant memory, osmotically ingested somehow or another in my expeditions. Deep South of the United States, unless I was very much mistaken. The Smoky Mountains of Tennessee.

The trouble with time travel in my wonderful bus is the fresh hell it plays on the suspension. Oh, it hadn't half been tempting to introduce asphalt into numerous planetary histories over the years, which would have saved several lovely vinyl records from being scratched, too. However, with the laws of space and time and all that nonsense, it was easier just to get a tune-up at the local galactic body shop from some strapping young space mechanic. Kept Tom happy, too, the cheeky pet.

The bumping of the bus, however, made a wonderful chugging rhythm as I drummed my fingers on the steering wheel. I could hear the lyrics and melodies coalescing in my head as we drove, inspiring me to sing a few improvised lines, until Tom bellowed at me to stop.

'I'll have you know I stood in for Loretta Lynn at the Grand Ole Opry in 1965,' I retorted. 'I was so good even Conway Twitty didn't notice.'

Tom mumbled something in reply about being blind on moonshine.

The other trouble one has in an incongruous time machine was usually the looks and stares from bewildered locals as it chuntered along, especially in early industrial time zones like this. Not just early industrial, but evangelical and superstitious as well, if some of the early LP covers I'd seen were anything to go by. I quickly fumbled in the dashboard and found a gaudy string of rosary beads connected to a large plastic crucifix, and hung it from the rear-view mirror.

A few locals stopped and stared in wonder as I drove, probably expecting me to be here from interstate to hawk my wares. I stared back in wonderment at the height of the hair on two ladies frozen mid-conversation. Lord help the ozone layer with all that hairspray. What was that phrase again? The higher the hair, the closer to God. Far from being breathless at their beauty, He'd probably be choking from the fumes.

The doors opened with a hiss, and a pair of cowboy-booted legs descended to the dusty street. Tom raised a hand to his eyes, squinting in the bright sunlight, even under the brim of an ill-fitting cowboy hat.

'Ooph,' he grunted and stumbled as Iris tumbled out the doors behind him, cloaked in a long-sleeved dress with glittering white wings under the sleeves.

'Watch it, chuck,' she cried. Iris surveyed the quaint street. A butcher's and general store to the left, with a horse tied outside lapping at a steel pail of water. To the right, a small building with an old-fashioned petrol bowser outside. A Studebaker puttered past in the distance, a tail of thick grey exhaust trailing behind.

'Texas tea,' Tom breathed.

Their attention was drawn to the jangling of a bell above the door of the general store. Tom gaped. Out strutted a handsome man with chaps over his jeans and plaid shirt, a cowboy hat atop a square-jawed face with a tidy dark beard.

'Oh, my,' Tom squeaked, catching the man's eye and looking down quickly. His own outfit looked like a cheap Hallowe'en western get-up.

Tom looked up again as the man came towards them along the street. His face was so handsome it almost shone.

'I saw him first, Iris,' Tom muttered under his breath.

Iris scowled. 'That cowboy is about as genuine as my Ship is a bus. Chaps are supposed to be chapped, not polished,' she muttered, before smiling and raising her voice as the man approached.

'Howdy, pardner!' she hollered, in a faux Southern accent.

Tom winced in embarrassment.

'Can I help you, sir?' the cowboy drawled. Tom looked up and caught his eye.

'Joshua?' came a surprised voice. Iris, Tom and Joshua turned. A young girl in her teens stood there, mouth agape. 'Is that really you? You done scrubbed up real well. Why, you've even trimmed your beard. I thought that was your pride and joy!'

Joshua grinned. His teeth were a luminous white. Dolly couldn't believe the makeover her friend had. Usually he looked like a hobo.

Again Tom noticed his skin almost had a metallic sheen. Even Iris noticed.

'Hello, Miss Dolly,' Joshua said warmly. 'How's that latest song comin' along?'

'Why, it's plum pitiful,' said Dolly. 'About another boy gone breakin' my heart.'

Joshua shook his head. 'Well, I'm sure a pretty young thing like you will have no worries finding a decent man. Meantime I'm about to ask this pretty young thing out on a date.' Joshua turned back to the bus.

Iris giggled and looked abashed. 'Why, how forward.'

'Not you, ma'am.' Joshua doffed his hat and put a hand out to Tom.

Tom stared agape.

'Fancy a root beer?'

Iris opened her mouth to say something and Tom interjected quickly.

'Yes!' He took the cowboy's hand. 'Don't wait up,' he said sideways to Iris, and the two men walked towards a local bar.

Dolly and Iris stared in amazement.

'Now, I know I get my decades mixed up, but that's awfully bold behaviour for 1959,' Iris said.

'That ain't the half of it, ma'am,' Dolly said. 'Everyone's acting completely nuts.'

Iris thought of the metallic sheen on Joshua's face and began to worry. The Vainglory was affecting the locals even faster than she expected. 'Is that so?'

Dolly grabbed Iris's hand. 'I'll show you. It all started when I saw your magic bus flying through the air.'

Iris frowned. 'Oh, heck,' she muttered. 'You forget you saw that.'

Dolly chuckled. 'I won't tell nobody if you tell me what's going on! I like your plastic gems,' she added.

Iris feigned shock, allowing herself to be pulled down the road towards some more of the shops. 'Plastic, indeed!'

Dolly suddenly paused. 'Can you hear that?'

Iris stopped. The town was quiet—too quiet. Even the cicadas had stopped their electric guitar drone. But there was something. Iris strained to listen. Her hearing wasn't what it used to be. It sounded like children.

'Quick, behind here,' Dolly cried. She pulled Iris behind a large horse trough. They ducked down, Iris careful to lift her outfit away from the mud.

From around the corner, a crowd of children came in rows of two, led by Dolly's teacher, Ms Hutton, who moved stiffly, still wearing the moth-eaten ball gown from earlier, but her face shining in the midday sun. The children were all humming, their faces silver and their eyes a bright white.

Dolly gasped. 'That's Judy!' Her friend was among the children, shuffling forward. Iris raised a bejewelled finger to her lips. Dolly's eyes welled with tears. 'Not Judy.'

Iris laid a comforting hand on Dolly's arm. 'We can undo this,' she whispered. 'Trust me.'

The children passed, humming eerily.

'They're singing my song,' Dolly breathed. '"Puppy Love". I wrote it just last spring!'

Iris nodded. 'Clever girl! That shows how much they admire you,' she said quietly. 'They want to emulate you. The Vainglory's got its hooks into them.'

Dolly blushed. 'That didn't stop them teasing me.'

The children filed away around the corner, the eerie humming subsiding.

Iris stood, lifting Dolly up with her. 'That usually just means they're jealous. Come on. We've got to follow them!'

'Can we take the bus?' Dolly asked eagerly.

'I'm afraid I can't risk that blob getting its grubby protuberances on it. We're just lucky we've landed somewhere out of the way.'

'Well, that is true,' Dolly nodded. 'Nothing much ever happens in Sevier County. Where did you get a flying bus, anyhow?' she added excitedly. 'You'll just *have* to show the others. Nobody believed me. They put it down to my imagination again.'

Iris chuckled heartily. 'Tell you what, chuck,' she said. 'I'll take you for a special ride if you promise not to tell anyone. After we find the—the star.'

Dolly nodded sagely, with a wisdom beyond her years. 'The shooting star I saw, that's what's causing everyone to act so strange?'

'That it is, luvvie,' Iris said. 'The Vainglories are a scoundrel of a race. I've seen entire monasteries in drag by nightfall when one of them drops in. They bring out secret desires, magnify hidden feelings.'

'That doesn't sound so bad,' Dolly said. 'I think more people should let themselves feel what they truly feel.'

Iris nodded. 'That's all well and good, dear, but this one's got caught in my temporal slipstream. It shouldn't be here in this time and place. Heaven knows what would become of Earth if I don't stop it. If left too long, there'll be no more amber waves of grain, no more...' Iris looked at a sign as they passed, 'Sevier County, no more America.'

'Iris!' came a muffled cry to the right. 'Mmmm-nnggg!'

'That's coming from the saloon,' Dolly cried. She pulled Iris over to a corner pub. She paused before the doors. 'I shouldn't really be going in here, Papa would kill me.'

'I think this time we can make an exception,' Iris said, and burst through the doors. Dolly looked around guiltily and followed.

Slumped over the bar, Dolly noticed, was Jackson Moses, the local bartender, snoring loudly, his silvery jaw wide open with a puddle of drool forming around an empty spirits bottle. Next to the bar was Tom, caught mid-embrace with Joshua, his tongue caught between the frozen lumberjack's teeth.

'What the devil,' Iris stormed. 'We've only been here five minutes.'

'Woob you kinely helb,' Tom said, 'Mah tongue is shtuck.'

Iris stormed over and tapped Joshua on the shoulder. Her finger struck an unnaturally hard surface under the flannel cloth. Joshua didn't respond. She reached up and prised open the man's jaws. They moved slightly, enough for Tom to stumble back and land on his backside.

Dolly tittered despite herself. Far be it from her to judge why two men were kissing—she grew up around farms, she had seen all sorts of things. She knew sometimes the birds loved the birds and the bees loved the bees as much as they loved each other.

'We don't have much time,' Iris said. 'Get yourself together and—'

'What the devil!' boomed a voice behind them. They spun around. Dolly saw her father standing silhouetted in the doorway. 'Dolly Rebecca! What are you doing in here?'

Dolly looked terrified. Iris stepped forward. 'I can explain, Mr..?'

'Parton,' the man said.

Tom stopped rubbing his jaw and looked at the girl in sudden realisation. He looked to Iris, whose eyes lit up. She nodded slightly, then composed herself.

'Mr Parton,' she said haughtily, 'your daughter has been showing me around your town. I'm here on important business.'

'Recruitin', Madam?' he said sarcastically, looking up and down at her outfit.

'I'll have you know I'm here to save your town, this fine town of...' Iris flailed.

'Sevierville!' Tom gasped. 'This is Sevier County!'

'Sevierville!' Iris finished with a flourish. 'You're all in mortal danger.'

'It's true, Papa,' Dolly said.

'You'll be in mortal danger when you get home, girl!' he said then softened. 'Meantime I need your help.' He thrust a Bible into her hands. 'Your Grandpa Owens is possessed by Satan himself.'

Dolly gasped. 'Grandpa Owens? What do you mean?'

'The old church,' Mr Parton said. 'Caton's Chapel. The village is flocking to it like pigeons to bread, and your grandpa's in there snake-handling, and your brothers are in there too.' He turned to Iris reluctantly. 'Are you a Christian woman?'

'Well, there was that one time in Jerusalem—ooh!' Iris was interrupted by Tom standing on her foot.

'She meant Jerusalem in New York,' Tom said sheepishly. 'We are indeed, er, soldiers of the Lord.'

'Follow me,' Mr Parton growled. 'We have to get to the church.'

'Can we take the bus now?' Dolly begged.

Iris was about to decline again but saw the little girl's eyes shining. 'It should be ready now. But no flying,' she added.

Dolly ran for the door excitedly.

'Flying?' said Mr Parton, confused.

As Iris, Tom and Dolly clambered aboard the bus, Mr Parton examined it from the outside.

'Putney Common?' he read aloud, as he circled the vehicle.

Iris pumped the clutch savagely as the engine spluttered and choked. It roared into life. 'Hop on, chuck,' she cried.

Mr Parton hoisted himself into the door-well.

Inside, Dolly squealed with excitement as she saw the colourful costumes flung askew over the interior from their earlier crash-landing. She picked up a sequinned jacket and grinned broadly, slipping her arms into its oversized sleeves and spinning in front of a mirror.

Tom grinned, too. 'Well, I'd say you can keep it, but I think you've already got one,' he said.

Dolly stared uncomprehendingly, then realisation dawned. 'My coat of many colours!' Her eyes narrowed. 'Just a dog-gone minute. How did you know about that?'

Tom shrugged. 'A little bird told me,' he said. 'A little sparrow, even,' he added quietly.

Dolly turned back to the mirror. Tom threw a feather boa at her. She laughed and embraced it, posing and twirling.

Iris glanced in the rear-view mirror as Mr Parton directed her down the main street of the town and towards the old church. 'Tom, chuck me that cassette tape, will you, love?' she cried. 'On the ledge.'

Tom picked up the tape sitting on a shelf above the mirror. He looked at the faded writing—"Iris's country compilation". He flipped it over and skim-read the messily written biro track listing. Side two was fine. Side one, however, was a dangerous anachronism in the making.

'Stick to side two,' Tom cried as he threw the tape to Iris, who thrust it into the stereo on the dashboard. The Dixie Chicks began to lilt over the rumble of the bus, singing a cover of *Power in the Blood.*

Dolly squealed. 'I know this one!' She began to sing in front of the mirror, posing in Iris's over-sized outfit as Tom slapped his knee in time.

As the bus turned the corner, the old church became visible. Hiding among trees like a stray animal, it was battered and abandoned, one of the main doors barely hanging on.

'This is the place,' Mr Parton growled, still holding onto the pole in the bus doorway as the road outside rushed by. 'Though it hasn't been a house of God for years.'

'Oh, Papa,' Dolly sighed, 'It will always be a house of God. Everywhere is.'

As they got closer, the rising and falling sound of whooping, clapping and singing became audible. 'Well, it's certainly a house of something Godawful right now,' Iris said. 'I think we've found your shooting star, young lady.'

The scene inside was chaos.

The broken old pews were kicked aside as the local Sevierville residents danced, clapped and testified, facing the dilapidated old stage at the head of the church. They spun and jerked, some speaking in tongues, others silent in ecstatic reverie, swaying with arms outstretched. Iris noticed their faces were all shining, some more silver than others as the Vainglory took hold. Even as she watched, one of the revellers froze in place, their body stiffening with hands outreached, face cast in a rictus of worship.

At the front of the church on the stage danced Dolly's Grandfather Owens, speaking in tongues, holding writhing silver snakes in his hands. They wound around his arms, connecting him to the quivering blob propped on the pulpit, gleaming like a large ball of pure mercury.

Mr Parton pulled a small tattered Bible from his pocket and advanced toward the stage, ducking as the maddened townsfolk writhed around him.

'St. Michael the Archangel, defend me in battle,' he began. Grandfather Owens stopped his babbling and his head snapped towards his son-in-law, eyes gleaming. 'Be our protection against the malice and snares of the Devil...'

One of the silver snakes unravelled from Grandfather Owens's arms and arced through the air, extending its length to wrap around Mr Parton's torso.

'May God rebuke you!' Mr Parton gasped, but as the snake tightened around him, his words joined the discordant harmony of tongues that burst forth from the townsfolk around him, and his skin took on the familiar silver sheen afflicting them all.

'Daddy!' Dolly cried in horror and began to rush forward. Tom caught her arm, and Iris stepped forward instead. Dolly clapped her hands over ears as the choir gabbled and yapped and hooted.

'Enough!' Iris cried.

The babble of tongues silenced. The townsfolk all turned in unison to look at Iris, their eyes blank pools of silver. Dolly took her hands off her ears and clung to Tom. Iris kept her attention on Grandfather Owens.

'You!' A voice came from within him, deep and plummy. 'How did you follow me here?' It was the Vainglory using Owens as its mouthpiece.

'I know your lot,' Iris said. 'Always leaving a trail of... well, actually, fabulousness wherever you go. It's not hard to follow. And far be it from me to judge, but you need to stay in your own time zone. This world's not quite ready to deal with the likes of you yet.'

'And who are you to decide that?' the Vainglory replied.

'Take it from one who knows a lot more about being fabulous than you,' Iris said haughtily.

'Nobody knows more about fabulous than my people,' the Vainglory retorted indignantly. 'It is our entire purpose, to spread our shine throughout the cosmos!'

Grandfather Owens raised an arm. One of the silver tentacles whipped through the air and scooped Iris up. She squirmed and pushed at her captor, to no avail. The metallic-looking tentacle was rubbery in texture and gripped firm.

'Iris!' Tom cried in horror.

Dolly ran forward, standing in front of her father, frozen in the embrace of another silver tentacle. 'Put her down!' she cried.

The body of her grandfather turned to face her. The face appeared quizzical as the Vainglory delved into the memories of the elderly preacher.

'My darling granddaughter, Dolly Rebecca,' it began.

Dolly stamped her feet and put her hands on her hips. 'You ain't my granddaddy! Get out of his body at once!'

The Vainglory snarled. Another tentacle whipped into the air with a crack and dove through the air towards Dolly. She stood firm. The protuberance zoomed towards her, but recoiled as it came close.

'What?!' the Vainglory gasped. The snake-like arm withdrew slightly and tried again, but to no avail. It was as if there were an invisible barrier around the young girl. 'Why can't I reach you?'

Iris stared in amazement. 'Of course! You can't affect her because she has no hidden fabulousness.'

Dolly turned to Iris, crestfallen. 'I don't?' she said sadly.

The snake sensed a weakness and curled itself around Dolly.

'Not hidden, no!' exclaimed Iris. 'And it never will be! You're Dolly Parton! Your fabulousness is never far from the surface! The Vainglory can't control you because you've got more than it does! It just wants to freeze you and capture your spark, like a butterfly pinned to a board. You want to share it with everyone!'

Dolly's face burst into a grin as bright as the light of a clear blue morning. She turned back to her stricken grandfather. The snake arm withdrew from around her. She reached up and grasped the tentacle like a rope. With her free arm, she reached out and grasped the other tentacle around her father and shook it roughly. It came loose and unravelled from his body. He slumped unconscious to the floor, the silver sheen draining from his face, which returned to its weathered Southern tan.

Holding the silver snakes like the reins of a horse and carriage, Dolly advanced on the stage.

'I'm not gonna say a prayer to scare you off because you're not even scary enough to be the Devil,' she said. 'You're just a big, mean, vain bully! Let my granddaddy go!'

Dolly cracked the silver reins. With a gargled cry the Vainglory released its control of her grandfather, unravelling its appendages. Like her father before, Grandfather Owens slumped unconscious to the floor. The appendage holding Iris unravelled and retracted with whiplash speed. Around them, the townsfolk all quietened, their silver glint fading as, one by one, they slumped to the floor unconscious.

'Thank goodness,' Iris breathed. 'Any longer and they'd have frozen that way forever.'

'I could have found a use for Joshua,' Tom replied. Iris shot him a withering look.

As Dolly climbed the stairs, the Vainglory quivered and began to shrink. The closer she got to it, the smaller it became, until it was the size of a basketball. Soon all that was left was a singular spherical blob on the lectern, barely the size of a chicken's egg.

'As I live and breathe,' Iris said. She and Tom followed Dolly to the pulpit.

'What's wrong with it?' Tom queried.

'It's like two fighting fish,' Iris said. 'You could never put two of these blobs together. They'd outdo each other to death. Like some sort of interstellar Eurovision, with poor innocent bystanders back-up dancing themselves to oblivion. I think this young lady's even more powerful than that.'

'It just can't stand the competition,' Dolly grinned. She reached out to touch it.

'No!' Iris cried, but it was too late.

Dolly touched the blob, which exploded with a flash, and everything went dark.

Much later, Dolly awoke on the bus. She sat up with a gasp. 'Mama, I just had the strangest dream!' She looked around. 'It wasn't a dream.'

Tom was pouring himself a gin at the front of the bus. Iris was sewing something, sitting on the couch across from her. It was a coat covered in what looked like gems.

'Thank heavens you're all right. I don't know how I would have corrected history if you'd left us. How's your head, young lady?' Iris grinned.

Dolly smiled. 'Quite fine, thank you, ma'am.' A panicked look came over her face. 'Papa! And Granddaddy!'

'They're fine,' Tom said, closing the dashboard liquor cabinet. 'Everyone will be back to normal when you get home.'

Dolly relaxed a little. 'What's that you're making?'

'A gin and tonic,' Tom replied.

'Not you,' Iris hollered over her shoulder. 'It's a coat for you. I know how ever fond you are of them. Of course, it won't be your favourite coat, I know that much.'

'Are those real diamonds?' Dolly gasped.

Iris chuckled. She pulled the needle through and snapped off the thread. She handed the jacket to the young girl and took a fresh glass of gin from Tom.

'No, but they'll be the most precious rhinestones on Earth for many a century,' Iris said. 'It's what's left of that nasty blob.'

Dolly slipped on the jacket and lifted her arms one by one, admiring the sparkling gems. 'It's beautiful!'

Iris smiled. 'I have a feeling Earth won't be troubled by the Vainglory for as long as you're wearing this,' she said.

'But why didn't it affect you?' Dolly asked.

'Oh, don't get me wrong, I'm quite fabulous myself,' she chortled. Tom harrumphed light-heartedly as he selected a cassette. 'Look out the window, chuck,' she told the young girl.

Dolly reached forward and pulled aside the curtain to reveal a brilliant starscape—and planet Earth hanging in space.

She gasped. 'This must be a dream,' she said, shaking her head.

'Not a dream,' Iris said. 'And it's up to you to keep on shining.'

Dolly grinned. 'All the world's a stage.'

Tom sighed wistfully, thinking of Joshua. He took a deep gulp of gin and tonic.

'And all the men are players.'

The Haberdasher's Tale
(or Never Trust a Hat with a Perfect Fit)
Brendan Jones

With the Parson's words heavy in my mind,
Arose from the tradesmen a noise unkind.
My intent to halt the tales and the vice
Stalled by the haberdasher in a trice–
His disturbance was clear, but words were not;
I called to him, "Fellow, be not so hot!
These bawdy tales we tell of woe and shame
Are profanity 'gainst God's sacred name."
The Parson stirred true, the nun shrunk silent,
But the swarthy hatmaker's voice did vent,
"You're all in danger, but you can't see why!
Death is coming for us all from the sky.
Do not stop the tales, great poet, I beg,
For I swear I am not pulling your leg."
The party grew silent in hushed awe
As the dark haberdasher spake once more.
"Do not prevent me from telling my tale.
Heed me not, and we'll be below the shale."

From this point, I'll allow the boy his role
His tale of wonder, his face like coal–
"Yeah, thanks, Chaucer mate. They got it—I'm black.
No time to harp on, so please shut your crack.
My story is terrifying, you will see
Timing is crucial, so listen to me.
You chose this journey to honour your God
While I'm here cos of a mardy great sod.
…I start my tale on Siri Minima
Look left in the sky—see that faint glimmer?
Around that green star, a world just like yours
With Physicians, good Knights, Butchers and Whores."

Incensed, the Wife of Bath cried in distress
The giggling Knight got a slap where he dressed.

You, Mrs Bath, would be snugly at home
With the Minimans in their froth and their foam.
The Great Mardy Sod, named Iris, did land
On Siri Minima for a drink; and
Cos she wanted to visit an old flame.
Don't get excited—it's always the same.
They're mad, or she is, so it's left to me
To sort which is which, but this time, you see
We were wrong, dead wrong. Her old friend had changed.
"Oh Iris," he cried, "Are you really back?"
Then he was upon her, like Liza on crack
I tried to tell her but she'd never listen
Not when there's tall, dark blokes to be kissin'.

She left the bar fast, vanish'd in the night.
Now, the tavern's patrons *were* a queer sight.
Queerer than you lot, and that says something
Queerer than me, and that's quite a rum thing.
They turned all to face me, as do you now,
But slack-jawed, knock-kneed, like a herd of daft cows.
They lunged as one force—I fell off me chair!
One touched my knee, while another, my hair.
"Iris!" I cursed, as she'd left me alone–
You can't stop her when that dog gets her bone.
I slammed my daiquiri hard on a nose
The dazed heads tilted—their bodies now froze.
I crawled backwards fast, the door out of sight,
When a male voice spoke—mellow and bright.

"Hello, dear man," he cooed as he tilted,
"It looks like your friend has left you all jilted.
Come sit with us til she's back, if you please–
We have wine to spare, some grapes and ripe cheese."

I looked 'round the room, and my stomach churned–
No-one else faced me, and no-one's eyes burned
Deep into my head. Had I but dreamed it?
Looking to the voice—his smile a slight slit,
with eyes enticing. So, taking his hand
I was led to a table near the band.
His name was Jeflik—with a small snub nose,
A green fedora—my interest arose.
And the wine did flow, with cheese a'plenty–
I knew in the morn, I'd need a venti.

Jeflik kept my glass topped up—and what's more
Evinced me to table, and to the floor
The minutes slipped by, Iris quite forgot–
To be blunt, dear pilgrims, Jeflik was hot.
So when I noticed his hand on my knee
Did I object? No chance—I let it be.
The band played softer, my head found its rest–
Jelflik's own developed, pillowy chest.
I spare no blushes of my tradesmen friends–
The Wife of Bath is aware of my ends.
She is not alone, so pick up your jaws.
Pilgrims, I kissed him, and tightened my claws.
If Iris was to leave me abandoned,
I would leave with horizons expanded.

Here's my first moral—traveller, be cautious
Many hands joined me—I felt quite nauseous.
On my right, Luki and Tanni did smile
On my left, two hefty men meanwhile
Grabbed each a thigh. Ah! This must be, I thought,
What a Christmas Turkey felt, so it ought.
I was not keen for so great a stuffing
But found myself entangled in huffing
Unearthly beings in a rainbow of hues–
Were orgies this world's payment for one's dues?

I'm no prude in terms of four in a bed
But not tonight—there's an ache in my head.
Slurring, I offered to pay for the wine–
Snap! All heads tilted, all eyes fixed on mine.

The pawing stopped dead, as time itself gasped.
Jeflik broke the air, as his high voice rasped,
"Kiss me again, and the others all too
With such little time, so many to do!"
All five still upon me, those queued behind,
Breathless mouths gaping for my flesh to find.
My free hand twisted, uselessly flailing,
Summoning help, but totally failing.
When slapping and pinching proved fruitless too
I resigned to the trick that porn stars do;
Faced with a minger? Close your eyes and think
He's really Bruce Lee, and not a green fink.
A new hand appeared, and quickly I felt
An expert begin to undo my belt.

My hand did fall. In a moment of luck
I brushed Jeflik's head, his tongue did untuck
And leave my mouth. They recoiled in pain.
I was relieved, aggrieved—but in the main
T'was glad of the freedom—all well and good–
But none recoil from me, and nor they should.
I jumped up and ran, my tender pride bruised,
Both from rejection and having been used.
Jeflik lurched forward, desperate and pale,
"Run, stranger," he urged, "Don't stop, don't fail–"
Then Luki returned the hat to his head–
He straightened his back and smiled as I fled.
The nerve—why had he called me a stranger?
My heart panged as I escaped to danger.

Thinking as my feet pounded the cobbles–

A sex-pest planet? I've lost my marbles.
This lot would shag at the drop of a hat–
Oh. Oh bugger. I hadn't thought of that.
I'll tell you later Chaucer, mate. You might
Not believe it now. But this sexy blight
Had a cause both bizarre and macabre.
I saw then as I looked back on the bar,
As the group fanned wide to search for me
Each, to a greater or lesser degree,
Wore a hat—trilbies, fascinators, caps
Were they all part of this erotic trap?
My fears confirmed as I ran to the bus–
More hats, and a sight at which I did cuss.

Against the windows, the body whipped red,
Was tied poor Iris a gag on her head.
I needn't have been bashful of swearing
She'd chewed through the gag and was tearing
Her old friend a new one—but I was scared
That he revelled in the abuse she bared.
"I'll tell you another thing, chuck," she cried,
"This old girl's off limits to you—denied!
Tom—run love! They've gone flippin' barmy–
They're whoring us out to an 'ole army!"
I must thank Iris, because until then,
I hadn't been seen, but luck has to end.
The choice was being plain hogtied or bagged
So I stepped forward and chose to be shagged.

I draped myself upon Iris's friend–
His name was Parn—a Mars/Peladon blend.
"I'm flattered, Parn, by love so expressive–
But why is everyone so attentive?
Iris and I've travelled both wide and far;
Despite my good looks, a grope in a car
Is the best I can usually manage–

So unless you have a nearby garage
I figure there's something else happening."
I stroked his cocked hat, feeding his craving
And got a reply—the same cooing grate
With which Jeflik had lured me to his plate.
"We cannot feel as humanoids do–
We possess what we need to feel—you!"

"We Minimans," said Parn, "have minds alone.
No sweat glands or sinew, blood, skin, or bone.
Our knowledge and science are unsurpassed–
But lacking sex is a pain in the arse."
Or not, I thought, in this case, but hushed
And with my chin his developed chest brushed.
"But these fragile forms are almost spent
After only three weeks of fun most bent.
We must find new bodies, new grounds to breed,
To enjoy—it's sensation we need.
We have found it in you, we think, dear man.
To Earth we will spread—that is our plan!"
He clutched me close, as I saw, with dread
Jeflik approach, with a hat for my head.

"My darling," I crooned, unconvincingly,
"What's with all the hats? I'll come willingly."
Parn laughed, squeezed tighter, "There's nothing to fear.
We ARE the hats, Tom—I thought that was clear?
We can't bonk or breed—we have to be made
First comes the fun, then as you start to fade,
You will make more of us; we'll start anew.
There is no limit of who we can do.
Your bus is the bridgehead—all is prepared.
With flattery, Iris's mind was shared."
The thought of shagging til death was quite bad;
To end making hats was even more sad.
But that it could happen to all the world?

Every dog, cat, man, boy, woman and girl?

"Tom! You ruddy fool!" Iris, irate, cried.
"You can't let them win—we'll be dead inside!"
The silly bint thought I was taken in–
But I'm a good actor, or it was the gin.
A swift knee to Parn, I dove for the bus,
And switched on the tea-mat with no more fuss.
(Iris's idea—it finds tea nearby
And takes you to it—it was worth a try)
That's how I came here—to forewarn you all.
Give me your hats or the planet will fall
The tale ends not here—it's still going on.
Do as I say or the hats will have won!

And so ends the dark haberdasher's tale–
No it doesn't—I just said it didn't–
A strange telling, which did rather fail–
Chaucer, how long have you been wearing that hat?
To provide a moral to our party–
Come to think of it, how does a pink sombrero come to be in Fourteenth Century England?
Or indeed, any form of clarity.
Oh hell.
Now, we'll dispense with ridiculous verse
If you don't mind—in our view, it's a curse.
Knight, Squire, Yeoman– hold and bind him fast
He shall join us now or else breathe his last.
You hatless fool, Tom. Did you not expect
Us to use a time ship to full effect?
A time portal was easy to open–
The journey swift, our resolve unbroken.
Tracking your travels, we arrived afore–
The plans are made for our planet of whores!

Where better to start than these archetypes?

Clergy, tradesmen, artists, writers and knights–
They will spread from this trip, back to their homes
Our stiff Minimans to then, this world, roam.
'Til then, we must ration ourselves steadfast–
Not wear out our threads, nor hosts to the last.
Lady Bath drew rota, with times and places,
And positions, with up or down faces.
The wagons contain not just food and drink,
But scores of thirsty hats, desperate to sink
Upon the heads of sensitive bodies–
Settling for the night after their toddies.
To live, to feel, to possess such form–
Let the orgies commence; let the hats swarm!

"I think you've forgot, chuck, who's in charge here!"
Iris, lit by headlights, betrayed no fear
"You forget yourself, mate, but panic not–
The salve for any cockup, I got!
They say size means nowt, but you've not met me!
Look up, Sombrero—D'ya see what I see?"
Of course! On the planet, Iris was hatless–
A mishap with Panda, gin, a mattress–
Now, its broad-flowered brim plain to see
The flowers half dying, mind, but oh she
Had eyes all on her, as was her favour.
Twisting her hat brim with flair and flavour
She cried, "I'm your leader, Iris Wildthyme–
Queen of the Headjobs!" Now that's quite a line.

The effect was electric and shocking
Chaucer scratched his head, Bath her stocking
"Did you know the Head was coming?" he asked.
"No!" replied she, in the brim's shadow basked.
"The form so wonderful and befitting–
It must be she, and we're just unwitting!"
Iris moved among them, my gizzard froze–

Possessed or a saviour—with friends or foes?
"'Ere, now, ducks—time for an aperitif–
This bird's had more sex than good old Sir Cliff!
That reminds me –" And so Iris went on
Enthralling the hats—I made myself gone
Back into the bus. Had Iris a plan?
If she had, I must help—I was her man!

"Down deep in the jungle," Iris explained,
"I had Tiny Tim, but never complained!"
Of course—Iris is distracting the hats
So among their pigeons I'll throw some cats!
You're sure about that line? Panda, shut up.
What would you know—you were hid in a cup!
They were all laughing when I found the box;
Iris was now on a story of Lox
"I said 'My dear girl, Friday's time for fish!'
Ariel can't sing, but she's quite a dish!"
I hoped I was right, and made for the door–
She was now on her footballers' top four.
If I was wrong, I'd be shagged to death.
There's worse ways to go, but don't hold your breath.

While I crept through the dry bushes nearby
Iris talked of Twiggy in a layby.
We locked eyes—a glance, a moment of truth–
I slipped, broke a branch, and near lost a tooth.
The sound broke the spell. I was caught again,
Sat by the fire among the tradesmen.
Resigned, I settled on the Weaver's chest
If I was shagged to death, he was the best.
As I nuzzled, Iris cooed with a glare,
"I'm glad you returned him with gentle care!
That hat box holds the rest of our number.
We'll put one on him, and end its slumber!"
The Weaver's tight biceps held me like lead–

Then, like a flash, was a hat on my head.

"Oh horror! Oh woe!" I heard myself cry
"My Minimans—we must act now or die!
The sun of Earth can destroy us in time
If we stay too long in its golden shine.
The sun has hurt us, but safe in the moon
We must swap with the other hats, and soon!"
The effect was quick—the hat box opened
And hats were swapped with panic unspoken.
I gave out the last, and sealed the old in,
Iris cracked open her mouth with a din.
"Tom, you clever sod, you understood fine!
They're trapped in that old dress-ups box of mine!
It's a hat box prison, where they're all sent–
I hope their pins all get thoroughly bent."

Here's where we leave, with a poet in charge.
That's right, Panda here—alive and at large!
Sorry I've not been about, but, you know–
A hat lacks a hooter to punch—ho ho!
We took the pilgrims the rest of the way,
Tom showed the Weaver the meaning of 'Gay'.
A jump back to leave some tea at the Inn–
To bring Tom back to this time, to begin.
The tales were done, Chaucer lamented
While in his mind, new stories cemented.
Strange worlds, queer folk, unearthly desires–
So Iris had to put out some fires.
"Sorry Chuck, I don't think so, cos you see–
A sci-fi poet? Crap, if you ask me."

The Exploding Somewhat Inevitable

Philip Marsh

Hello there my luvvies! Iris Wildthyme here, adventuress of the space lanes and timelines, setting down the details of another of the outrageous adventures that make up my existence on the transtemporal plane. Expect courage, danger, daring-do, and to meet one of the 20th century's greatest artists.

The story… no… *adventure* I'm going to relate to you now involved some of the hippest and most famous people in 1960s New York. As you'll all know by now, I do love a good party. At this point in our travels, Panda (Oh, she mentions me at last!) and I had recently had a narrow escape from the planet of the Blood-sucking Horrors, and before that we had had to run hot-foot from the Slow-moving Terror of Tetra 5. So, as you can probably guess, we were both feeling the need for liquid refreshment and a right good knees-up. There is a place where the most stylish and creative people in one of the most stylish and creative cities go to hang out. Naturally, I have always fitted right in. So, I set the co-ordinates and went to pick out one of me best frocks.

(Hello. Panda here. Iris has decided that she hasn't got the patience to type these memoirs up, and so has left the job of deciphering her appalling handwriting and sorting out her syntax to me. On the plus side, it means I can correct some of the errors and exaggerations that she's bound to include. Honestly, that woman can't cross an empty road without making an adventure out of it later. Anyway, I'm sure I'll be popping up every so often to set the record straight when her imagination (or alcohol-induced amnesia) gets the better of her, as I have perfect recall of the events she is about to relate. But for now I'll let her get on with telling the story. Ta-ta!)

When I'm in the mood for a good bohemian party one of my favourite places to drop into is 1960s New York. Or rather, one particular place in 1960s New York—the fifth floor of 231 East 47th Street in Midtown Manhattan, any time between 1964 and 1967. Now, one of the perks of being a time traveller is being able to go to the same spots every night like regular patrons, but have glamorous adventures in-between. Though you do have to be careful not to arrive on the same night that you've visited in the past—after all, you might be wearing the same outfit as yourself, and that would be very embarrassing. Also, it's good temporal etiquette to try and visit places in the right order—there's nothing worse than accidentally telling someone about the events at a fabulous party or a blood-curdling escapade they've not actually had yet because you've gotten your dates mixed up. Luckily, I have a natural flair for avoiding trouble of this sort and can generally trust the bus to land me on the right day.

We landed on the roof—much more discreet than having a London double-decker bus appear in the Manhattan streets—and let ourselves into the building via the access hatch, before taking the lift down to the fifth floor. When I stepped out of the lift I took Panda out of my handbag and put him on the floor—he might crawl out of parties but he always likes to walk in (The cheek of the woman!). As usual of an evening, the party was in full swing. As we entered the floor that was known as The Factory, the silver foil covering the walls threw back our distorted reflections. As always there was no-one checking invitations because there were none—anyone was free to come. Of course, only the coolest, hippest, and most with-it people wanted to come due to its reputation as a hang-out for the wildest party goers. I was, of course, utterly at home.

And what a crowd there was! Girls with their hair as scandalously short as their skirts, boys with theirs scandalously long, and indeterminates who wore ambiguity like it was the first time they'd ever felt certain. Rock 'n' Roll pumped through the air, and people danced with little care for decency or the sensibilities of the world outside this enclave. One man danced whilst cracking a whip (he was understandably given a wide berth). Others sat around talking, wearing sunglasses even though they were indoors.

And then… there he was! Through the crowd, his bright blonde hair catching my eye like a beacon. One of the greatest artists of the 20th century—black leather jacket, skinny white top with black stripes running across, just as I'd seen him in the photographs. I elbowed my way through the crowd and waved to get his attention.

‘Coo-ee! Andy me love. Over ‘ere!’

Andy Warhol looked up, took in the sight of me in my spectacular outfit (sequins have always brought out the best in me) and from the look on his face I could tell that he was especially stunned by my sense of fashion that evening. As I made my way towards him the crowd parted and all these members of the “IT crowd” stared at me, unable to believe what they were seeing.

‘Oh… hello Iris,’ he said, in that slightly nervous way of his, but I saw through his manner and knew that he was delighted to see me.

And then we had a lovely and insightful little chat about his art while Panda seemed more interested in trying, unsuccessfully, to pick up women. Probably for the best as Panda’s taste in art is a little… suspect at times.

(*What? No, let me re-phrase that. WHAT???* That isn’t what happened at all. *My* taste in art is suspect? This from a woman who, when she first went to see the Mona Lisa in the Louvre loudly exclaimed, “Drunk as a skunk, you can see it in the eyes.” Has she forgotten my career as a well-respected and widely-published art critic? What nonsense. As for her comment about me trying to pick up women, I think she’s just annoyed that a group of delightful ladies (called, if I heard them right, Eddie, Candy and Nicko) all but fought each other for my attentions. Andy Warhol, in contrast, was somewhat less enamoured of *her*. Perhaps she thinks that I was too distracted by the lovely ladies in question to notice, but I saw and heard the whole thing, and will write it as it *actually* happened.

‘Now then, Andy,’ Iris said, grabbing a hand that he had been too taken aback by her fashion sense to offer to her, ‘so good to see you again. Feels like it’s been *ages*. I visited a big exhibition of your work in the early twenty-first century recently. They had all your most famous pieces. The weirdly-coloured Marilyn Monroe pictures. That soup tin. Those floating silver pillows—love ‘em. Not very practical on Earth of course, but you could sell them by the bucket-load to the Floaters of the Zero-G City. I could put you in contact if you like. Make you a fortune.’

She paused for a moment, a look of concern on her face. 'Er... you have already done all of those haven't you? I've not gone and dropped a temporal clanger?')

Warhol was so excited to see me that he couldn't even let me finish saying hello before he was offering me the opportunity to be the subject of one of his "movie portraits". (I think it was the first thing he could think of to get rid of her). And so, with Panda focused on impressing the ladies, I was led by one of the world's greatest ever artists to be turned into a work of art by his own, gifted hands. Admittedly, I was a little disappointed that in this case his "hands" were essentially replaced by a movie camera on a tripod with a chair in front of it, but the idea is the thing isn't it? Andy indicated for me to sit in the chair and moved behind the camera.

'Now,' he said. 'I want you to just sit and look into this camera, okay? I'll turn the camera on, and I won't even be here. I want you to just look into it, like it's taking your picture rather than making a movie and you're posing. It'll be great, I think. So, just stay sat there and don't move off the chair, okay?' Then he set the camera running and walked swiftly back to the party, obviously concerned that his other guests would be jealous of the amount of time he was spending with me.

I looked into the lens of the camera, grateful for my natural poise and ability to pose even when given no time to prepare. It meant being away from the party, but it's not everyone who can say they have been turned into a work of art by a major artist, and to sit in the exact chair in front of the exact camera that so many of the most important artists of the time and place had sat. And anyway, I thought, it's nice to get away. I had wanted to get away from the party, hadn't I?

I immediately realised that something was wrong. Me, wanting to get away from a party? When did that ever happen? No-one loves a knees-up more than me. And that was the whole reason I'd brought myself and Panda here in the first place.

Who are you? I thought, sending the question outwards telepathically.

You can hear us? You have no idea how much of a relief that is, Iris Wildthyme.

I can feel you scanning my thoughts you sneaky-boots, and I'll put a stop to it. You can't attempt to read someone who has had as much experience of telepathic communication as me and expect me not to be able to block you. So, I'll ask you again.

Who are you? And why are you trying to make me leave this party before I've even gotten the slightest bit squiffy?

We find ourselves in a desperate situation Iris Wildthyme, and had despaired of ever finding someone who could help us. Your arrival gives us new hope.

What's with all this "we" and "us"? Who are you?

We are the Photons. We exist on the visual spectrum in clusters of linked individuals. One of our clusters was exploring this part of the galaxy. They reached this planet but we lost contact. We were dispatched to find out what happened to them. We picked up a muffled signal which we traced to this city, and to this building.

So you sneaked inside to take a butcher's for yourself… I mean, yourselves.

Oh, that we had. Instead we made a fundamental mistake. We thought our chances of success greater if we contacted the authorities on this landmass to request their assistance. At first they welcomed us, but when we sent part of our self out as an ambassador we did not return. We felt our pain as they experimented on us—this after we had revealed to them how to enable us to manifest so that they could communicate with us.

Well didn't you try to get them… I mean, yourself back?

We have no power in this realm. We are unable to interact with what the natives of this planet call the physical world. The only way we can have agency is to impose ourselves on suitable material that can store our consciousness.

Like camera film.

Exactly. We can be stored on the film and use it as a bridge into the physical world. But we are extremely limited in action even then. This is why it is fortunate that you arrived—with your powers of telepathy it was easy to scan your mind and know of your likely good intentions.

That's all well and good, but you've still not explained how you came to be in this 'ere artists' studio.

When we realised that the authorities would not help us, we decided we must take matters into our own wavelengths. By some good fortune we cannot explain, we received a sudden increase in the signal from our comrades' ship and were able to trace it here. We observed that the people here seemed to commune with this device so we transferred ourselves into the film. And then we tried to communicate, but until now we have been unsuccessful.

Well, now that you've explained how you got here, what exactly do you want me to help you to do?

We must complete our mission. We must locate the missing ship and rescue the crew. Once we have found them, we can return to our own dimension and be free of this strange place. And you seem to be the very person to help us!

Yes, I do seem to be rather on your... er... wave-length.

So will you help us? You must help us, you are our only hope.

Hmm. How do I know that's all you want though? How do I know that once I get you out of there you won't turn out to be some kind of great Evil from The Dawn of Time whatsit? Or a great slobbering beast that'll drool all over me sparkly outfit?

You don't. But from what we saw of your mind Iris Wildthyme, you're not sure, and if there's any doubt in your hearts you won't be able to tolerate the thought of innocent creatures trapped as we are, and you'll take the risk.

I stood up and walked over to the camera and switched it off. I had to admit that this was a bit of a puzzler. I mean, any ship that could come into a space like The Factory and not be noticed must be pretty small. Luckily, on this occasion there were two geniuses in the vicinity rather than just the one, so I was confident that with the help of good old Andy, I could get to the bottom of this whole thing.

(Panda here again. I've not interrupted the narrative here to quibble with Iris's comment about being the only genius around most of the time—although I *could*—but rather to let you know what was going on whilst Iris was in communion with the creature in the camera.

Having delighted the charming ladies with my breathtaking analysis of our host's art for some time, they decided to go and powder their noses. My attention having the chance to wander, I took in the wider scene of the party. I have to say in my career as an art critic I have attended many functions at galleries and studios and have seen a lot of things and met many different kinds of people, but the crowd at The Factory were certainly unique. Bright young things—beautiful, fashionable, but mostly on the cheap, and with an attitude that made all of them look like they were wearing those wrap-around sunglasses even when they weren't. The art itself may have been far from classical, but at least I could tell what was art and what was furniture—not like the time I went to that exhibition launch party and fell asleep after one too many glasses of champers on a bed that turned out to be the major exhibit. I still feel the embarrassment to this day.

Anyway, I digress. Having travelled for many years with Iris on the bus, I have come to own a highly-honed sense of perception where trouble is concerned. I can spot a suspicious character a mile off, and on this evening something was troubling me. Or rather, *someone*. I couldn't quite place him at first, but I knew that someone there—apart from Iris and myself—didn't belong but was doing a good job of keeping in the background. Not that that should have been difficult at this party, stuffed to the rafters as it was with the greatest collection of outsiders and eccentrics in this of all cities. But in the end, that was what gave him away. When I finally managed to spot him it was because he'd tried a little too hard to fit in, without fully understanding what it was that he was trying to fit in *to*. Every element of his clothing was right enough, but it looked more like a beatnik uniform made up by someone who had read an article about bohemians in *Life* or *Time* than something someone would genuinely wear. At first I wondered if he was just someone new on the scene, but something about his general demeanour suggested otherwise.

I subtly studied him. He moved around the room, always in the background, never involved in any conversations but always close enough to overhear them, positioning himself on the edge of small groups, which made him appear to be part of them to anyone who might notice him. Clearly, this was a practiced technique in information-gathering and infiltration but my experienced eye could spot even the smallest details.

And then there was the moment when he tripped over someone's leg and his wig fell off, revealing an official short-back-and-sides beneath the unruly mop. I accept that this is a somewhat heavy-handed clue, but it was only because of my perceptiveness that I happened to be watching him the moment it happened—he responded so quickly in putting the wig back that no-one else even noticed.

I asked Nicko if she knew who he was or if she had seen him before.

'Noooo,' she intoned Germanically, sounding as though she were channelling the answer from the other side. 'I have nott seeeeen him beforrrre. But Arndy alllllways has new peeeople at his parties. It's how he likes eeeeeet. He calls eeeeeet open houuuuze.'

It didn't take a time traveller to realise that sometimes having an open house policy was a risky business. I was about to go and start a conversation with him to see if I could get any information out of him, when—)

I strode back into the party, looking for Andy. Such was my obvious determination and natural authority (and an unfortunate collision with a small table) that everyone instantly stopped talking and looked at me.

'Where's Andy?' I cried.

'I think he's hiding behind a curtain,' Panda replied.

Andy stepped forward, clearly somewhat in awe of me. 'Er… hi,' he said.

'Andy,' I said, 'I need a private word with you right now. You too Panda.'

(As Iris led Andy Warhol from the room I looked around for the interloper but he had disappeared).

Andy and Panda followed, hot on my heels, back to the room with the video camera.

'Now then Andy,' I said, 'you might want to sit yourself down because I have something big to tell you. When I sat in front of that camera, something very odd happened. I heard a voice.'

Panda made a comment about the amount I'd had to drink but I ignored him.

'Now, hear me out. The voice wasn't spoken aloud in the room, it was beamed telepathically into my brain by an intelligence that was imprinted into the film in the camera. Whilst the camera was on and aimed at me, the intelligence was able to communicate thanks to my exceptional telepathic skills. It was an *alien* intelligence. As in, not of this world. Now, Andy, what do you have to say to that?'

'Oh…' he replied. 'Gosh.'

I must admit that I had expected something more by way of reaction from one of the decade's greatest artists, but it was better than outright dismissal or complete panic, I suppose.

'It's made a nest in the film in your movie camera, says it's looking for a scout ship of its own kind that went missing in these parts. Seems convinced that it's somewhere in The Factory. Do you know anything about it?' I gave him my best stern look. 'Andy, if you're involved in some cosmic shenanigans that you shouldn't be, you'd best tell me everything because I'm the only person who can possibly help. Be honest now.'

'No… no not at all. Golly.'

'Good. Because we need to help them. They've already lost part of their crew when they made the mistake of approaching the authorities. They probably kidnapped it to try to get technological secrets I'll bet. So it's up to us to prove to them that not everyone on this planet is so unfriendly. Right then. We need to carry out a top-to-bottom search of this place. Only problem is, I'm not exactly sure what we're looking for or how we'll recognise it when we find it.'

'Sounds like art,' said Andy. 'Shall we get started?'

(Say what you like about producing art like a factory-made product, it did mean that everyone who worked there was used to having to get organised and to put their backs into some work when it was required. Andy walked back into the party and clapped his hands. Someone turned the music off, and all eyes turned towards him.

'Now, everyone. There's something I need you all to help me with. Think of it as a game. There's something hidden in The Factory, something that shouldn't be here. And I want you all to try and find it.'

'Andy,' drawled one of the young men in wrap-around shades, 'how are we supposed to know what's not supposed to be here in *this* place?'

'Well, that's the challenge isn't it? Come on now Lou, get searching, and when you find anything you think it might be, holler nice and loud.'

Much to my surprise, even the proto-goths got up and started looking. In fact, there was only one person who didn't instantly join the search, instead moving stealthily towards the exit.

You're ahead of me on this, aren't you?

Yes, it was the man I had spotted earlier, and he'd obviously seen enough. Iris would have said I was being paranoid but I had a hunch, and when a panda has a hunch he has to follow it. So, I let him leave and then slipped out after him.

I saw his back as the lift doors closed behind him, and a moment later it started to descend. There was no way I could catch him by going down the stairs and if I waited for the lift to come back he would have disappeared into the night. Suddenly, I realised what I had to do.

I ran back into the room and pulled at the trouser leg of the first person I bumped into. I was slightly taken aback to realise it was the snarly youth in the shades who Andy had referred to as Lou, but this was no time for nerves.

'I need you to get one of the floating silver pillow things for me,' I said. He looked at me askance for a moment. 'Quickly, it's urgent!'

He shrugged and walked away, coming back a moment later with the object.

I led him to the nearest window. 'Would you mind terribly opening that for me?'

He shrugged again (I got the impression he did that a lot) and opened it for me. 'Now, if you'd be so good as to help me onto the windowsill and hand me the pillow?'

He reached down and picked me up, placing me next to the open window, then handing me the pillow. I took hold of the string that was attached to it, the pillow floating above my head. I looked out the window down into the street and sure enough, there was the suspicious little fellow making his way along the pavement.

Right then, I thought to myself, taking a deep breath. *Here we go.*

With a tremendous amount of personal courage, I leapt out of the open window.

I must have cut an extremely heroic, dashing figure, as I fell five floors towards terra firma, my descent slowed by the floating pillow. I even found myself whistling the theme music to *The A-Team* but realised it was undignified so I stopped.

I landed gracefully and let go of the pillow which floated back to the open window and was caught by the snarly youth. I waved to let him know my daring stunt had been successful (and to show how unruffled I was by the whole thing) and then set off in hot pursuit through the mean streets of Manhattan. If only I'd had a fedora and trench coat!

Eventually we arrived at what appeared to be a former thrift store, now boarded up. The man went round the back, and made his way up the fire escape. Once at the top, he gave three firm knocks with a deliberate gap between them, and the door opened, allowing him entry. I walked around the shop (trying not to think about how filthy the fur on my feet must have been getting) and looked for a way in. Luckily, I discovered that a small window of opportunity (haha!) had been left open. There was some abandoned cardboard around the back, which I pulled around to make into a platform from which I could reach the window ledge, and clambered into the shop.

Inside, the building still contained signs of its previous incarnation—the serving bar, shelving units and even an old-fashioned till. But there were clear signs of its new purpose. Items of surprisingly advanced technological equipment had been installed. In the middle of the room, on a table, pointing at a white screen to which all the technological gubbins was connected, was a projector. I had an immediate hunch as to what this was all for.

I could hear voices from the floor above through the ceiling. The man from the party was doing most of the talking, explaining to whoever else was up there that they had been right and that the missing aliens *were* at The Factory (or, "at the freak house" as he so charmingly put it). When he told them that a full search was going on for the missing ship, an older and more authoritative voice (think mine but with an American accent) replied;

'Then we've no choice. We'll have to raid the place. Now.'

I knew I had no time to lose. I had to free the alien prisoner, and get back to The Factory to warn them. There was only one way to do it in the time I had. I placed both paws on the projector stand and pushed. It was a large stand (well, compared to me) and it took all the strength in my short but strong arms to tip it. But tip it I did, and the projector came crashing down onto the floor. My cover immediately blown, I scooped up the roll of film from inside the projector and made for the window as the sound of heavy footsteps came pounding down the stairs into the shop.

'Oh Lord,' said the man from The Factory. 'It's that panda!'

'That *what?*' asked his superior, but I was too busy running as fast as my legs would carry me to hear the response.

I got back to the main road and as luck would have it I saw a car approaching. I held out my paw but realising that I didn't have a thumb I abandoned the traditional hitchhiker sign, and just jumped up and down waving my paw in the air instead. The car pulled up and a man with long dark hair and straggly beard looked out of his window.

'Hey,' he said, 'you need a ride little guy?'

In truth I was pretty sure that he had been indulging in more than just egg cream this evening but frankly I didn't have much choice.

'231 East 47th Street, and step on it!' I shouted.

'Dude, I have been waiting my whole life for someone to say that to me. Get on in.' And with that he reached down and lifted me in through the window, before putting his foot down on the accelerator just as the two men who were chasing me reached the sidewalk).

I have to admit, what with all the searching going on I didn't miss Panda straight away, but eventually I realised that I should have bumped into him in the midst of all the other people searching. An unkind part of my mind thought that maybe he'd passed out after a few drinks too many and was snoozing away in some dark corner, but I soon dismissed the thought that my friend would simply duck out when there was vital work to be done—and besides, we'd checked all the corners, dark and light, and he'd not been in any of them. I was worried, but there was nothing I could do for the moment except find the ship and hope that Panda turned up again soon. However it was clear that we were now searching for the sake of it—there was no sign of the missing ship. There was only one option left to me. I went back to the camera, switched it on and took my place in front of it.

Have you found it? Have you found our comrades?

Not a sign of them I'm afraid, chuck. Can you give us any clues at all? Do you have any idea what it might look like in the physical realm?

The physical realm? But we thought you understood.

Understood what?

We cannot have what you call a physical form unless we imprint ourselves on a suitable host material.

You mean, if the ship is here, it must be on film or some such material, like you are?

Correct.

Oh lummy, we've been looking in totally the wrong place. I thought a ship would have its own existence and it was just the crew that needed the film. Right, that gives us new places to check. Oh, and how long exactly was it that it went missing, in human terms if you can?

It took us several Earth months to arrive after their signal disappeared. That is all we can tell you.

Right. Don't you worry, I'll find them for you in two shakes of a lamb's tale, I thought brightly, hiding the follow up thought, *if we're very, very lucky.*

I switched the camera off and went back to the others. They had stopped searching and were waiting for further instructions.

'Okay,' I said, 'listen up. We've been looking in the wrong place. The thing we're looking for isn't a physical object at all. It's something that's been hidden on some film footage stored somewhere in The Factory.'

'But we have lots of film around,' said Andy, 'we make films all the time.'

'Then we'll have to narrow it down,' I replied. 'Apparently the ship... er... thing arrived a few months ago. If I'm right, it arrived while you were making one of your films and accidentally got sucked into the film itself. Now, have you noticed any unusual things happen while you've been making films?'

'*Everything* that happens during our films is unusual, that's the point of them.'

'Okay, well... anything more unusual than you expected?'

'No, not really...' His voice trailed off and suddenly the look on his face changed and I knew he'd thought of something. 'But, I think I know which film it is most likely to be.' He turned to one of the thoroughly bemused-looking party-goers. 'Paul, would you mind finding the original film rolls of *Empire* please?' He turned back to me. 'We filmed the Empire State Building for twenty-four hours last year. If an alien spaceship was going to get trapped in a roll of my film, it's most likely to have happened then because of the amount of time we were filming and because of the amount of open space that was always in shot. It shouldn't be hard to find, we only screened it last week.'

'That would explain why the rescue ship was suddenly able to detect them! Great thinking Andy. Your film would have acted like a net, and the ship would have gotten caught up in it. And to think some people say you're not a proper genius. I mean, er... jealous people who don't know anything about art, obviously.'

'Er... okay. And I think I might have thought of a way to reunite our little space friends. Little Joe, be a dear and bring out the film projectors, would you? We're going to have an impromptu screening.'

And just as it looked like one problem was about to be solved, the other resolved itself. We didn't hear the lift arrive on the fifth floor but we certainly noticed the black and white blur that shot into the middle of the room, carrying a roll of film. Unfortunately, I was about to discover that this little resolved problem was about to introduce an even bigger one.

('Panda!' said Iris, clearly delighted and relieved to see me. 'Where have you been? And what's that you've got? We think we've found the scout ship so... no! It can't be!'

I was still breathing heavily from my heroic exertions. 'It (gasp) ruddy (gasp) well (gasp) is.' And I handed the roll to Iris. 'The one taken prisoner by the government, I think you'll find.'

'But where did you find it.'

'No time for that now. We've got company.'

'Oh,' she said, indicating the others in the room, 'they know all about it.'

'Not *them*. There's at least two of them following me and they'll be here any moment, plus they called for back-up. I don't know if they're the FBI, the Men in Black or film enthusiasts prepared to go to extraordinary lengths, but they're on their way and they want the scout ship and all our other alien friends.'

'Golly,' said Andy. 'Then here's what we'll do.')

'Lou,' Andy said to one of the group in all black and shades. 'You know those very long introductory improvisational songs you drive people away from concerts with? Could you play one of those for us please? As loud and long as you can.'

The group all went to a collection of guitars leant against a wall, and started connecting them to the amps, while the blonde woman who had been chatting to Panda—Nicky, I think her name was—went to the microphone whilst holding a tambourine. At that moment, Paul and Little Joe came in carrying projectors. 'Would you put them next to the movie portrait camera please? Angle them so that the projections overlay on each other. Wonderful. Now, we need to play the *Empire* footage, the movie portrait of Iris and the film Panda brought us, all at the same time. That should bring all the space people into the same beam of light and allow them to make contact with each other. Could you set that up please?'

(I believe Iris's comment at this point was something along the lines of a rather flummoxed, 'Oh... er... yes, the Photons need to be in the same contact ... er ...beam. Absolutely.')

Paul and Little Joe placed the projectors on the floor and pointed them towards a bare white wall before spooling the video tapes into the machinery. The projectors soon started to hum and after a moment the familiar shape of the Empire State Building appeared in grainy black and white—but all too soon we heard the determined knock that is common to law enforcement agencies across the Universe.

'Are you ready?' he asked the band. They nodded. 'Okay then. When I put my hand on my head, start playing.'

And then Andy walked to the main door and opened it. Facing him were several large men, dressed in regulation dark suits and straight ties, dark glasses and scowls.

'Can I help you?' Andy asked them.

'We need to search this place for... illegal aliens,' said the leader of the group, holding up a piece of paper that was probably a warrant.

'Oh, really? Well, we have no aliens of any sort here. We're just a group of friends having a little party.'

'Nevertheless, we insist on coming in.'

'Oh gosh. Well then, I guess you better had.' And he placed his hand on top of his head as though about to run his fingers through his hair.

Instantly a cacophony of noise sprang up through the speakers. The sound of a viola scythed through the air, riding over the top of guitars and drums so loud that the walls and floor started shaking. Little did the agents know, but it was the sound of the future coming out of the speakers, every strum and crash like a wave knocking the forces of squaredom back.

The men in suits pushed past Warhol and made their way into the room, but their steps were sluggish and slow, their hands raised as though they were fighting their way through a hurricane that no-one else could feel.

I looked around at the projections all running over each other in unison and moved in front of them. Panda came to join me, ready to defend the aliens. The intruders made their way slowly towards us—proving that they understood the importance of the projections and film. And as slowly as they were moving, they would reach the projectors eventually. I didn't know what Panda and I could do against them but we had to try.

Then, just as I was beginning to despair, the rest of the Factory regulars came forward and joined us to form a barrier. I wasn't really sure if they had bought into the story of the aliens, whether they were protecting Andy's films, or just hated the authorities and wanted to obstruct them in any way possible. But we stood ready to repel them. When the agents got too close, a heavy beat on the over-turned drum would bend them double, or the screech of the viola would flash out like a lasso, pulling them off their feet. The agents kept coming, but the line held. The lead agent made one last attempt, hurling himself at us, arms outstretched to reach the projectors behind us. For a moment I thought he was going to make it. But then, Andy appeared behind us.

'Oh, hello,' he said, as though to an unexpected but welcome guest. 'Do you mind if I take your picture?' And he held his camera up into the agent's face and pressed the button—prompting the flash to go off right into his eyes. The shock made the agent stagger back and he joined the rest of his men on the floor.

Iris! said the voice of the rescue vessel inside my mind.

Have you found them?

Yes!

Blimey. That was quick. There's twenty-four hours of footage for you to look through.

We were able to signal to each other once we were in the same beam of light and unify. We are whole again and can leave.

Then go! I dunno if we can keep these squares back much longer.
Thank you, Iris. We go.

The telepathic connection snapped, and I knew they had gone. I waved at Andy and he understood. He turned to the band and moved his hands in a sideways cutting motion and the music abruptly stopped. The agents, who had seconds before been struggling to put one foot in front of the other, snapped out of it so fast that some of them fell over with sudden, unexpected momentum.

'I'm sorry,' said Andy to the agent in charge. 'They do play a little loud but aren't they fabulous?'

'Sir,' said one of the agents, holding out a device that didn't belong to this century (and that they'd probably got from the alien that Panda sprung from captivity), 'there's no sign now. They're not here,' he said, slipping the device back into his pocket.

'Oh dear,' said Andy. 'Have you made a mistake? Well, these things can happen.'

The agent in charge glared. I walked over to his subordinate and put my arm around his shoulder. 'Never mind, chuck, eh? Why don't you stay for the rest of the party. The band'll be striking up again any moment.'

The agent looked terrified at the prospect and then relieved when his superior, deliberately ignoring Warhol, turned to his men and said, 'Okay boys, let's go.'

They filed out, not even glancing at the Factory entourage as they went. Clearly, they thought this hippie beatnik scum too below them to deserve their attention. Good riddance, I say.

'Well,' said Panda, 'have they gone?'

'Oh yes,' I said. 'Off to explore more friendly places, I should think.'

'You did notice that they had alien technology, didn't you?'

'What, this?' I said, producing the scanning device that the agent had been holding. 'I picked his pocket on the way out. Can't have technology like this lying around in the 1960s.'

'But they've got machines in a secret base a few blocks from here. I saw it when I rescued their ambassador.'

'Then I think we need to pay it a little visit before we go. If we nip back five minutes in the bus we can collect it all up before they get back there.'

'Are you going?' asked Andy. Poor love, I could tell he was desperate for us to stay.

'Yes, sorry but duty calls. You carry on your party without us. Don't worry chuck, we'll be back to pay you another visit soon.'

He was so excited by this prospect that all he could say was 'Oh.' And then the band started up again. I couldn't quite make out all the words because of the volume but it was something about a heroine. I don't like to brag, but I'm pretty sure it was about me.

The Brightest Stars in the Demimonde

Matthew Bright

Buckle up, luvvies—have I got a story to tell *you!*

It's been quite the whirlwind couple of trips, I have to say. It started with me up to me nugs in trouble, as per usual, cast cruelly into the coldest, darkest of prisons—Bow Street, 1870 to be precise—and left to rot for eternity, never mind their "sleep it off til morning". Me, the motherly wouldn't-hurt-a-fly type! Shame on them, I say. The cell wasn't half parky, I don't mind telling you, and this particular crevice in time and space weren't much padded for them of the criminal nature. Not that was what I was, of course, but righteous indignation in the face of wrongful incarceration doesn't do much for keeping your extremities or your bum from going numb.

But you're not here to listen to the Collected Bellyachings of Iris Wildthyme (unless you are, in which case you'll be after the unabridged version, available now from all good galactic bookstores), so allow me to speed the story along to the point where things got interesting.

It started with—

—Lights. Gaslights, a battalion of them, illuminating the cell in a stark, all-seeing glare, the kind of light that pierces through pearl powder and rouge, and picks out every harsh line, every infinitesimal hair below the surface, every masculine pore. It is an unforgiving spotlight into which our main players are thrust.

Allow us a moment to introduce them:

First, always first, Miss Stella Boulton, the younger, elegant in a scarlet evening dress, face delicately painted, lace-fringed muslin shawl wrapped tight around her head. Second, always second, Miss Fanny Graham, stouter and yet still striking, matronly brows at odds with her carefree flaxen curls, her dark-green crinoline rumpled and muddied.

Despite their position centre-stage in this melodrama, they had the air of actors after the curtains have come down, their clothing merely costume, their hair and makeup simply window-dressing, the braggadocio of performance turned into transparent play-acting; in perhaps more practical words, they looked like little boys caught by their father playing dress-up in their mother's wardrobe.

In this harshest of spotlights, they quailed.

The constabulary closed around them, jackals and wolves behind their ring of lights, champing at the bit to witness the spectacle.

One stepped forward. 'Remove your clothes,' he said, and his voice was the kind that pierces through muslin and silk and crinoline.

Layer by layer, Miss Stella Boulton and Miss Fanny Graham shed their dress, kid boots, crinolines, and the flannel petticoats that lay beneath, revealing the short stays and padded bosoms of Ernest Boulton and Frederick William Park.

The officer tilted his head. 'You,' he said, pointing his nightstick at Stella. 'Are you wearing drawers?' When Stella didn't respond apart from a nervous nod of the head, he motioned at her. 'Take them off.'

Reluctantly, tears pricking the makeup at the edge of her eyes, Stella obeyed, casting aside her undergarments and standing before them naked, patently male but with the face of a beautiful woman.

The jackals jeered and howled, as jackals are wont to do.

'As you were,' said the man with the voice, and waved away his men and their gaslights. The crowd dispersed, the spotlight dimmed; the officer locked the cell door behind him, and melted away into the gloom.

In what little light remained, Fanny and Stella stooped to gather their scattered clothing and began to dress themselves in something resembling decency, feebly pulling silk over flannel. They avoided each other's eyes, heads down, focusing on their task with the deliberate attention of those who know that completing the task at hand is all that keeps them from breaking down.

As she struggled to fasten her dress, Fanny cracked. She sank down to her knees, covered her face, and emitted a single, plaintive sob. It reverberated from the prison walls, magnified to ghastly enormity before fading away at last.

Stella knelt beside her, and rested her forehead on the crown of Fanny's head, dislodging the hairpiece yet further. 'Dear sister,' she said, and then again: 'Dear sister,' but this time the words were choked with her own tears.

From out of the darkness, a voice interjected.

'Ohhhhhhhhhhhhhh,' it said, 'there was a young man of St. Paul's...'

Disturbed by the loud interruption, the sisters looked up, squinting through the bars of their cell in the direction from which the voice came.

'... who possessed the most useless of b—'

All around the air was suddenly inhabited by a deafening chiming; somewhere very nearby a church was marking the hour, and a cloud must have passed from the moon because a silver light flooded the prison through the narrow window. It illuminated the cell opposite them, revealing a woman laid on her back, an enormous hat covering her face. She was dressed in an assortment of ragtag, bedraggled clothing, and from the smell of her had apparently been bathing in beer.

'He went to the Strand, and managed a stand, and t—'

A loud, final chime.

'—off in the stalls!' the woman concluded and cackled to herself. 'Thank you, thank you,' she said. 'I'm here all week, and probably longer at this bleedin' rate.'

Stella climbed to her feet and approached the bars wearily. 'Well,' she remarked, arching an eyebrow. 'I think we know what *you're* in for.'

The woman grinned. 'Ayyyyyy, now look at that,' she said. 'Did you see that?' She gave no indication of how, with her hat fully covering her face, she could have seen anything herself, but this didn't seem to give her any pause. 'Your back, all nice and straight, and that hand on the hip. And that lip curl—ooh *yes!* Good on you, lady. Don't let the buggers get you down.'

'Didn't you see?' said Fanny. She had stayed squatted on her haunches in the corner of the cell, less interested in their companion than Stella. She sounded defeated, and very, very tired. 'We're no ladies, are we?'

Stella sat down beside her. 'Apparently not, dear sister.'

'Awww, no, now, I'll not be having any of that,' said the woman across the way. She rummaged in her pocket and produced a small silver flask, and tossed it without looking through the bars. It ricocheted, and skittered to a halt at the feet of the sisters. 'Here, take a nip of that, it'll perk you right up.'

Stella retrieved the flask, unscrewed the top and sniffed it suspiciously. She winced.

'Oi,' said the woman sharply. 'That's gin from the fields of the planet Thursday, don't you go turning your nose up, thank you *very* much.'

Stella took first a sip, then a glug, and passed it to her sister, who swigged without caution.

'Why,' said Fanny, her lips moistened with gin, gleaming a red that in another situation might have been seductive, 'did they make us strip to our nothings, while you are over there secreting away bottles of liquor.'

The woman in the other cell waved a hand dismissively. 'Oh, that silky-voiced officer of yours wouldn't dare put a hand on me, or he'd find out what I've *really* got hiding in me bloomers.'

'Oh,' said Stella, and then, '*Oh*.'

There was a clatter in the doorway, and a sudden light as the door opened. As if summoned, the officer appeared, lit by the guttering flame of a lantern. 'Less of the commotion, I'll have you mind.'

'I'll cause as much commotion as I like,' said the woman in the other cell. 'It's practically my stock-in trade. Go on—hop it.'

The officer pursed his lips for a second, then apparently decided it wasn't worth the bother. He swept his gaze over the sisters as he turned back, and caught sight of the flask. 'Is that liquor? Hand it over.'

'Oi!' The woman in the other cell threw aside her hat and sat up, looking furious. 'That's mine, that is.'

'Not anymore,' said the officer, and departed.

'Well that's the last straw,' said the woman, and glowered. 'The cad, stealing a lady's booze like that. I'd like to see *him* fight the distillery dragons on Thursday and get away with a barrel on his back. Bloody priceless, that was.'

'Who *is* he?'

The woman jumped, as if she'd forgotten there were others in the room. 'Him? Never mind him. He's just the Antagonist. Every story's gotta have one, or it's not a proper story, and he's ours. Well, yours mostly, but ours for now, while our paths are *entwined*, as they say.'

Stella grimaced; she looked pale, frailer than she had moments ago while comforting her sister. 'He's a horrible man.' She looked down. 'He scares me,' she said, barely audible.

'Hey now,' said the woman. 'I already told you—I'll be having none of that. You there—both of you. Stand up! That's it. Now do that thing, the hand on the hip thing, that's it, luvvie. Arch your back. That's more like it. You look...'

She trailed off. Finally, she shook herself, and smiled. 'You look grand, the pair of you.'

The sisters held their poses, breath swelling their chests. Stella jutted her chin defiantly outwards. Fanny smoothed the waist of her dress, breathed in and heaved her bosom. Then they caught each other's eye, and began to laugh.

'That's it,' said the woman. 'Does a body good to hear laughter.'

The laugh faded from Stella's lips. 'Laughter is all well and good,' she said, 'but it won't get us out of this cell.'

The woman bent down to retrieve her hat and plonked it on her head at a jaunty angle. 'What do you want out of the cell for?' she said. 'Where would you go?'

'Anywhere,' said Stella. 'Anywhere at all—anywhere that officer isn't, or any of his men. I'd run away right this second if I could.'

'Me too,' said Fanny. She sighed wistfully. 'Freedom, except for some metal and locks—what are you doing?'

The woman was rooting in her bloomers again, and the sisters exchanged looks, realising that it was entirely possible—for all her jovial bonhomie—that she could easily be a lunatic, a possibility all but confirmed when she wheeled around brandishing a corkscrew and screeching: 'Never fear, auntie's here!'

There was a long moment in which nothing happened, and the triumphant grin died on the woman's face. She tapped the corkscrew hard against the palm of her hand, there was a glint of light, a strange whirring noise, and then—

Then the chains were made loose.

The woman scooted across to them and pulled open their cell door. The padlock fell away, clanking, and rolled into a corner.

'Hello girls,' she said, extending a grimy hand. 'Allow me to introduce myself, I'm—'

'Iris Wildthyme!' she said. 'You'll see all my papers are in order.'

The ticket officer was red-faced and panicked. 'Yes, but what about—?'

'The bus? What about it. I've paid my fare, even paid my extra baggage fee and everything. Look, the paper says so.' She waved it in his face.

'Yes, ma'am, but... I don't think we normally cover such a *large* item... ma'am,' he added again, lamely.

'Well clearly you do, otherwise I wouldn't have been permitted to bring it on board at dock, now would I? Unless you think I just materialised out of nowhere?'

'No...' he said weakly. 'But...'

'Go check with the Captain,' said Iris blithely. 'In the meantime, I'll be showing my sisters—er, daughters—here around the boat. Take good care of her.'

She patted the Number 22's rear hubcap and strode away, clicking her fingers for her charges to follow, leaving the ticket officer to wonder exactly how he'd failed to notice a London bus parked on the top deck of England's biggest cruise liner for the last thirteen days.

'Where *are* we?' asked Stella, struggling to keep up with their new guide. Everything that had happened in the last twenty minutes was proving very confusing, from the way all the prison locks had mysteriously opened, to the bizarre red machine she had been bundled inside, to how the outside had melted into blue light before finally solidifying into their new surroundings.

'The *Arcadia*,' said Iris, pointing to where the name was spelt out in a wide curve on a white wall. 'But your real question is *when*, and I'd say from the taste of the wind about 1958, but I'm never too good on that sort of thing. Failed the air-tasting class at the Academy.'

'What do you mean *when*...'

'Just, y'know, *when*. Come on.'

Giving them no more time for questions, she dashed onwards. For their part, Fanny and Stella found themselves shell-shocked by the opulence they found themselves amongst. Under the starry early-evening sky, lit by lamps, the cruise ship seemed like a floating faerieland, a phantasmagoria of filigree and fluorescence a world away from their grime and gaslight. They gawped, openly, even as Iris dragged them bodily along the decks, haring along with no apparent concern for either her fellow passengers or no-entry signs. She shouldered them through a door marked "ship crew only", vanishing into the gloomy interior, skidding to a halt only when she realised she had lost her companions.

She retraced her steps, and found them stood at the doorway, leaning over the railing. Below them the full expanse of the main deck was in evidence, its centrepiece a large, square swimming pool rippling with reflected pinpoints of light. Around it, people reclined, in tasteful swimwear, waited upon by men in blazers and ties carrying brightly-coloured drinks in tall glasses. Everybody in sight *gleamed*: primped, tucked and expensive.

Stella was marvelling at how beautiful everyone looked. Fanny, ever the more practical, was wondering how they kept the water warm enough to bathe at night.

'Iris,' Stella said, looking back and smiling. 'I don't know how you brought us to this place—or time, if that's what this is—but this is *wonderful*. If we were ever going to run away to somewhere... I mean, thank you!'

'Ay?' Iris's face crinkled in confusion. 'You what?'

'This ship! It's every luxury my sister and I have ever dreamed of.'

Iris blinked, as if she was only just now noticing the ship behind them. She peered over the railing. 'Them lot?' She sighed, and shook her head with exaggerated disappointment. 'Have you ladies learned nothing in your time? You should know by now, the party's never at the front door. You want to have a good time, you gotta get *backstage*. Now come on.'

She grabbed them each by the wrist and hauled them down the corridor, brooking no argument. Here the walls were noticeably less well-kept, with cracked off-white paint, and there was barely space to walk two abreast.

Somewhere, there was music.

'And where there's music, there's dancing,' declared Iris. 'On the double!'

Like a pig sniffing out truffles, she led them through the warren of corridors to a set of double-doors, above which the word "MESS" was stencilled in fading letters. On the other side of it could be heard the sound of Eartha Kitt. 'You 'ear that?' she said. 'To me, that old girl's voice is like catnip to an old tom—c'mon!'

She threw open the doors and dived into what lay on the other side.

If it was an officer's mess, it bore no resemblance to anything Fanny and Stella might have expected. For a start, there was an awful lot of silks hung about the place, and an awful lot of dresses. Fanny and Stella were pitched into what felt like a taffeta ocean. Their guide dived freely into this tossing sea, screeching, 'Mine's a gin and tonic, Richard!' as she accosted a tall, moustachioed man in a ballgown. He kissed her exuberantly on either cheek, and reached for a bottle. 'Iris, my darling—it's been so long! But you came for my show!' But what this show might be was lost on Fanny or Stella as they vanished beneath the surface of the ocean themselves, finding themselves swept by the current amongst a crowd of men in varying degrees of dress—from effervescent evening gowns to slinky, silky kimonos. Some wore wigs, some wore makeup, some both; jawlines were sharp, eyelashes long, ruffles were everywhere, and laughter broke in waves on the shore.

'At least you've come dressed for the part,' said one, plucking at Stella's stays. She slapped his hand away, though not before she had noticed a very particular twinkle in his eye. 'A basque is rather old school but with those hips, it'd be a crime not to!'

Fanny, meanwhile, had fetched up near the punch bowl, being ministered to by a waiter in a purple nightdress. 'Oh, honey,' he said, 'your makeup is *disgraceful*—have you been crying in a rainstorm all night?'

'Not so far wrong,' Fanny said. 'You wouldn't *believe*—'

'Oh, I'm sure I would,' said the waiter. 'I'll believe anything, me. Here—let me help you out.' He produced a compact from his pocket and leaned in close to apply fresh makeup to Fanny's tear-streaked face.

As if it was only moments, an hour vanished, and then another. Some men came, some men went, but Fanny and Stella stayed in the midst of it all. There was gin, and wine, and singing, and when the door opened there was no stiffening of limbs, or nervousness as to who might enter. Despite Iris's earlier explanation, it was still quite beyond Fanny and Stella where or when they had fetched up, but through slivers of conversation they began to build a picture. These were the crew of the *Arcadia*, waiters, entertainers, cooks and the like, who had signed up to travel aboard the fleet of cruise ships owned by P&O.

Iris watched them carefully, in quiet moments between bouts of merriment. She noted the sisters move slowly from the self-conscious theatrical enjoyment that masks a great discomfort, into a comfortable, unaffected cheer, and she glowed with satisfaction at a job well done. She necked half a glass of gin and smiled to herself; Auntie Iris strikes again.

'Surely,' said Stella at one point, perched on the knee of a burly sailor who had taken something of a shine to her, 'you can't all be... y'know?'

'Friends of Mrs King?'

'I haven't the faintest idea who Mrs King is, but... if I infer your meaning correctly?'

The man whom Iris had greeted first, Richard, took it upon himself to answer. 'Not all of us,' he said. 'Not all of us on the ship, at any rate. I'm sure the rest of them are off sobbing themselves to sleep in their dull little cabins while we inverts over here rule the roost and play our records. And anyone who wants to come and rub shoulders—or whatever else they like—with us down here are more than welcome.'

'It's like running away,' the burly man said. 'Running away and joining the circus!'

Fanny said, 'But what about home? Surely you aren't like this at home?'

Richard laughed. 'Depends who you ask,' he said. 'Me? I've got a wife in Torquay. Let that be whatever answer you like.'

Stella looked around from face to face. 'So you're all... this place is... you're only... *free* when you're out on the sea?'

Richard winced. 'Freedom is a tricky word,' he said. 'After all, this isn't really running away. The ship gets to port and turns right back around and sails home.'

'But,' said the burly man, 'then it leaves again.'

'I see,' said Stella. She had the sad look of a child who has just learned that their beloved dog didn't really go to live on the farm.

'Well, this *is* getting maudlin,' interjected Iris. She staggered into the circle, clutching a half-empty (though Iris thought of it as half-full) bottle. 'We'd best liven things up, don'tcha think? Hey, girls—I know a thing. How about you teach these boys how to chirrup?'

'What's chirruping?'

Stella roused herself. 'Where we come from,' she said, 'it's a thing we do to show we're... available, shall we say, and interested.' She pressed her lips together and fluttered them, emitting a loud sucking noise. 'Like so!'

The sailors attempted to imitate her, with varying degrees of success.

'It's vulgar of course,' her sister noted, 'and so naturally Stel is an expert.'

Stella leapt up and took centre stage, pulling an exaggerated face and letting loose a barrage of chirrups. She strode towards one of the sailors seated a little out of the throng; he had a thick, handsome face and looked a little nervous as she approached. She chirruped again, leaning in, her hands on his thighs, spitting the final repeat of her chirrup with a purposeful, suggestive force.

There was a pregnant moment of nothingness, and then the sailor kissed her on the mouth. The assembled ladies of the sea cheered raucously, which was when—

—when—

—when Stella saw him. The Antagonist. The officer from the cells, the man who had stripped her clothing from her, and left her naked to be inspected and catalogued and reported on. He was there but a moment, glimpsed between shoulders, but that split second opened a hole in her belly from which a hollow, shuddering panic spilled out, impossible to dam back up.

Her glass fell from between wooden fingers, rolling across the floor. She stumbled back. Blood was roaring in her veins as if her own body was shouting at her, and she felt irrationally angry, at the betrayal it was enacting upon her. It was only a face, probably a mistake, and here she was acting like a—

'Stel?' Fanny was on her knees in front of Stella, one hand supporting her lolling head. 'Dear sister, are you not well?'

'It's nothing. I thought I saw...'

'Who?'

Fanny's face was set with concern, the frivolity immediately cast aside. There was an awkwardness between them, a painful sense of unreality; this was not how they were meant to be. Fanny as the worrywart, the nervous one, and Stella the free spirit who could swish away her concerns and pull her along in her brilliantine wake.

Though after all—look where that had landed them. But no, that was not a charitable thought.

'I thought I saw *him*, the officer who arrested us. Who made me... but don't trouble, Fanny—

'You saw him?' Fanny looked around for Iris. 'Iris! *Iris!* Have you seen Iris?'

'Yes, but I'm sure it was just—'

'Either way, just look at you, we can't be having you shaking like this, can we? Come on, take my arm—we'll find Iris, and we'll—Iris!'

Iris blinked at them, having been entirely unaware of anything untoward happening as she danced the robot to *There Ain't Nothing Like A Dame*. 'What's up, luvvies?'

'We have to go. Stel, she saw the... *the man*, and now she's... well, she's like this.'

Iris looked her up and down. 'Just the sweats, by the looks of her. When you say you saw *the man*, do you mean...?'

'The Antagonist—is that what you called him?'

Iris pursed her lips. 'I see. And you want to what—run away again?'

Fanny gripped her sister's waist. 'Yes,' she said. 'Emphatically yes.'

Iris sniffed, and downed the remains of her glass. 'Who am I to argue?' she said. 'Let's be having yous then.'

'Okay, I hold my hands up,' said Iris. 'It might have been the gin doing the thinking. See, what I thought was, a bit of "it gets better" would do you girls the power of good, but I tend not to think much beyond four walls and a bar, you see. So here was me thinking "let's show them a party" but the thing about parties is that they have to end, and everyone has to go home.'

'Unless you have an omnibus that travels in time and space,' said Fanny.

'Even then,' said Iris.

She cranked the parking brake on the Number 22, and craned to look at her rather nervy passengers.

'The one exception,' she said, 'is an Irridican party.'

There was a rapping at the door, and Iris swung the door open. A short, purple person stood at the bottom of the steps, his eyes barely peering over them. Aside from his colour, the most noticeable thing about him was his clipboard, which was mainly of interest as it was the only thing he was wearing.

'You're late,' the person said, 'but not to worry. I'm Jask-wah-thurtoria, the nineteenth-and-two-thirds, and I will be your undresser for today's ceremonies. Do I have permission to board?'

Iris beamed. 'You most certainly do, Jask-wah-thurtoria. You come right on in!'

Jask-wah-thurtoria leaped up into the Number 22 and, without apparent concern, began to remove Iris's clothes.

'So as I was saying,' Iris said, lifting her arms to grant Jask-wah-thurtoria better access, 'I didn't go far *enough.* I skipped a few decades ahead, went for some glitz and glamour, but nothing had changed. And then it struck me—an Irridican wedding, just the ticket! See, on Irridica, their primary economy is parties. The party literally never stops—people come here from all over the galaxy to party. There's about a hundred versions of me, knocking around the place, at one time or another. And a wedding is the biggest of their parties, but *this* one even more so.'

Her cardigan fell away, revealing several more layers beneath. Jask-wah-thurtoria barely masked a sigh.

Stella, nursing the cup of tea Iris had provided (enhanced by a nip from Iris's "special flask"), looked unimpressed. 'Iris, what exactly is he doing to you?'

'Well,' said Iris, 'what Jask-wah-thurtoria is doing is ceremonially undressing me, seeing as all Irridican wedding ceremonies are held naked as we came. But where you're going wrong there is when you said he. Jask-wah-thurtoria is actually a nye—is that right?'

Jask-wah-thurtoria nodded curtly; nye was looking at Iris's blouse and wondering how it could have so many buttons, what business it had being six layers below the last blouse nye'd removed, and why there seemed to be a duffle-coat beneath it.

'Irridican's have thirteen genders,' said Iris. 'Plus fractions. Until today, anyway. Today's a special wedding—it's a royal one! Honorary Voo-shaw-lagward is marrying gos childhood sweetheart Honorary Xin-skye-fareva, and that alone would be cause for celebration, but gor has also decided that gor is actually a jo. Or has been all along.'

'I have absolutely no idea what you're talking about,' Stella said. 'Are you even speaking English?'

'Technically, no,' said Iris, 'but that's a whole different kettle of fish, but anyway—short version is, Irridicans *did* have thirteen genders, but in about an hour and a half, they'll have fourteen. Oh glorious day!'

'Oh glorious day!' echoed Jask-wah-thurtoria, and thumped nyeself twice on the chest.

'That sounds beastly confusing,' said Fanny.

'Not remotely,' said Iris. The last piece of her clothing, released from its pin, drifted free, and she span around, grinning broadly. 'And more importantly, it's time for the party.'

Jask-wah-thurtoria stepped back and admired his handiwork. Nye popped his head out of the bus, and returned carrying a round loop of what appeared to be rope, though it glowed a calming, iridescent white. 'Your ceremonial robe, ma'am.' Iris accepted it, and looped it around her neck. Despite its name, it concealed nothing, but when it touched her skin it began to glow a cheery crimson.

Jask-wah-thurtoria turned to Fanny and Stella. 'Who's next?'

Fanny felt Stella stiffen beside her. 'Oh, no, thank you,' she said. 'I think we'd rather stay in our dresses, if you don't mind.'

Jask-wah-thurtoria looked scandalised.

'Now then,' said Iris, 'thing is, at an Irridican wedding we must shed all of our outer accoutrements and present ourselves free and unburdened. It's symbolic.'

'I'd really rather not,' said Stella, curtly. She was thinking of the officer in the cell, and the jackals who howled when she pulled off her clothes.

'Well in that case, not to worry!' said Iris. 'But I've got me face on now, so if you don't mind, I'll go take a nosey at the ceremony myself. I'll be back before you know it. Jask-wah-thurtoria—lead the way!'

Nye jumped down ahead of her, guiding her off the bus. The door swung shut behind them.

The sisters looked at each other.

'It wouldn't be the same as when—' said Fanny.

'I know,' said Stella.

A few moments passed.

'Thirteen genders,' said Stella.

'Fourteen,' said Fanny.

The bus settled, creaking. It sounded tired, but content.

'Which would you say we are?' said Fanny.

'Depends who you ask,' said Stella.

Somewhere, something ticked inside the Number 22, just a little faster than seconds should sound.

'I'll do it if—' said Stella.

'Fine,' said Fanny.

Fabrics hit the floor, one by one.

'Do you feel free and unburdened?'

'I never feel less free when I'm only wearing my skin.'

A long, *long* pause.

'Shall we anyway?'

'Yes, sister dear, we shall.'

When they exited the Number 22, they found Iris waiting for them, leaned against the front wheel. 'Knew you'd come,' she said. 'Here, Jask-wah-thurtoria left you these.'

They strung the white robes around their necks, each lit up a different colour; Stella's nude body was cast a fierce, opal blue, and Fanny's a deep, vibrant green.

Which was how the wedding of Voo-shaw-lagward and Xin-skye-fareva included as its witnesses Iris Wildthyme of the Clockworks, and Fanny Park and Stella Boulton of Bloomsbury, London. The wedding itself was an affair such as Fanny and Stella had rarely witnessed, bigger even than their imaginations could have given credit for, taking place in an enormous stadium thronged with every race in the galaxy, observing from an endless array of floating bubbles that suspended them in mid-air despite no visible physical ground upon which to stand. They witnessed the happy couple ride in on the traditional cloud-ships, witnessed them sing their vow-cantatas (a little overlong and slushy, but who can blame them?), witnessed them consume a slice each of the ritual marriage pie, witnessed the final moment in which they both hooked their robes to the roof of the stadium, their bubble-ship's fading away, and the robes unspooling as they descended, entwining with each other until both merged into one, single colour.

'I declare you skal and jo!' announced the officiator, and the stadium burst into applause.

'It was a beautiful ceremony,' said Stella, dabbing at tears that threatened to upset her makeup all over again.

Iris snuffled into a hanky that she had produced from... well, who knows where, and sometimes it was best not to question. 'I wish them every happiness,' she said. 'Fact, I went ahead and checked, and they live to the grand old age of eleventy-hundred together.'

'Is that a real number?'

'Who knows,' said Iris. 'Probably. Let's say it is.'

Fanny's robe had started to glow red, and moments later so did Stella's. Fanny looked over at her sister, alarmed. 'Iris, what's happening—is something wrong?'

Iris giggled. 'Wrong? Course not, don't be silly! It's a red alert—and you know what that means!'

'Danger?'

'No, not here. Red means it's time to dance.'

The stadium lights had dimmed, and all around them robes were turning red, casting the entire space a vivid, neon scarlet. Down from the ceiling of the hall it began to rain stars, streaking golden stars, the kind that a long way away and a long time ago, Fanny and Stella might have wished upon.

'Come on,' Iris said, grabbing them. 'Dance!'

There was a music throbbing up now, and the bubble-ships were starting to sway and move with it—they crashed into each other and began to merge. Theirs collided with a neighbour's, and Stella found herself engulfed in the embrace of an elephantine creature, weeping openly from its seven eyes, tilting its tusks aside to avoid goring her.

And so they danced as the bubbles crashed and merged until the stadium was one big dancefloor. The music rose, pulsing, racing, quite different from the music that Fanny and Stella were used to but thrilling in its novelty. At first they danced awkwardly, unsure how to move to the unfamiliar rhythm, until they realised that nobody else did either, and that they were surrounded by thousands of nude bodies in all shapes and sizes, dancing to their own tune. There was no drink at this party, nothing imbibed to grease the wheels, but there seemed to be something in the air that made all of that unnecessary, and soon Fanny and Stella were both lost—lost to the music, lost to the dancing, lost in the present without even the slightest sting of memory.

Iris watched them, and felt, for the second time, proud of herself. This time, she thought, it had worked. She was a clockmaker, one so finely tuned to the gears and movements of the heart that with a few gentle tweaks she had been able to make something broken tick again.

The sisters danced apart, then together, then apart again. Inadvertently, in the course of a few scant hours, they had become Victorian England's foremost experts in alien anatomy, but so multitudinous were the new sights that the wedding had exposed them to that they were barely absorbing a single detail.

At length they found one another again, dancing close.

'Dear sister, you look happy!'

The one pressed against the other. 'I am, dear sister, I—'

And then the one saw the other see the officer—the Antagonist—advancing through the crowd. The music's pulse raced, threatened to burst open her very heart, and the hole in her belly split its weak stitches and the panic burst out again. Pain bloomed in her knees and she realised she had fallen to the ground.

'Iris!' called Fanny. 'Iris—!'

Fanny knelt, once again, by her sister in the back of the Number 22. Stella was turned away from her, back arched. The sharp points of her spine stuck out violently through the fabric. Fanny ran her fingers soothingly down Stella's back, plucking anxiously at the dress's loose threads. Her sister breathed in, a shuddery, teary breath that tightened as she exhaled.

'Here,' said Fanny, and she draped a shawl around Stella's head, tucking it tight.

Outside the windows of the Number 22, a blue vortex of nothingness and time was spinning, and Stella stared miserably out into it. 'No matter how far we go,' she whispered, 'he follows us.'

Brakes squealed, and the bus came to a halt. The vortex solidified into *home.*

Outside was a London square, late autumn. A thick smog was rolling in, but in its murky depths could be made out the familiar bustle the sisters were accustomed to; broughams swerved around the bus, busy men stormed by pressing their toppers to their heads, women clutched their shawls tight against the creeping cold. Somewhere above, the sun was being swallowed whole, barely visible as anything but a watery globe through the mist.

'Iris...' Fanny cast a worried glance at her sister, and craned to peer into the driver's seat. 'I thought we could go to—well, I don't know. Somewhere else. Not back home. I confess that I don't quite understand my sister's state; she has never been one to fall apart so. In fact, it is usually quite the opposite, and I confess I usually rely on her to calm my *own* hysterias. She is the strong one, and I the weak.'

Iris fussed with the parking brake. 'Run away again, ay?'

'I don't see why not.'

'Well first up, a lesson from your Auntie Iris. Your sister and you—it's not weakness. In another time they'd have a name for it, but put plainly, you've had a shock, and the shock is gonna keep on going. I don't blame you. Your sister keeps seeing a face that reminds her of that shock, and going a bit giddy. And don't you think you've escaped it either—you've got her to be thinking of right now, and so it's easier to push all that nonsense away. But it'll come back around, sometime when you're least expecting it, and you're all on your own. Gin, that's my recommendation, but there's plenty would disagree.' She retrieved her hat and plonked it on her head. 'Apparently, I'm an *enabler*,' she said.

She yanked a lever, and the door creaked open. 'Thing is—I haven't brought you home. I know it looks like it, but I thought I'd take you on a little detour first. Go on—get your skirts on. Can't go out with your nethers all on show like that.'

And some minutes later:

'Welcome,' said Iris Wildthyme, 'to Empireland.'

She explained as she led them across the square.

'Nostalgia's a funny thing,' she said. 'Your hometown might seem like a pretty grim place to grow up, but give it forty years and you find yourself knocking round a museum looking at exhibits of your privy and telling everyone how grand it was when you had to go piddle with the spiders in the cold. Give it a hundred years, and people will be queuing up to give it a go in the name of *hauthenticity*. That's what's happened right here—

sometime a couple of centuries after you, they bulldozed Milton Keynes and built Empireland, a perfect replica of Victorian London, itchy clothing, piss-pots and cholera, the lot. People pay to come and live with historical accuracy!' She waved around. 'What do you think? You're the experts, after all.'

Fanny and Stella, for the third time in a short space of time, gawped, though the effect of Empireland was markedly different from the previous destinations they had encountered on their grand tour. Instead, it had the strange effect of a dream, in which every detail is right but somehow completely wrong.

'The newspapers aren't right,' said Stella. 'With all those big headlines. We didn't have those.'

'And the air smells clean,' added Fanny.

'Yeah, well, people have gotten used to a certain level of comfort that even authenticity can't change,' said Iris. 'That's people for you. But what I really wanted to show you... is this.'

It was the pub, the Dalston Arms.

'My god,' said Stella. 'It looks just like *our* Dalston Arms.'

'Come on in,' said Iris, and pushed open the door. A bell tinkled above, vibrating on a coil of metal. The bar was crowded, full of people dressed altogether more fancifully that the kind of clientele Fanny and Stella were used to in the real version of the Arms, and so they presumed they must be Empireland visitors. But they had no time to inspect any of them too closely, for what immediately caught the eye—of anyone entering, but especially the sisters—were the two women in the centre of the bar.

A circle was cleared around them, and they were singing raucously, accompanied on the piano by a squat, sweating man who thumped away at the keys with carefree abandon and little-to-no musical talent.

'Why,' breathed Stella, 'it's—'

'Us.'

The song finished, to applause. Some of the guests clinked together tankards of ale, froth spraying.

'Why thank you, thank you,' said the taller, prettier of the pair. 'You don't know what your applause means to us, you really don't. Allow me introduce myself—I am Miss Stella, and this is my dearest sister, Miss Fanny.'

There was more cheering, and the two women dipped shallow curtseys.

'You might have heard of us,' Stella continued. 'We're rather *notorious*, you see—the infamous he-she girls of London! Those beastly policemen stormed into the Strand Theatre—a den of iniquity, no less!—and stole us away. Had the nerve to suggest we were no real ladies—can you imagine?'

She winked theatrically at the crowd, who roared with laughter.

'My sister and I, we were aghast, of course. We couldn't believe we'd been impugned by such absurd and frivolous notions. So shocked by the allegations were we that my sister even swooned dead away—right into the inspector's lap, she did. But not even *that* could save us!'

The Fanny in the spotlight—this Empireland Fanny—dabbed her lips exaggeratedly and winked. It seemed to be her part in this charade to be silent, only occasionally mugging to the crowd.

'And we became sensations,' continued her sister. 'Monsters! Freaks! Perverts! It's enough to make you want to grab your pitchforks and get yourself all hot and bothered. They sang *songs* about us—do you want to hear one? Well, maybe in a minute. Patience! See, I need to make sure of a few things first.' She circled the room, fixing her patrons with an iron stare, one by one.

'Are you here to jeer?' she said. 'Are you here to catcall, or laugh? Somehow I doubt it—if you were here to laugh at a man in a dress, you'd have to do a good lot of laughing at yourselves.'

She paused before a guest in a vivid purple gown; to Stella and Fanny's eyes it was wildly unfashionable, but presumably with the distance of several centuries the vagaries of fashion had merged. 'You look beautiful, darling, by the way.' She stroked the woman's cheek for a moment, then blew her a kiss, and turned back to the crowd. 'If that's not it, why, could it be—' She affected a gasp. 'Could it be some of you are rather *partial* to a lady with a little bit extra?' She looked around. 'No,' she said, 'that *couldn't* be it.'

The crowd laughed, jostling each other. The guest in purple adjusted her hat.

'Very well then,' said the Stella in the spotlight. 'I shall take it on trust that you are here to sing *with* my sister and I, and I shall even let you into a little secret. Now, I'm trusting your good selves here as this is rather painful for my sister and I. That song they sang, well, it isn't altogether flattering. Some might argue it's even downright insulting. But my sister and I—we actually rather *like* it. Would you like to sing it with us?'

The crowd roared with approval and stamped their feet. The piano struck up, tunelessly. 'Take it away, sister dear,' said the Empireland Stella.

The other Fanny spread her arms wide, took a deep breath, and launched into the song. 'Ohhhhhhhhh, there was an old person of Sark, who buggered a pig in the dark—*join in!*—the swine in surprise, murmured "God blast your eyes"—*altogether now...!*'

The crowd raised their tankards and with one voice shouted back, '*Do you take me for Boulton and Park!*'

Fanny snatched a pint-pot from a guest and knocked it back. 'Again!' she cried. 'There was an old person of Sark...'

Jostled this way and that by the crowd, the real Fanny and Stella had been thrust together, with Iris sandwiched between them, craning to look up at them. She beamed, clearly pleased with herself.

'So, whaddya think?' she said.

'That song is hideous,' Fanny said. 'Suggesting that we, well...'

'Well, don't you?' Iris said.

'Well, yes, but even so—we don't want everyone *singing* about it. It's vulgar!'

'A bit of vulgarity never killed anyone,' said Iris, 'and it saved a good few others. What about you?' She wriggled around to face Stella.

'Is that meant to be us?' she said. 'Is this what's going to happen us? Are we going to become a laughing stock? Is that what those dreadful police officers are going to do to us?'

Iris looked around. 'I don't see any laughing stocks,' she said. 'I see you ladies, with all these men in the palm of your hand, still here after centuries. And I sure as hell don't see any of them police officers who can say the same—do you?'

The song, after four repetitions, had come to an end, the pianist thumping out an atonal set of closing chords. The crowd applauded, and the sisters curtseyed. 'Now then, would anyone else like to sing? Perhaps another of our "he-she's"—now's your chance, to perform with the great Fanny and Stella, and there's not many who can say that!'

'Except half of London,' someone heckled from the crowd, and Fanny chirruped at them in acknowledgement.

'How about you ladies? My word, look at the attention to detail!' And Fanny and Stella found themselves suddenly the attention of the *other* Fanny and Stella. 'I really must commend you on your historically accurate presentation, ladies. Of course, you're no match for us as the *real* exhibit —' they mugged for the audience '– but nonetheless, *brava*. Will you sing for us?'

'No, no thank you.' The sisters shrank back.

'Oh, for goodness sake.' Iris squirmed out from between them. 'I'll do it,' she said. 'Do you have *Any Old Iron*?'

'We certainly do. What's your name, dear?'

'Me? I'm Iris bloody Wildthyme and you're about to get a treat people have paid millions to see in other galaxies. Just gimme a minute.'

She turned back to Fanny and Stella. 'Now listen here,' she said, sotto voce, 'there's jackals everywhere. There always are. Look around—look at the faces. Look carefully. I bet you'll see—yes, there it is, I saw it in your eyes. That's him, isn't it—the Antagonist? You just saw his face. Except it wasn't, and it hasn't been all the other times, but that hardly matters. You'll probably be seeing his face in many others to come. Me, I see faces in every crowd I find myself in, life as long as mine.'

The pianist struck up a tune—if it could be called that—and looked expectantly at Iris. She held up a finger. 'Hold yer horses a second,' she said. 'I'm dispensing life lessons.' To the sisters she continued: 'Ridicule and derision? *Pah!* I've had my fair share of that. People love me, but people hate me just as much. There's plenty who think I'm nowt but a cheap trick. But I knew as soon as I saw you girls, all bedraggled and beaten down in that mucky cell, there was something your Auntie Iris could teach you.' She pointed behind her. 'Those girls out there—did you see the way they sang that song? They took all that nonsense—and they made it armour. And *they're* the ones who are still here, still remembered.'

The pianist played the introduction again, pointedly—the crowd began calling, chanting her name: 'Iris! Iris! Iris!'

'You have one song to decide,' she said. 'We can carry on running away—I'll take you to the bordello-domes of Gladatrix III, or the Emporiums on Armanii Major. Wherever you want to go. Or I can take you back to Bow Street police station, on the twenty-eights of April 1870, and you can face the limericks. Just remember —' The crowd chanting her name were getting impatient. 'Just remember—drag, at the heart of it, is nothing more than putting on a really, *really* brave face.'

And then Iris sang.

—Lights, flaring on.

'Another one to join you,' said the officer. A key turned in a lock; a gate opened; a third body was thrust into the cell.

'Hugh!' The sisters leapt to embrace the man, then, remembering their observer, quickly released him.

'Fanny, Stella—thank the Lord! Are you unhurt?'

'Yes, we're fine, we're fine...'

'They told me I wasn't under arrest, but I couldn't leave you here all alone so I insisted, and then they asked me for my address and I wouldn't tell and, well, long story short, it looks like you have a cellmate.'

The door slammed shut.

'You *gentlemen* enjoy your night,' said the officer—the Antagonist, the face that had chased Fanny and Stella across time and space—and he looked the three in his cell up and down for just a fraction, just the tiniest millisecond, too long. Then he was gone.

'It's been quite a night,' said Hugh. 'But fear not, I'm sure it'll be over soon. There's really nothing to hold you on, it's just a lark, after all. A prank. It'll all be smoothed over in the morning.'

'I think not,' said Stella. 'I fear we're about to become a national spectacle, Hugh, darling.'

'Oh, don't stay that,' said Hugh, looking alarmed. 'Brave faces, girls!'

The sisters looked at each other, then to the empty cell opposite. They gripped each other's hands.

'That,' said Stella, smiling wanly at her sister, 'is precisely what we are doing.'

Starstation to Starstation

Jon Wesley Huff

From the journals of Iris Wildthyme, Transtemporal Adventuress Extraordinaire

Dear Diary,

Well, it happened again. I was stumbling home from a party at Roger's place in the West End (I've mentioned Roger before, haven't I? If not, I should at some point.), and fell right through a temporospatial doorway. Earth is positively littered with them, and thanks to my body being soaked with chronitons or some such, I seem to trigger them at the drop of a hat. You've got a few options when you find yourself suddenly transported through space and time, don't you? Me, I go right for the nearest bar. Although, in this case, what I found wasn't *quite* a bar…

'Do you have something to drink? A *proper* drink?' asked Iris, looking down in disgust at the carbonated concoction that had been placed in front of her. It tasted of berries and herbs, but certainly not of alcohol. The bartender, whose skin was beige with the slightest tint of blue, widened his eyes.

'Not sure what you mean, mum,' he said.

'Just my luck,' said Iris, harrumphing to herself. She looked around the bar again, and realized what she had perceived at first as a prim, subdued crowd was actually something more terrifying. It was a completely *sober* crowd. The city she'd found herself in was rather bland—all brutalist architecture and people milling about in gray woolen suits—but through the fog of the aftermath of the previous night's celebrations, she hadn't realized the truth of where she was.

'So, no alcohol, then?' Iris asked wearily, hoping against hope her instincts weren't correct this time. Suddenly the bag on her shoulder felt very heavy. The bartender looked shocked.

'O-of course not, mum. No alcohol permitted during working hours,' he said.

'And, let me guess, working hours never end?' Iris didn't wait for the man to answer. She knew the score. She made her way to one of the terminals set into the wall at the far side of the bar and tapped a few buttons to confirm her suspicions.

She was on a corporate planet, owned by the Brocti Corporation, to be exact—a whole world dedicated to whatever soul-grinding pursuits the company saw fit. Filled with men and women constantly wired on stims or cybernetically-enhanced with sleep-pulse tech so they could stay awake and work, work, work.

Iris found her need for a drink rising as she sat heavily in an uncomfortable little chair next to a group of drones drinking their fizzy drinks and discussing today's efficiency reports. As she sat, however, something thudded against the side of the table. She reached into the red velvet lining of her jacket, and pulled out something so wonderful she could have almost wept. It was a tall, and very full, bottle of gin. Which, she remembered, she'd nicked from Roger's drinks cabinet right before she left. Her eyes went wide with joy.

'You beauty, you!' she exclaimed as she gave the bottle a kiss. One of the corporate drones, a compact woman with a tint of orange to her skin, looked at her. Instead of the sniffy look of contempt Iris expected, however, there was a spark of intrigue in the woman's eyes. 'Want a nip?'

From the journals of Iris Wildthyme

So, that's how the whole thing started. One nip led to two, and then before I knew it that whole, beautiful bottle was empty. Whatever race these multi-hued people belonged to, they couldn't hold their liquor, that I can tell you. In short, I was having a blast...

'Miss, you're going to have to come with us,' came a voice from behind Iris.

Iris turned from the stumbling laughter of the bar's patrons, and saw that the thin, raspy voice belonged to a very tall man—who had a subtle green tint to his skin—dressed in a soft gray onesie. Next to him was a smaller, pudgier man in a matching onesie, who had yellow, bulging eyes but whose skin was tinged red. If it had not been for the gleaming silver badges on their left breasts and the shiny black caps on their heads, Iris would have had no clue the men were some sort of law enforcement officers at all.

'Well, chuck,' said Iris unsteadily, suddenly aware of her newly-rekindled intoxication. 'That may be a bif diplicult. A bit difficult, rather. Although I'm not opposed to being carried!'

'My name is Officer Danning,' said the taller man, 'and this is my partner, Officer Borol. And we… well…' Danning looked to Borol, hoping he might have the right words. Borol, for his part, just shrugged.

'You two boys all right?' asked Iris, blinking her eyes and straightening herself up, forcing herself to feel soberer than she actually was.

'It's just that, well, you're *intoxicated*, aren't you?' asked Danning, nearly whispering the word. Iris couldn't help but laugh in their faces. The crowd in the bar joined in her laughter, although they weren't paying enough attention to understand what the cause was. Danning waved a device at Iris, and whatever readings popped up on its little screen made him do a double take.

'I've had a little nip, yes. Well, we all have. But isn't that grand? Isn't life boring enough as it is? Still, I suppose I should get going. I do need to figure out a way home.'

'I'm afraid that won't do at all,' said Borol, moving quickly to block her way out of the bar. He removed an object from his belt. It looked vaguely like a cudgel, but it was soft and flopped to one side like a bag full of beans.

'Don't worry, chuck, happens to everyone,' said Iris. The joke didn't go over well.

'You're coming with us, Miss,' said Danning, his voice turning from flatly professional to distinctly chilly. Despite the fact that they didn't look very threatening, Iris found her annoyance at the situation sobering her up.

'Now, look you two. I know you've got a job here and all, but I'm really in no mood. Not today. Let's just skip to the part where you chase me around, lock me up, I escape, and so on. Why don't we go off and grab a quick dr— er, a nice cuppa and have a laugh?' She knew from the look in the policemen's eyes that, sadly, this tactic wasn't going to work.

'No need to worry about any tiresome chases, Miss. At the Brocti Corporation, efficiency is kind. You'll go straight into the dispersal chamber. No fuss, no muss, no pain,' said Borol, who actually smiled somewhat benevolently at this, as if he was doing her a favor.

'What am I being charged with?' Iris snapped.

'Public intoxication, of course, ma'am,' said Danning.

'And disruption of the Brocti Corporation work shift,' said Borol.

'And the sentence for that is… dispersal? *Death*?'

'Ah, no, as you should be well aware from your Brocti employee handbook, ma'am,' said Danning, shaking his head in disdain, 'both those offenses are just cause for dismissal.'

'The death sentence is for conducting non-allied business activities on a Brocti Corporation-owned facility,' said Borol.

'But I haven't conducted any business at all,' said Iris, confused. She looked down at her outfit for a moment, grew angry, and continued, 'I'm not some lady of the night, if that's what you're thinking!'

'Believe me, that was the furthest thing from my mind,' said Danning. 'That charge relates to the dissemination of alcoholic substances.' As if to punctuate his point, the thin, orange-hued woman slumped off her chair and fell to the floor with a heavy thump.

'Well, it's not like I was charging, though I probably should have. They cleaned me clear out!'

'Ah, the old "free sample" trick,' said Borol, his thick and slightly phlegmy voice a contrast to his partner's. Iris finally had enough.

'Is that your baton, over there on the floor?' she asked Danning, staring past him. As she hoped, both Danning and his partner looked away briefly. It was the opening she needed. She bolted away from the two officers, her heels clicking against the smooth metal of the bar's floor, and pushed through the door to the outside.

'H-hey, wait!' Danning shouted after her. He looked at Officer Borol, who had also been too shocked to react immediately. Their eyes narrowed, and they ran after the woman.

Iris ducked into an alleyway, but everything was so well lit here. The entire city was smooth walls of concrete and steel, with soft lights that outlined the shape of nearly everything. Identical hover cars glided past noiselessly, their drivers obscured by tinted windows. In fact, all the windows here were tinted, which made the place feel eerily empty. If it weren't for the passersby she apologized to as she barreled past, she would have thought the city was empty. They looked at her with their mouths agape, her disruptively colorful presence a contrast to the surrounding gray world. The only color to be found at all, really, were the multitude of hues that tinted their skins.

Iris took off her shoes, deciding her feet were safe on the impossibly clean and smooth ground of the city, so that their loud clicking wouldn't give away her position. Still, the two policemen were right behind her. She ducked quickly into a small side passage between a building and the elevated track for some sort of monorail. Unfortunately, in her haste, she ran right into the back of a man carrying a brown paper bag, causing him to lose his grip and send the contents flying.

From the journals of Iris Wildthyme

This was, of course, embarrassing, but I was running for my life. Whatever momentary embarrassment I felt was immediately overtaken by surprise as the man turned around. He had a long, angular face with prominent cheekbones. It was a face I thought I knew well. The man before me looked very much like a musician friend of mine. We'd had a jolly good time of it back in the '70s, I even helped out on an album or two. Actually, let's just say his Berlin period would have been his Boise, Idaho period if I'd not steered him right.

Well, here he was again on this alien world, a hundred years or so in the past. Except, well… his skin was a bright blue. Not the pale tinge of everyone else on the planet I'd seen. The blue of his skin reminded me of the Caribbean — clear and bright. And, like my friend, he had irises of two different colors. Except one was bright red and the other bright yellow. It was so striking and so strange-and-frankly-impossible, that I couldn't help but vocalize the question in my head.

'David?' Iris asked.

'Who?' The man was picking up his scattered items and putting them back in his bag. He looked at her like she was an interesting puzzle, his eyes searching hers instead of paying attention to what he was doing.

There was a grace and ease to his movements, and a sly smile at the corner of his lips. 'I'm afraid I don't know a "David."'

'What is your name, then? And if you say "Jean" I'm walking right back to those cops.'

'It's Dovan, actually. Dovan Binderwall,' said the man.

'Oh, I think you'll want to workshop that a bit more, mate.'

'It's worked pretty well, so far,' said the man, his eyebrows contorting into a scowl that was immediately betrayed by his smile.

'Sorry. You… look like an old friend,' said Iris. She gathered her wits, and helped the man gather the things he'd dropped, which included a roll of tickets, some candles, a strange squishy fruit the color of a Robin's egg, a pack of something called Moo-glix, and what looked an awful lot like a kazoo.

'Miss! Miss!' Came a familiar, thin and raspy voice that echoed off the metallic panels lining the alley. It sounded some distance away, but not far enough away for Iris's liking. 'Don't make this hard on any of us!'

'In a spot of trouble?' Dovan asked, his eyes still probing.

'Yes, apparently I broke a law somewhere along the way, and I've only been here a half hour! Which, come to think of it, isn't my shortest time.'

'Oh, I know their type. All rules and floppy sticks.' Dovan grinned mischievously. 'Come with me. I know somewhere you can hang out until we can get this sorted.' Iris sighed in relief. It was always nice to run into someone on an alien planet who didn't want to lock you up.

'As a come-on I've heard worse, I suppose,' she said.

'I was thinking somewhere more *public*.'

'Cheeky. I'm game, chuck,' said Iris with a wink.

'I have a performance, actually. Now shush. This takes a little concentration.'

Dovan stuck his hand into the open air in front of them, and to Iris's surprise it seemed to part the air itself. He widened the gap and pushed it aside, as if it were an invisible curtain.

'Ooh, a dimensional bubble?' Iris asked as she walked through the gap.

'Yes! On the nose the first go. It's called—somewhat unimaginatively, I suppose—The Bubble,' he said.

The Bubble couldn't have been more different than the sterility of the city they'd just left. Where the city outside was brutal and monolithic, this was more shambolic, buildings with large irregular stones of red, gray, and ochre. Warm yellow lights lit the streets and emanated from windows covered in tattered green awnings. It even smelled like a real city, all sickly sweetness, and choking fumes. Iris found herself in another alleyway, but the darkness felt cozy, as her feet shuffled through the trash littering the floor. She could hear the laughter and chatter of voices coming from the street ahead of her.

'Can Officers Dull and Boring get in?' Iris asked.

'There's an official portal to The Bubble a couple miles away. So it'll take them a little bit longer than the backdoor we just used,' said Dovan.

'This place isn't half bad.' Iris kicked a discarded bottle approvingly. 'Granted, it's a total mess and the place we just left is a pretty low bar but…'

'I'm fairly proud of it. This sort of curated disarray doesn't happen overnight,' said Dovan.

'This is your doing?'

'About thirty years ago, the Brocti Corporation bought the whole planet, despite my opposition. They covered the whole thing in concrete and metal and turned it into the central hub of their company. They call it "Starstation" now. But I'd grown... *attached* to the planet. They let me create The Bubble so me and my fellow compatriots could have a place away from the Starstation that we could really call home. It was the easiest way to keep us from being a pain, I suppose. I think, officially, I'm noted as "Artist in Residence" here,' said Dovan, his smile caught somewhere between wryness and bitterness.

'So you're not from here, chuck? Or, I mean, whatever planet this used to be?'

'I was born here. But I'm not exactly *from* here.'

Suddenly Dovan stopped in front of a rusted metal door in the side of a building, accessible only by a rickety metal staircase. 'Well, if you don't mind… actually even if you do mind… I have something I really need to get to in here.'

'Well, dropped like a sack of potatoes then. Men. Typical. Blue or green or yellow, it's all the same. It seems my pursuers have lost the scent, anyway. I should probably try to figure out how I'm getting back home…,' said Iris, looking around at the alien city that surrounded her.

The vivid colors were more comforting than the dull sterility that had greeted her outside Dovan's bubble, but it was no less foreign.

'I didn't mean to send you on your way. In fact, it'd be quite nice if you stayed and saw the show.' The man's voice was soft and his eyes darted slightly to the side, as if he was suddenly embarrassed by the invitation. It was so at odds with the quiet confidence he exuded in general, Iris found it as endearing as she did familiar.

'Well, of course, luvvie, I'd never turn down a show,' Iris said with a smile. 'Are you some sort of… musician?'

'No, no, nothing like that. Right! Well, the entrance is just around the corner there. Off you pop,' said Dovan, giving her a playful wink before disappearing behind what Iris figured must have been the stage door.

Iris walked down the dark alley, the flash of neon beckoning her forward, and the sickly sweetness of rotting trash filling her nose. She stuffed her hands into her coat as a strange feeling washed over her. The reality of where she was fell away, if only for a moment, and she felt like she was back at 23 Heddon Street. It was a miserably wet January day. She, David and Becka were on their way to a party, but David needed to get the album cover taken care of and Brian was available. She'd shied David away from the photos of him coming out of the phone booth, at least. She preferred the close-ups herself, but the shot they chose worked too. Her memory of that London felt as far away from the London she'd just left as this alien planet. She sighed wistfully. Alleys and memories, connecting through time and space...

Meanwhile, one dimensional pocket away, Officers Danning and Borol inspected the area where Iris and Dovan had been moments before.

'Are you sure she came this way?' asked Borol.

'She's not hard to track, with her heels clacking all over the place,' snapped Danning, his nostrils sniffing, trying to discern what he was smelling.

'Maybe she jumped on the monorail?' said Borol. Looked up at the track suspended above them. Danning followed his gaze and scowled.

'Oh, yes. She just jumped thirty feet in the air onto a moving monorail. That seems perfectly logical.'

'Well, you're hardly providing any ideas yourself!'

'Well, if you'd just shut your ugly yellow maw for two seconds and let me think,' said Danning, sniffing the air once again.

'Do you have a cold?' asked Borol.

'That smell. It's faint. But unmistakable. The putrid stench of The Bubble.'

'Ahhhh, yeah, I've got it now,' said Borol. 'You think she escaped into there? But we're miles from the entrance.'

'Unless you're Dovan. She's just the sort of lost cause he'd be attracted to.'

'Well, then. You and I should take a trip there ourselves. Teach Dovan a lesson about the rule of law,' said Borol, suddenly standing up straighter as a sneer played across his lips.

'Agreed,' said Danning. 'But first, I think we should make a little stop…'

Inside the Skizax Club there was music playing—something jangly and atonal—coming from unseen speakers. Dovan said that music wasn't really his thing but hadn't had the chance to explain what *was*. The place was packed, but Iris immediately felt amongst her own people. Smoke gathered into one aggregate cloud over the club, contributing to the solidity of the light beams as they searched the interior. The chatter was a boisterous roar, only broken by the clanking of glass as people made toasts or sat their cocktails down drunkenly. Everyone was dressed in bold colors, strange angles, and oversized hats. It all seemed heavenly.

'Hey, Toodleoo,' called a voice that seemed aimed at Iris, and somehow managed to cut through the noise of the crowd. Iris found the source of the voice in the form of an older woman in a startling yellow dress seated at a small round table. Her dress seemed more like a sculpture than a garment, drifting up in smooth curves toward her left shoulder. Her hat was similarly sculptural, a series of swirls trying to escape the woman's head. She had fuzzy pink hair and thick, yellow-framed glasses that popped against the blue of her skin.

'Yes, that's right, Toodleoo. *You*!' exclaimed the woman, presenting the empty chair next to her to emphasize her point.

'Thank you, dear,' said Iris, happy to be off her feet.

'No fretting, sister,' said the other woman. 'You had that look in your eyes. That long day look. My name's Mercy, by the by.'

'Pleased to meet you, Mercy. And yes, it has been a day. And a night and a day before that.' Mercy let out a girlish giggle. 'I'm Iris.'

'Sounds like you need a drink,' said Mercy. She pushed a button on the table and a drink materialized in front of Iris. 'My treat, of course.'

'At last. It's been a half hour or so since my last, which was about twenty-nine minutes too long.' Iris gave the concoction, a swirling green and blue thing that bubbled and fizzed pleasantly against her nose, an exploratory sip. It tasted of cardamom, juniper, and strawberries with just a hint of summer. And it burned at the back of her throat. She knocked the glass back and let the rest flow into her in one gulp before setting the glass back down. 'Right. I'll take another one of those.' Mercy giggled again, and pushed the button, causing another identical drink to appear.

'So you a fan of Dovan's?' asked Mercy.

'Ooh yes! Absolutely. Most talented… Though… I've never actually heard… well, whatever he does,' Iris said. Mercy's jaw dropped and her eyes bulged.

'How did you end up in here then?' she asked.

'Well, I just ran into him a bit ago outside and—'

'You met him? Think you could get me backstage to meet him too?'

'So I take it you're a fan, then?' asked Iris, trying to avoid the question.

'A fan to the max,' said Mercy, her smile growing as wide as her face. 'Oh, he's just brilliant. No one can do what he does. No one.'

'What, exactly, does he do?'

'Quantum poetry. The most gorgeous, life-changing quantum poetry,' said Mercy, hugging herself, closing her eyes, and tilting her head to the side as if lost in Dovan's artistry.

Danning and Borol stopped at the heavy door of the armory. Danning placed his palm on the control pad as Borol looked around nervously. The computer let out a low chime as it scanned it.

'You sure about this? This stuff…' started Borol, before lowering his voice to a whisper. 'This stuff is just supposed to be for planetary invasion.'

'True,' said Danning as the door slid open, the computer satisfied with his identity. 'But did the woman look like she was from around here? Did she act like she was? As far as we know she could be some sort of... advance force, threatening our way of life.'

'But maybe it's a bit much?' Borol asked. Danning took two armored vests off the wall and handed one to Borol. He took a pistol and a large laser rifle as well. He stared down the scope of the rifle and smiled.

'Shock and awe, my good man. Shock and awe. We aren't going to fire a shot. I just want to put the woman in her place. And for some people it just takes a little—'

'Shock and awe.' Borol took a pistol of his own off the wall and nodded his head approvingly.

The lights in the club lowered, and the music cut off. In that instant, the crowd quieted to a whisper. Dovan was about to take the stage. Iris searched the cloudy blackness on either side of the spotlit stage—a circle with a silver wall backing. But Dovan was not to be seen.

Suddenly, two tones sounded—deep and rumbling and so loud it shook Iris to her bones. The notes droned on as the light began to shimmer across the silver-backed stage. Iris was nearly blinded by the reflected light, but soon realized that the changing light was due to the stage itself moving. It was rotating, and what she had at first perceived as the stage backing was simply a partition bisecting a circular stage. The other side was revealed slowly—first, there were pulsing purple and blue lights. And then Iris could see the chair, metallic and brutal in its architecture: sharp angles and flat planes. The lights danced on either side of it.

Dovan sat in the chair, on his head a smooth crown of metal that connected to what looked like two large tuning forks on either side of the chair back. He smiled theatrically at the crowd, and Iris was amazed at the change in him. And yet, never had he seemed more like her friend. The man she'd met less than an hour ago was quiet on the outside but had a reserve of confidence and certainty that shone through his mismatched eyes. The man before her seemed like his twin. He sat upon the chair like a king on his throne, welcoming his loyal subjects—confident and sure and very nearly haughty. Yet, in his eyes shimmered a playful and quiet knowingness. Iris couldn't help but smile, nearly matching the one on Mercy's face.

Dovan closed his eyes, and the musical drone stopped abruptly. It was silent.

'Crossing,' said Dovan. His intonation was bold and direct. Mercy gave out a gasp. Iris moved forward in her seat.

'Marked,' said Dovan.

'Vital.'

'Breaking.'

'Zone,' he said, intoning each word with importance and purpose. Iris tried to put the words together in her head, but nothing particularly sensible or even profound seemed to result.

'Swizzle.'

From the journals of Iris Wildthyme

Okay, luvvies, so, before this goes too far, I guess I should explain.

This went on for about an hour, at which I slumped in my seat further and further, the novelty having long worn off, I can tell you. I tried to sneak looks at the people around me. All of whom, like Mercy, were completely enraptured. It was only later that I really understood what I was watching, although I can't say that I particularly liked it. The chair, you see, was quantum-entangled with similar chairs in other worlds or dimensions. And each quantum poet recited a part of the poem, all at the same time, their minds intertwined by the chairs. If you were the sort of being who was pan-dimensional or ex-spatial or could perceive along those lines, I was told, the results were quite stirring and beautiful. If, like everyone in that club that night, you were not… well, it was an acquired taste.

We were just about to slide into hour two of this, and I was considering going back to the sterile city beyond The Bubble and throwing myself at the feet of Officers Dull and Boring, when the decision was entirely taken from me. The two coppers burst into the club, still resplendent in their pajama-uniforms, but now with added armor-padding, helmets, and guns. Though, really, this only made them look more like toddlers playing dress-up.

'Attention Bubble citizens, we are Officers Danning and Borol with the SPDF,' said the taller of the two policemen through a small mic attached to his vest, amplifying his voice through hidden speakers. 'Remain calm and remain seated. We have a warrant for the arrest of Miss Eros Windertile. Miss Windertile, please put your hands in the air, slowly rise from your seat, and don't make any trouble.'

Iris felt a great deal less guilty about not remembering the two officer's names after that particular mangling of her own. She tried to figure out if there were any quick exits. Mercy caught her gaze, and instantly intuited that Iris must be the woman the two officers were looking for. To her credit, she said nothing. Fortunately, the darkness of the club and the brightness of the spotlight must have kept the officers from seeing Iris immediately. That, and Iris's bold, wide-brimmed hat was almost muted in this crowd. This time Danning and Borol brandished wicked-looking weaponry, a far cry from the soft little batons they'd had before. Clearly, Iris (or Eros, as the case may be) had been branded a deadly threat. *Drunk and dangerous, no doubt,* thought Iris ruefully. Little did they know an hour of quantum poetry had sobered her right up.

As for Dovan, he was still entranced in his own performance, his eyes fixed on some faraway point.

'Cob,' he said, much to Iris's puzzlement, as the last word he'd said was "conflagration." For the first time in her long life, Iris wished she had pan-dimensional senses.

'Miss Windertile, we assure you that you will be taken in with a minimum of physical injury. You will be treated fairly, and euthanized painlessly,' said Borol. This was hardly reassuring.

'What,' said Dovan.

As the two cops swept their flashlights and laser pistols through the crowd, Mercy slowly took off her hat.

'Officer Borol is correct, Miss Windertile. We're just doing our jobs, ma'am,' said Danning. Suddenly, he grabbed one of the club patrons by the shoulder and whirled him around. The crowd gasped.

'Are,' said Dovan.

'M-my apologies, sir,' said Danning to the small grey-skinned alien with large, luminous blue eyes wearing a wide-brimmed hat not unlike Iris's. Iris decided it actually looked a little better on him.

'Mixelfraggle pajax!' exclaimed the alien, in a high-pitched squeal before angrily turning away.

'You,' said Dovan.

Mercy passed her hat to Iris, as the two officers were busy trying to calm the little grey alien. She mouthed the words 'You are *so* going to get me a meet and greet' as she gave her the hat, to which Iris could only nod her assent. Iris slowly removed her own hat, and put Mercy's on instead. It was far too large, and settled so far down it nearly covered her eyes, which was fine by Iris. The more hidden the better.

'Doing,' said Dovan.

It was in that instant that Iris, Mercy, and some of the other club members realized that something had changed about Dovan's poem. Danning and Borol saw the shift in the crowd's attention, causing them to look at the stage once more. Dovan was standing now, disconnected from the Quantum Entangler. His eyes—one red and one yellow—were wide. His hand was stretched out, his finger pointing. The look on his face was a mixture of anger and surprise.

'In my club,' he said, finishing the sentence Iris only now realized he'd been saying as he pulled himself out of his trance.

'Mr Dovan, apologies from the Starstation Police Defense Force, but the administration will not allow you to harbor a fugitive,' said Borol, his voice cracking.

'You, nor your laughable organization, nor the "administration" of Starstation have any authority here,' bellowed Dovan.

Danning straightened himself a little. Even through the protective screen of his helmet, Iris could see his stare grow harder. Suddenly, he was pointing his pistol directly at Dovan.

'The administration of Starstation begs to differ,' he said. '*I* beg to differ.' Mercy let out a gasp that only made it halfway out her throat before turning into a dry croak. Iris had seen Danning's type before. Just because a man was pathetic, it didn't make him any less dangerous.

'Okay, okay,' said Iris, taking off Mercy's hat and standing. 'The jig is up.'

Borol pointed his weapon at her, but Danning kept his pointed at Dovan. 'You've caused us a great deal of annoyance, Miss Windertile,' said Borol.

'Well, first of all, it's Wildthyme. W-I-L-D… look, I'll just write it out for you. Secondly, I really haven't meant to cause anyone any trouble whatsoever. I'm just the one who drew the short straw and fell through a portal in space and time. It happens a lot to me, chuck. Now, sure, I was a little tipsy—'

'Your blood alcohol level was 2.37% percent. Which for many sentient beings would be fatal,' said Danning.

'I was a *little* tipsy. You'll find my constitution is heartier than most, thank you very much,' continued Iris, her voice harder. 'That being said, I really am just looking for a way home. Well, back to my bus. Well, I was planning on looking for a way back to my bus. Once I'd finished being bor—' Sensing Dovan appear at her side she quickly changed course, said, 'Er, I mean challenged, yes, by emotional, socially relevant poetry.'

'As far as I'm concerned, Miss Wildthyme's transgression was far less severe than your own, officers,' said Dovan, his tone sharp and commanding. 'As you've interrupted an important piece involving four beings across space and across dimensions, before the Grand Viziary of Doxxus.' Danning and Borol looked around, their faces scrunched up in confusion. Iris herself was only hanging on by a thin thread.

'AND WE ARE NOT PLEASED,' boomed a voice from nowhere. Or, to be more precise, a chorus of voices that spoke in unison, which seemed to emerge from *within* Iris's brain in a way that made her grab her head in pain and confusion. Judging by the reactions of everyone around her, except Dovan, the voice (which, Iris supposed, must belong to the pan-dimensional audience of the Grand Viziary of Doxxus) had a similar effect on them as well.

'Bloody hell,' said Borol, steadying himself on a table.

'WE ARE NOT PLEASED AT ALL,' said the voice again.

Iris crumpled a bit more from the pain of it, and saw that Mercy had fallen to the floor beside her. Before she could turn to help the woman, however, she felt someone grasp her hand. She turned to see it was Dovan, who looked at her with a sly smile.

'Time to run, I think,' he said. And they did just that. Iris heard the commotion of the other club-goers, and the shouts of Danning and Borol as well, but she didn't look back and didn't really even register what they were saying.

They'd run a few blocks further into The Bubble before stopping to catch their breath.

'I seem to have made a right mess of it,' said Iris, trying to work out a stitch in her side. It had been a while since she'd had to run for her life, she realized, as she massaged the cramp.

'Nonsense, it's been a nice change of pace,' he said. 'I've been here quite some time, and to be honest it can get a little bland. The people of the Starstation—well, you've met them. And even the people of The Bubble… well, their non-conformity is very conformist. I'm trying my best to open their eyes, but a hundred years in and I'm just making headway.'

'A hundred years?!' asked Iris, realizing that she knew very little about her new friend, as familiar as he might seem. But before Dovan could elaborate, two laser beams cut through the darkness of the alley they'd paused in.

'Are those imbeciles actually shooting at us! Show yourself you pajama-wearing, limp-batoned little—' started Iris, before another laser bolt hummed through the darkness.

'Okay, enough playing around,' said Danning. He and Borol walked toward Dovan and Iris slowly, keeping their weapons leveled, not taking their eyes off them.

'This really does seem unnecessary,' said Iris. 'Get me to a portal and I'll be out of your hair, lickety-split.'

'I'm afraid that's not an option now, Miss Winder… *Wildthyme*,' said Borol. His voice was calm and authoritative. But there was an undercurrent there as well. A hesitation that Danning didn't seem to possess.

'Now come along like a good corporate citizen,' said Danning, who holstered his smaller laser pistol and instead gripped the over-sized rifle that had been slung over his shoulder, pointing it at Iris and Dovan.

'Well, I'm not an employee, chuck,' said Iris. 'And your weapon isn't going to do much with the safety lock on.'

'Nice try, Miss Wildthyme. But you're not going to distract us this time,' said Danning. Danning felt a small prod at his side. He glanced over to see it was Borol's elbow, nudging him gently.

'It does look like your safety might be on,' Borol whispered.

'It is not,' Danning hissed through is teeth. 'Green light means it's good to fire.'

'No, it doesn't. Green light means it's safely locked.' Borol grunted, annoyed, reached for the rifle and, with one hand, slid the button near the trigger to the right until it glowed a deep red.

Danning tried to yank it out of his hand. 'You idiot, you just turned the safety *on*! And keep your meaty paws off my equipment!'

As the two men fought, Iris and Dovan started to inch away from them. Dovan nodded in the direction of a dark alley a few feet away. But neither of them got very far. Danning gave the rifle one last yank to pry it free from Borol's grip. Borol's finger squeezed the trigger involuntarily, and an arc of green energy shot forth. Dovan pushed Iris out of the way before she could even react and took the brunt of the laser blast to his chest. He crumpled to the pavement, but Iris was there to catch him.

'Oh no,' said Borol. He took off his helmet, threw it away and went to Dovan's side. 'It… it just went off. You saw it. *You saw it*,' said Borol. He removed a medical kit from the armored vest he was wearing. He started to apply gauze to the wound, but even Iris could tell it wasn't going to do much.

'What have you done?' Borol asked Danning, who was looking at Dovan in horror. Danning had no response, so Borol turned his attention back to Iris and Dovan. 'We aren't even supposed to have this equipment. It's for planetary invasions. We just wanted to scare you. Get you to cooperate so we could get home before it got too late. We've never even…' Borol looked at his gloved hands, now covered in thick rivulets of Dovan's blood, and found he couldn't continue. Iris was about to say something—maybe something comforting, maybe something scathing, she hadn't quite decided—when the ground shook with a ferocity that almost sent Iris tumbling. It was enough to send Danning off-kilter and he fell to his knees.

'What was that?' Iris asked.

'My fault, I fear,' said Dovan.

'How could the ground shaking possibly be your fault?'

'My people… we're… wanderers of a sort. Our physical bodies die on one planet, we travel through the stars in our native energy form, and then take on a new body and a new life elsewhere,' Dovan said, the strain of staying conscious clear in his voice. Borol wrapped more gauze around Dovan's wounded torso, but it seemed to soak through with blood faster than he could wrap it.

'Just be still, Dovan. These officers… they'll get an ambulance or something. You can explain it all to me later,' said Iris.

Borol looked up from his work, and satisfied he'd done all he could, followed Iris's advice. He stepped away a few paces to let Iris and Dovan talk while he called in an emergency vehicle. Suspecting, as Iris did, that these were probably Dovan's last few moments.

'I don't think there's going to be a later, Iris,' said Dovan with a sad smile. 'Which is unfortunate because now the Grand Viziary of Doxxus is going to really be in a tiff.' The ground shook again, and the sudden jolt made Dovan cry out in pain. Iris looked over at Borol, who simply nodded his head, letting her know the ambulance was on the way. Iris decided keeping Dovan talking might be for the best, if for no other reason to keep him awake and alert.

'That doesn't explain the ground shaking, chuck,' said Iris.

'Oh, yes. I was getting to that. Just… what with the dying and all…' Dovan tried to smile but it turned into a wince of pain. 'My people, when they find a home, take root. It's just a side effect of our presence. We become ingrained in the worlds we inhabit. You see, I couldn't just leave when the planet was turned into the Starstation. But living here with these people would have driven me mad. So I put all my energy into The Bubble. A place the free-minded could come and play in... to express themselves. But it all depends… on me to maintain it. The quantum poetry… it was payment for the Grand Viziary. They were to keep The Bubble going, when I decided to leave.'

'No you, no Bubble?' Iris asked. Dovan didn't respond. His eyes were closed. Iris's heart skipped a beat. She shook the man a little more firmly.

'Dovan. Come on, don't be boring. This is boring. Death is boring. Me, trying to not get you to die. That's boring, right? Right?'

Dovan's eyes fluttered. His mouth twitched at the corner, as if trying to smile. Tears began to trickle at the corner of her eyes.

At that second, there was a rumbling. Iris thought for sure it was The Bubble, ready to become permanently undone. But the rumbling sounded far off at first, growing steadily in volume. Iris recognized the sound the instant a portal of blazing light opened before her, illuminating the whole back-alley tableau. She by Dovan's side. Borol standing helpless a few paces away. Danning on his knees, mute and unmoving from shock.

'Iris!' said a familiar voice, a small fuzzy shape emerging from the portal. 'You've been a real pain in the arse this time.'

'Panda?' Iris asked with a gasp, wiping the tears from her eyes.

'Well who else is going to go to the trouble of securing a highly-advanced portal genera—' he started, before being cut off by Iris, who had leapt up from Dovan's side and grabbed the portal generator (a whirring box of lights and moving doo-dads) right out of Panda's soft little hand.

'Yes, yes. Details. Later,' said Iris as she punched the buttons on the crude little machine, closed the portal that Panda had just come through, and opened a new one.

'Slow the hell down, Iris! If you just—' Iris jumped into the new portal, which sealed itself shut behind her, '—tell me… what's… huh.' Panda looked around him, sighed, sat down, and took out his whisky flask. 'It's just been one of those days, I guess.' He didn't have the cap off before another portal appeared, and Iris bolted out with a spray can in her hand. The ground around them was shaking with some regularity now.

'Will you please just let me finish one—'

'Shut it, Panda!' said Iris, as she raced past him and back to Dovan.

'Hold on there, luvvie,' she said as she took the cap off the spray can and sprayed it right into Dovan's wound. It released a blue foam that grew fluffier and fluffier as it filled the blaster hole in Dovan's chest.

'What's that?' Panda asked, having toddled over to inspect the spray can in Iris's hand. There was a white label on the silver can, with the name of the product in bold red letters, followed by a small novella's worth of legal text. 'Phixitol?'

'Yes. Haven't you heard of it? Or seen the signs on the side of the space lanes?' Iris said, much calmer now as she watched the foam bubble. 'They used to space them out every few light-years so you could see them if you were traveling at impulse. Each one had a little part of the message. The one I remember best went: "Head wound big. Head wound small. Phixitol will Phixitol."

Dovan let out a large gasp as he bolted upright. He ran his hand over his chest, feeling the edges of his singed shirt. The wound itself, however, was gone.

'That's… that's incredible!' Officer Danning exclaimed, finally shaken out of his stupor and rushing toward Dovan, offering his hand to help the man up.

'No, Incredi-Ball does something quite different,' said Iris.

'A genuine miracle,' said Borol, with astonishment.

'Well, matter-knitting nanites, technically, but to the corporate mind it's all the same, really,' said Iris, giving Dovan's shoulder a friendly squeeze.

'Awfully convenient,' said Panda gruffly, taking a swig from his flask. Iris whirled around, her eyes wide and furious.

'*Convenient?* This is the last can of Phixitol in existence! It took me three months just to track it down,' said Iris.

'Well, pardon me,' said Panda raising his paws in defeat. 'I suppose I, the person who made this all possible, will just go over here and be quiet.'

'That's the idea, Panda,' said Iris, her dark mood passing.

'Thank you, Iris. I can't… well, I can't begin to repay you,' Dovan said. He took the spray can from her hand and looked at it in wonder. 'And here I thought I'd seen a little bit of everything over my lifetimes.'

'Well, this portal gizmo isn't mine. Actually, I'm not sure where Panda got it from,' said Iris. Panda opened his fuzz-lined mouth to answer, but Iris waved him off. '*Details*. You can tell me over a glass of gin later, if I still care.'

'Well, I'm just so grateful. I'm—both of us are… I guess we got a little… caught up,' said Danning, having shed his armor so that only the soft gray onesie he called a uniform remained.

'Thankfully I've had a few months to cool off. So, no hard feelings here. I guess if I lived where you did, I'd get caught up in a little excitement too,' said Iris.

'No hard feelings here, either, mate. Now that the hole in my chest's gone, I mean. In fact, since you two are here, you're welcome to spend a little time in The Bubble if you'd like,' said Dovan with a smile. 'Of course, the guns and armor are *not* welcome.'

'Well, what do you say?' Officer Borol asked Danning, a grin starting to form on his face.

'It did look a bit… intriguing back there,' said Danning, a similar grin forming on his own.

'Go back to the club, tell them everything's all right, and Dovan said to set you up with a Sunset Special.' With that, the two officers waved their goodbyes and headed back to the club.

'Are you really okay with the cops palling around back at the club, like they didn't blow a hole in you? Seems like they should be punished somehow,' said Iris.

'Well, there are three more hours of quantum poetry left in the performance,' said Dovan with a wink.

'Wait, do you mean you know how awful it is?'

'Oh, it's the worst. But the Grand Viziary requires a quantum poem to be uttered every thirty days in order to maintain their multi-corporeality. Don't ask me to explain it, once things go quantum it's a grab bag of probability and sense.'

'Ahhh, got it. So you scratch their back...' said Iris.

'And *they* take over maintaining The Bubble while I seek out… new adventures,' said Dovan.

'Well, we'd better get back to our present day and place. My dogs are barking, and my feet are hurting too,' Iris said to Panda. Iris punched a few buttons, and the portal wibbled and reformed in front of them. Iris could smell the familiar scents of London wafting through it.

'Where is home, by the way?' Dovan asked, walking toward the portal with Iris and Panda.

'Oh, well, home's my bus, really,' said Iris, tugging on the brim of her red hat. 'But currently home is sitting on a little blue dot orbiting a little sun in the sticks of a galaxy they call the Milky Way. It's a fun little place, most of the time. You should come visit.'

'I might just,' said Dovan. He gave Iris a quick hug, which Iris suspected was a great show of affection from him, and watched as the twosome disappeared through the bright white light of the portal.

From the journals of Iris Wildthyme

Well, that's it then really. Today's little adventure. Well, the last few month's adventure. And today's adventure. Dating this diary entry could be madness if I were too literally minded. Thankfully, I'm not. A quick stop for a couple of curries from Prash's round the corner, and now we're in this little room I've rented in Soho, relaxing on the balcony with our feet up. It's not a bad life, diary. Not a bad life at all.

Iris put her diary down and took a bite of her takeout. Just then she noticed that the record player was making that scratchy-wooshy sound it does when the needle has ended up in the center of the record.

'Panda, be a dear and flip the vinyl, won't you?' Iris asked.

'We really need to hire some help. Maybe an intern,' he groused, although Iris heard the music start up once more, meaning he'd done as asked. He returned, hopped up into the chair beside Iris, and put his feet up on a thin stack of old books that he'd arranged as a makeshift footstool.

'Something nice about listening to a vinyl record. Something warm and familiar,' Iris said, blinking in the crisp cool air the night was bringing in.

'Well, at least it's a good record. I like his earlier stuff,' said Panda, sipping his whisky.

'Oh, I like all of it, myself. Maybe not his quantum poetry period,' said Iris with a chuckle. She relished the look on Panda's face as he stared at her, confused. He opened his mouth to ask, thought better of it, and took another swig of whisky. Iris smiled as she listened to her friend's voice coming through the speakers, singing of things strange, and beautiful, alien, and human.

The Magrs Conundrum!

Vivienne Fox

From the journals of Iris Wildthyme...?

So, there I was, luvvies, having a quiet pickle and a GinTastic Scrambler at one of the less raucous bars in the Seventh... wait, ... Ninth... no, Eleventh... oh some-numbered Cluster (bloody confusing as New New York street names!) when this bloke comes up to me and shoves a lurid paperback in me face!

'Oh. My. Good. Goddess,' he said, his eyes bulging, his skin shining iridescent frog-green under the mild lighting. 'You're her!'

I admit this had me a tad flummoxed, reader—a hearty greeting like that could mean any number of things in my experience. Not all of them having me ready a smile and whipping out the designer autograph pad. I managed to show him some teeth in what might be described as shy of a grimace.

'You're Iris. Iris Wildthyme!'

I goldfished for a moment.

He grinned, showing pointed teeth. 'Transtemporal Adventuress extra-Extraordinaire.'

'You missed an "extra", dearie,' I replied, then winced at my acknowledgement.

In excitement, his mouth dropped like a sideshow clown and he started to make this high pitched *squeeing*. Knowing I was in a nefarious part of the galaxy where my name might, mistakenly, be associated with gross thievery and dastardly shenanigan, I shushed him by snatching the book from his hand.

I popped my pen—a feathered Olympus Mons I always carried in case of the need for authoritative signatures—and was about to flip the tatty thing open when I noticed the cover.

It's me! All kitted out in baggy jumpers and a floppy hat, beckoning with a crooked finger like some mad ol' woman about to pop you in a cauldron for tea.

The Continuing Adventures of Iris Wildthyme, it said. *Bumper Issue*, it said. *Over 100 adventures*, it said, this in a big gold embossed sticker. Finally taking note of the book's title, I gave a good long laugh—*Iris Wildthyme & the Many-Tentacled Menace*. Then I saw its author.

My greatest fan wibbled a bit at my reaction, which was not favourable. His grin slipped.

I thrust the dog-eared paperback at him and said, 'Oright, luvvie. I'll give you the Wildthyme mark. But you tell me one thing: Who the flippin' heck is Paul Magrs?'

Manchester, Earth, December 2017

Tea, my dear reader, is a universal restorative. Especially when you've had the shock of your many-and-varied lives.

I'd tracked down this Mr Magrs, alleged novelist extraordinaire (I looked him up on the Googles where he had *quite* a following), to twenty-first century Earth. I parked the bus right outside his terrace to be downright intimidating, walked up the leaf-spilled walk, and rapped sharply with my umbrella on the red door. Ooh, I was spoiling for a fight, luvvies, ready to rail on about people stealing others' precious stories for their own gain. I rapped again and again and again and was about to knock on the front window when I heard a latch pop and the door click open. And bless me, dearies, but every word was snatched from my mouth. My jaw fell open like an old hinge.

For standing in the doorway, merely a foot high, and looking cross as a scarecrow, were only bloody Panda!

He sat me down in the colourful back room, on a tattered but comfy couch, and made me tea. Tea, I was to discover, was lifeblood in this strange house. It was a riot of colours—yellow and orange walls, plants trailing vines down bookshelves, a wall of DVD boxsets and CDs and lovely vinyl, covered in a dust that likely kept them in another age. For the house felt like a fantasy, dropped outside time, and something, dare I say it... magical happened here. And not just once but with some regularity. I could feel it in me waters.

Panda handed me the tea and sipped at a cup himself. Now I was calmer I noticed he was a bit different to the Panda I used to know. His fur was matted with age, and he did not smile. Though he did wear a rakish blue ribbon round his neck. All he'd said to me after my exclamation was, 'Oh. It's you. I knew this would happen,' and he sighed grandly, 'You'd best come in. Pot's still warm from the last brew.'

I watched him a while, trying to figure his mood, which was glum. Then I realised why I was here and anger fizzed up inside me gullet.

'Listen here, Panda! What the bloody heck are you doing in the home of this dastardly... novelist?'

It was the right thing to say. Panda stiffened and turned his beady black buttons on me. 'Don't you start, Iris Wildthyme. Don't you dare. I'll have you know Paul is a gentleman and a sweetheart—*and*,' he stressed when I harrumphed, 'if it weren't for him, you'd be a mere nudist with a colourful name.'

'I beg your pardon?' I replied, flummoxed at this last description. Then I twigged. Shook my head solemnly.

'He's 'ad you, hasn't he? Been whispering in your ear at night, no doubt. Convinced you—*you!* my dear and best Panda—that all these tales he's been scribbling are *his*!' I stamped my foot. 'Well they are *not*, oh no, luvvies. They are most definitely and most indubitably *mine*!'

Panda stared long and hard at me. His little eyes could be quite unnerving if he fixed you in a certain gaze. Eventually he said, 'You said "luvvies".'

'I did?'

He paused gravely. 'Who are the "luvvies", Iris?'

'What on—'

'Who are you talking to?'

I blustered and flushed. 'I've no idea what you're on about. Clearly too much tea. Now I've got a lovely gin here which you'd prefer...'

He sighed and knocked back the last of his tea. 'You're diarising again, aren't you? Completely incorrigible. Always at it, rain or shine. Even in the middle of conversations!'

I suddenly had the strop. 'And what of it, Panda?! They're *my* thoughts, written by me, not some mucky author who wants to put his stamp on it. I *won't* have them twisted and perverted by another.'

I expected him to rile, but Panda only shook his head. 'You have no idea, woman.' He leaned forward importantly. Reluctantly, I got down to his level. Panda cupped a paw to my ear and said, 'There's no easy way to say this. In a sense, Paul Magrs *is* you, Iris. You might even say he's the original.'

Now I'm not one for girlish faints, dearies, but the very idea that a male novelist could in any way be like your Auntie Iris had me in so many emotions—paroxysms of laughter, violent derision, wild hilarity—that they all cancelled one another out and wapped me to the floor quicker than a Gravitron.

Which was not the best of positions to be in to meet my nemesis.

I came to with a start, with a tickle of gin under my nose, to find a tumbler being held out to me. I looked beyond the glass to see a man of average height, grey-blonde hair parted in the centre and flopped like a louche college student, round glasses behind which mischievous, wise eyes twinkled, and a knowing smile tweaking the corners of his lips.

Never refuse a kind offer of gin, I say. I took the tumbler and swigged and felt it sluice down me gullet and stoke my dwindling fire.

'Hello Iris,' he said in a soft Northern accent, settling into the armchair Panda had previously occupied.

'You're him, aren't you?' I said.

'I might be,' he twinkled.

But deuced if I was to be bamboozled by a splash of booze (the very thought, dearies!) and a delinquent biographer. I pulled *The Many-Tentacled Menace* from a cardy pocket and waved its scruffy cover at him.

'Just what the bleedin' heck do you think you've been doing, mister? Typing up my diaries into neat, digestible adventures, eh? Oh, don't get me wrong—they're on target—complete with Panda and Tom and Jenny and Barbara and all me other companions, and you've got the tone right—I'll give you that—but... And it's a big but... Where's my whacking great copyright symbol and, more importantly, chuck, where's my whacking great royalty cheque?'

Mr Magrs sat there, one leg crossed over his knee, and looked me up and down, like I was some jelly come to tea. Then he beamed and leapt up, taking my hands. 'This is marvellous. Marvellous! You really are just like her. Everything I imagined, come to life.' He stepped back and surveyed me. 'My Iris.'

I was not impressed. 'Listen, chuck!' He giggled at that. 'I'm no one's Wildthyme.' Stopped when that sank in. 'Well, actually, of course, I'm quite a few hundred peoples' wild time... and I've got the fan mail to prove it. But—' I lost a bit of steam here at the thought of having to argue for my very existence. 'Look, luvvie. You can't just go about stealing other people's ideas. It takes the biscuit, it does, and that's not on cause *I'm* the one who always takes the biscuit.' I smacked my lips. 'First Law of Time.'

He frowned, and his face was like a boy who'd been told there were no Christmas presents this year. 'I thought Panda told you?' he said.

'Told me what?'

He rolled his eyes good-humouredly. 'Well, Iris, in the words of the walrus: "I am he as you are she as you are me."'

I stared at him, this man dressed in jeans and an ordinary plaid shirt, who was so composed and calm before me. I got a sense again of something magical and realised it was wafting from him, like a temporal perfume. I wanted to whack him with my handbag, dearies, that'd sort out his non-sequitur. But I'd left it on the bus. And a teeny bit of my brain found itself intrigued (which was always a bad sign). I shucked my annoyance like an oyster.

'If that's an explanation, I'm going to need more gin.'

Mr Magrs poured me another drink and took me up the dangerous precipice of stairs to the top floor, to his writer's room, the place where he imagined that he'd imagined every story he'd had about me (the bloody cheek!). It was a small room though it was filled with the bricolage of a creative mind: stuffed bookcases and more books spilling over tables, desks covered in drawings and sloppy paintboxes with mixed colours in the lids; mason jars with pencils and paintbrushes mingling like cats and dogs. He sat me down in a soft armchair by the window and piled my lap with books.

'There,' he said gently. 'Take a look at them, Iris. They're all about you—wonderful, glamourous, ratbag Iris in her big red bus, saving planets and wearing mad, cool costumes, and having a grand old time of it.' He crossed his arms. 'You can't tell me that's not how you'd like to be portrayed.'

I opened my mouth to give him a blast of disagreement. But then I listened to what he'd said. He had a fair point. I mean, I am glamourous and wonderful, and I do wear the height of fashions. And, mostly, I do have a lot of fun racketing about the Universe. I took a look at some of the books in my lap—hardbacks with gaily-painted covers of spaceships and monsters, and paperbacks with lurid colours and some pretty suspect likenesses of yours truly (some of 'em just can't get the hat right, nor the aristocratic bone structure). They might be stories with me in them, they might even be stories I'd lived, they may well be bloody stolen and written verbatim from my dear diaries. But... darn it! Didn't they look like they were *FUN*!

Mr Magrs saw me ruminating. 'People love you, Iris.' He gestured at the pile of books. 'You're famous—the best kind of famous. They want to live your stories.'

I slugged back the last of the gin.

His eyes slatted behind his glasses. 'You wouldn't take that away from them, would you?'

For a moment, I stopped, because, for a moment, I thought he'd tiptoed into my mind and knew what I was about to do. Because all this talk of people wanting to be in my skin was all well and good when *I* wrote about it but was a tad unnerving when others suggested they wanted to peel me away and slip in like a complicated metaphor. And I can't be havin' with none of that, no; put it on the plate simple. That's what one of my aunties used to say.

So I pulled out my slim pink blaster and aimed it at the nefarious author. 'Right, mister, enough of your silver tongue. You're coming with me. I'll show you the *real* Iris Wildthyme.'

I marched him out of that house quick smart and made for the bus.

Unfortunately, Panda had other ideas.

He met us on the bottom step of the bus with a glower and a sigh.

It was night and the gibbous moon loomed over us like a bad omen. The streetlamps lit his little button eyes an eerie pearl. I wasn't half knocked over with surprise, not to mention the uncanny way he had of opening the bus door without a key.

'Panda! What the blazes are you up to?'

'You can't, Iris,' he said, matter-of-fact.

Oh, that word! I hate that word! 'Just watch me, chuck!' And I shoved the oddly blithe, entirely untrembling author toward the bus.

Panda stiffened, his fur on end. 'Paul Magrs is a writer of great imagination, Iris. You cannot whisk him around the galaxy and show him wonders. They will become routine days to him. And then where will you be? Sales down, reader disinterest, Wildthyme merely a willfully strange name.' He leaned forward conspiratorially. 'Or is that what you intended?'

I looked at him, standing staunch on that step, and realised something had happened, some terrible horror that had changed my friend and made him all nervy and compliant and a little bit—yes, sorry Panda, love—ordinary. Frankly, it got me back up.

'What is wrong with you, Panda?! You were always first into the ruckus, ready for a tipple and a scandalous tale. Now, look at you! You're railing on about the reality doldrums... blah, blah, blah... mustn't touch, mustn't do that, mustn't take writers off into space for fear they'll get *too much inspiration*! Can you hear yourself, chuck?' I let that sink in a bit then I gave him a bit of a verbal shove. 'I know you always wanted to be a critic, but you know what they say about critics—they're only bitter about their failure. And I think you've been chewing that lemon a bit too long, love. Spit it out.'

Ooh, he was glaring mad, he was. His button eyes nearly popped. 'I'm sorry, Iris,' he eventually said through his anger. 'But I shan't let you ruin it all again. We have a steady life now, and we shan't be pulled back into your crazy and dangerous orbit. We like it here in this colourful house, with our garden, and the cat, and my solid work, days that go all in one line with breakfast and lunch and dinner! Nothing too scary to make a Panda's fur go *ruddy grey*!'

I ignored that cryptic comment. Continued with my gentle harassment: 'My Panda was so different, so full of life and rigmarole and wickedness. I mean, *you* could just be mistaken for a grumpy old toy bear.'

When Panda gets angry, dears, he starts to shake, his fur goes on end, and his little head goes on the side like a spinning top about to fall. It's why I can never play *Cluedo* with him (I always win).

I waited for the inevitable response.

'TOY bloody BEAR!' he cried, and a cat yowled in the night.

Then he leapt at me.

But I had me skirt up, caught him, and wrapped his little furry body in it, tying a quick knot. Giving Mr Magrs a smile—though he already had a brilliant one on, enjoying the show (rude!)—I bustled him onto the bus. He went with suspicious willingness. Amidst Panda's curses and furious wriggling, I closed the doors and pulled the satisfyingly chunky lever to dematerialise.

'All aboard for a wild time!' I cried.

And then we were off! Into the swirly, sexy vortex, into new adventures.

Manchester, Earth, Christmas Eve, 2017

Approximately (I don't do the counting, love; Paul can tell you exactly how many) eighty-seven adventures later, the bus materialised outside a little windblown street in Levenshulme. The doors opened and Paul scrambled down the stairs like a lover reunited. It was *not* a desperate run from your Auntie Iris. He'd had the time of his life. And what a charmer! He could have us supping from a king's table in no time, talk round torturers into letting us go with the price of a good story, even convince a sexual sea sponge from Siphilia to put away its lady bits. A wonder of a companion. Though, it must be said, sometimes it felt like I was his companion, what with him knowing exactly what I'd do in almost any situation. We've become firm friends, luvvies, and I even let him read my diaries. Course I had a few demands—remove all mention of my hair as straw-like being one, ensuring at least ten mentions of me being "glamourous" in every story, and a complete embargo on ever mentioning my age. Oh, and a smacking great copyright, too. © it there, at the bottom?

Panda was apoplectic when released from my skirt folds. I had to strap him into the baby seat and deny him gin until he saw reason. It was only after the first ten adventures that he deigned to come down off his high horse and actually have some fun. Revealing to me that he was only being a wet blanket cause I told him to, my last mysterious incarnation who wore all black and spouted ominous poetry (she sounds a dreary thing!) telling of some cataclysm if I took Paul away. Utter rubbish, of course, and I wouldn't put it past MIAOW to be behind the devious deed.

© Iris Wildthyme

'Right, then, shall we take the ham in and watch some telly?' asked Panda. He was wearing an elegant Santa-red fedora and a fashionable green vest with white piping.

'It *is* Christmas Eve,' I replied. 'Good excuse for a knees-up!'

Inside, we found Paul hugging his partner J—a wise, jolly bear of a man with a fearsome beard. J winked at me. I'd managed to get him a message not to worry about Paul and that we'd be back for tea on Christmas Eve. We popped some champers and cheered and went in to watch a new show on TV, a gorgeous little science-fiction Christmas special called *Iris Wildthyme & the Mars Conundrum.*

We screamed and jeered and whooped and flabbergasted at it. Afterwards, when the closing theme thundered on, Paul turned to me and said, 'See, Iris. Lots of tangled timelines, existing together, and everyone's happy.'

Well, not everyone, but they can lump it, chuck.

Which, naturally, was when the doorbell went. Paul answered it, and we heard a brief scuffle after a calm, female voice said, 'Are you Paul Magrs?' Presently, Paul stepped backwards into the room, arms raised. Followed by a glamourous woman, stick thin, with a honey-blonde bob, wearing a silver catsuit and huge pink boots with ridiculous but very cool heels. She stopped the instant she saw me.

'Oh no. Not you.' Then she noticed Panda. 'Oh no. Not him.'

Panda gave a momentous sigh. 'Dear God! This is going to happen again and again, isn't it?' He glared at the intruder. 'Right. There's only one way to sort out this malarkey.' He reached for his tiny mobile phone, flipped it open. 'We shall have to invite all your other selves for Christmas dinner.'

'Oh!' cried Paul. He grinned at me. 'I think I've written that one already!'

And he clinked my glass and we drank: to being fabulous, to strange stories, and to many more Wildthymes.

Untitled No. 22

Cody Schell

Iris stood in front of the Rothko with her father. It was a huge painting, as tall as a person, and almost touched the ground. It didn't feel like art, it felt like a big red confrontation that wouldn't explain itself. Her father awkwardly put his arm around her and pulled her close.

He whispered excitedly, 'Rothko never gave his paintings names. Only… it was the art dealers who made up stuff, names I mean, cause they needed to call them something just to sell them… anything!' He threw his other hand up, gesturing to the painting. 'Vague squares that wiggle and itch!' His fingers wiggled and itched. 'They float like moss but they're firm like bricks!' His hand made a wave motion, and then compacted into a fist. 'They're nothing…' He bit his thumb, '…they are everything!' His hand fanned out slowly, fully extended.

Iris turned her head so her dad couldn't see her rolling her eyes, but then turned back and smiled. 'Cool, dad!' She couldn't burst his balloon. He was just so excited. She wanted to move ahead and join Aunt Connie who had wandered off ten minutes previously.

'Let's buy a print of this one! To remember my day with my daughter.' He pulled her annoyingly close again. 'No! To remember OUR day!'

He was so enthusiastic about what a *lovely* day it was, but to be honest, Iris had been bored. Normally they got along wonderfully, but this was one thing she just didn't share with him. She didn't get it.

He grabbed both of her hands and held them in his, and looked into her eyes. 'I am going to buy this print so you can remember lying to me! I bet you feel bad about this now that I'm dead!'

Iris shook her head. 'No, Dad, it's not like that.' It was like that.

'Isn't it? You don't feel bad? That I'm so happy and you're just… flat inside?'

That was unfair. 'I am happy Dad. I love you. I just don't love this painting.'

'But you never told me that… and I always talked about how great this day was. For years afterwards! …and I was just… *oblivious*… to the fact you didn't share the feeling.'

'I know. Dad, I tried to understand. I tried to get it, tried to share it with you. But it's just a colored square, I don't understand how it can move you to tears. It's just… paint.'

'But honey, each other is all we have now that your mother is gone. I *need* you and I want to share a special bond.'

Iris wanted that too. 'We do! But dad, you can't just force this. We can't share everything…'

'Why not Iris? We are so alike.' His face was now in darkness, she couldn't see his eyes or hear his voice. She couldn't remember how he looked or how he sounded. It was just a memory of remembering how he looked and how he sounded.

'Iris, I'm dead and you're dead inside.'

She just wanted to see his eyes. She wanted to remember his eyes.

'We are so alike, Iris. You're going to do to yourself what I did. We are SO alike.'

Iris opened her eyes.

A new start, that's what she'd told herself.

Then why am I having the same old shitty dream I have all the time?

She felt the layers of sheets and blankets holding her down, holding in her heat, heavy layers of color and texture like the creamy bands of Jupiter. Every quilt and knitted blanket carried a memory of the various family members and loved ones who had gifted them, pretty much all gone now. Escaping the tug of sleep's gravity was not an easy thing, but she achieved escape velocity, just barely.

Like the vacuum of space, it was cold out here on the edge of the bed. She looked at the vacuum, the literal vacuum, that she'd never managed to put away the last time she used it, which was… who knows how long ago. On her way to the shower, Iris threw her dirty laundry on top of it, hoping to hide it forever.

The bathroom tiles were even icier, and she practically jumped into the stall before the pipes had a chance to push out hot water.

After getting dressed, Iris sat at the table and opened the newspaper comics. Most of them were awful, although it was incredibly amusing just *how* awful they were. They used the same jokes over and over again, monotonous musings on the tedium of Mondays, diets, and the mystifying nature of teenagers. They were entertaining—for the wrong reasons—and somehow comforting. She also liked the bright colors that weren't always precisely aligned. She didn't understand the printing process exactly, but she knew colors were printed from different plates. Sometimes the blue of Mary Worth's eyes would jump out half an inch from her face, and the blue water of the Charterstone apartment complex swimming pool was similarly unaligned, splashing free of its dimensions. It was as if the colors were hard to wrangle into place. They were jumpy, a bit wild. Like dad. Had been.

Iris's dad loved Silver Age comic books in a genuine way, not in the "ironic" hipster way. Not that he'd have used the word *comics*. He'd have been the first to draw a distinction between the newspaper "funnies" and *graphic novels*. In particular he'd loved the Flash, always rushing about in a red and yellow blur. Iris couldn't quite remember but there was something about running in a circle or vibrating molecules that allowed the Flash to travel in time. She imagined the printers "comic dots" were the molecules.

She tried to remember the name of the painter who was famous for turning these into paintings, but she couldn't stop thinking "Glockenspiel", which she knew was wrong. Her dad would have known.

When her mom died, her dad went a bit crazy. Collecting comics became an obsession. There's a fine line between being a collector and being a hoarder. He drained his life savings buying those things and he stopped taking care of himself. When Iris came to visit, it always frightened her seeing the empty stacks of shipping boxes by the door. Now his house was her house, and her childhood home was her adulthood home.

All those comics were still in boards and bags and boxes organized neatly in the basement. To him, they had represented a future made of magical dots and undomesticated colors. To her they were a sad reminder that her father was gone. She was probably being just as mental as he was, keeping those things around after his death. Somehow it seemed different than throwing out thousands of shoes or empty bottles or wrapping paper. They were books, and even more, they were *stories*. There was something her father saw in them, and they felt like a part of him.

She sighed. She worried that this was how it started for him, knowing holding onto objects was illogical, but doing it anyway. Maybe he'd passed on the genes for this compulsion. Good old dad.

Iris checked the time and quickly finished her cereal. Since she was alone, she slurped up some milk from her bowl. She would never drink the milk from her bowl in front of someone else, so in some ways there were advantages to living alone. She wasn't quite alone, there was Tom.

As was his ritual, he sat on the linoleum just inside the kitchen door, sleepily blinking his yellow eyes and waiting for her to share the milk. Sometimes in murkier mornings, Tom seemed to be just a pair of eyes, watching her eat. Iris poured the funny colored milk into his bowl before putting the dishes in the sink.

She could hear Tom lapping up the liquid as she hurried past her father's framed Rothko. She tried not to look at it, tried not to think about it, but failed every day not to think about it, and felt that same feeling every time she failed not to think about it, every day as she pulled the front door shut, locking it behind her.

She took a deep breath.

She hurried to her car. She hated being late for work but traffic in the school zone was always awful. She didn't mind it in the afternoon, but in the morning it was always a bit nerve-wracking trying not to, you know, run over kids or get stuck behind an ugly yellow school bus. And she felt bad for the crossing-guard, a woman built like a brick wall. Maybe they hired her because she looked like she could actually stop a vehicle with her body if she needed to.

Iris chided herself for not being very nice and consoled herself by telling herself she'd never *say* such a thing out loud. That made it not so bad.

It always took forever for the kids to empty the bus and cross the street. As had become her ritual, Iris pushed in the car's cigarette lighter. She didn't even smoke, but it had become a game to see what would happen first. This time, by the time the lighter popped out, the kids were *still* streaming out of the bus. She pulled out the lighter and held it steady, as she stared at the glowing red coil.

Something pulled her eyes to the right, and she looked to the empty soccer field. No practice until after school. She wouldn't see *him* until then, unless it was in the teacher's lounge. Although even that didn't usually happen. The coach's office also doubled as an unofficial "men's only" teacher's lounge in the part of the building with the gym. He'd be there now, perhaps trying on his Lycra wrestling singlet and running around like a superhero.

The driver of the car behind Iris honked his horn. She jumped. The lighter coil had faded to a cool grey and the bus, finally empty, had already pulled away. Iris waved an apology and pulled forward into the staff parking lot and hurried inside.

Home Economics class was outdated in some ways. Girls used to love the class and boys used to hate it. Now it seemed like most of the girls hated it too, since it cut into their texting and social media time, Snapface and Instashot, or whatever.

There were a few special boys who loved Home-Ec. Iris always made sure to befriend these special kids. She liked to think all kids were special, but some are more special than others. The gay boys were always her favorites. She took a shine to them and they to her. When they worked together on a pillow or a pie, and shared a smile over the finished project, successful or not, they both felt appreciated. A rare feeling for both of them.

Today was not a day with a highlight like the day of Rodrigo's unintentionally inappropriate pillow that had to be re-done. It passed uneventfully but slowly.

On her way home, Iris was on the same side of the road as the soccer field. She scanned the crowd and struggled to get a look at the coach. Who she had a bit of a crush on. Everyone did. She always wanted to make eye contact, wave hello, but she could only occasionally catch glimpses of his face. He never seemed to be looking *at her*. She could just see the back of his jersey in the school colors of blue and orange. JUAN was printed across his broad shoulders with a big 05 underneath it. Of course traffic was moving smoothly on the occasion when she wouldn't mind getting stuck in one place. That's always the way.

She looked in the rearview mirror and could see him talking to the French teacher, a big round woman. Iris had seen them talking a few times, but she was sure they were "only friends". It was interesting to imagine the two talking, both with such exotic accents. Who knows, maybe he was into that type, "big girls". She giggled to herself for being so… naughty!

It would be fine if Juan liked big girls, but Iris wasn't a big girl, so she hoped he had other tastes. Iris could see herself with Juan, a gym coach. Well, technically also the science teacher.

Could she date a soccer coach? Her mother always wanted her to marry a doctor and nagged her no end about it. Did other moms, non-TV-sit-com-moms, really do this? Her mother meant well, she just wanted Iris to be well taken care of when… if… something happened to her. But after a dozen matchmaking failures, Iris felt she could move on. Thankfully.

Back home, Iris opened the basement door. Tom seized the opportunity and rushed down the stairs ahead of her hoping to catch some mice in the act. The black cat quickly disappeared into the darkness below. Not sharing Tom's night vision, she flicked on the light switch and descended the stairs. She stopped at the bottom.

Time to do this.

The comic boxes filled the space like a hundred beehives. They were piled up on folding tables to keep them off the damp basement floor. Iris felt anxiety thinking about getting rid of them, but also felt anxious about simply opening them and looking at them, (almost as if they were actually beehives). Iris's anxiety wasn't a fear of imaginary bees.

She felt something soft run across her toes, followed by Tom. Iris wasn't normally afraid of mice, but instinctively jumped backwards, knocking a box off a table. The lid came off and the slick, plastic-covered comics spread out onto the floor like an alluvial fan.

Iris sighed. The floor was dry in that spot, but she couldn't just leave them and started collecting them up.

It seemed wrong not to put them back in the box facing the same way, and also wrong to put them in the wrong order. She looked closer at the covers. Fortunately, most of these had the same logo, they were the same book: *The Flash*. She only had to match up the numbers or months. Easy.

Iris turned a comic over in her hand to see the cover and stopped. This was the one. Probably the only issue she could actually recognize out of all of them. Despite the comic being valuable, her dad had taken it out of the protective plastic and showed it to Iris many times. This was the issue where the Flash learns his wife is still alive, in a new body in the future. Her name was Iris. Iris… something with a W too, but different. West? Yes, that was it, West. 'This is where I got your name, Iris. See?' She wondered if her Dad would have liked her to marry a scientist like the Flash. *He* was probably a doctor, of science anyway. A man obsessed with chemicals and molecules and time travel. She probably would, if such a man existed.

At that moment she doubted the existence of the right guy. She could get on by herself, she was smart and could pay the bills. She just wasn't sure she was enough to get anyone's attention. It was a combination that made her lean towards isolation.

Iris set that comic aside and shut the box. She would keep that one, but the rest would go.

She took it with her to school the next day. She handed it to one of her students, a kid named Tadaki. His eyes widened. She realized he probably thought it was a gift. 'Oh. Sorry, no, I wanted to show you this. I wanted to ask you something.'

'Okay.' Tadaki was one of her favorite students, of Japanese descent, but raised abroad. He spoke English with an unusual accent.

'I wanted to know where you buy your comics, and want to know if they buy them.'

'At Alpha Comics! Out by Canyon Lake. But they won't give you much for them, not even this one. You should do eBay.'

'That sounds… complicated.'

Tadaki reassured her that it wasn't and that someone could help her. She smiled. It was so sweet that he thought everyone had someone to help them. 'Sounds like a plan.' The bell rang.

'See ya, Miss W!!!'

Iris smiled, remembering this exchange with Tadaki as she pulled onto her street. There was a red glow, like the glow of the cigarette lighter, getting brighter.

A cop stopped her and she rolled down her window. 'Ma'am… you'll have to go a different way.'

She saw the trucks and the smoke. '…My house?!'

The next morning was cold again. Iris had stayed the night in the spare room at Jenny's place. The crossing guard she'd mocked had been so kind. Practically a total stranger. Everyone from the school had sent messages, just like when her dad died.

Almost nothing was left. Photos, clothes, blankets… oh, the quilts… they're all gone. Everything was wet and black and disgusting. The comics didn't burn, but they were soaked. Ruined.

It was surreal to be walking through the kitchen and still be outside. She considered sitting at the table for a moment, but everything was just too dirty. Tom's food dish was full of ash. Thank goodness the neighbors had taken him in.

She sighed. She knew she'd be more upset later. She assumed she'd be more upset. She was upset thinking about not being upset. 'There we go, I made it to the negative emotion eventually.'

Iris poked her head into the living room. *The only consolation I'll have is that that damn print will finally…*

The wall that the print hung on was untouched by flame. The plaster surface, the frame and the glass were covered in soot, but it was almost the only thing still intact. The sight of it threw Iris into a rage. Before she knew what she was doing she'd launched herself through the rubble to reach the object of her anger. She grabbed that damned Rothko and threw it across the room. The glass merely cracked, not shattered—unsatisfying. She picked up pieces of burnt wood and threw it at the thing, but her heart wasn't in it. She just didn't have the energy to deal with getting worked up.

She decided to just go over and sit on it. There. That'll teach it. It's unimportant. That will show it. She didn't even care about potential cuts from broken glass. Nope, it's just a place to sit, a dirty uncomfortable place to sit and it would just have to get used to her indifference. Any angry crying laughter was purely coincidental.

Iris's eyes locked onto the wall in front of her and she went blank. Where the print had hung was a rectangle of perfectly clean wall. It wasn't a *perfect* rectangle, it was blurry with soot along the edges. The color of the smooth pale blue wall was still vibrant just like it always had been and made the burnt carnage around it even more distressing in contrast.

It was just a patch of color, she told herself. But it was also a doorway to all her memories, all the time she spent in the house that was no longer there. It wasn't a doorway she could enter, but a window through which she could look with her mind's eye.

She sat staring at that fuzzy rectangle of blue, not sobbing but letting tears pool in her eyes. Each tear slowly reached the point of bursting the surface tension and ran down her cheek, slowly, one after another, for a few minutes.

Iris stood up and flipped the picture frame over, flipping the tabs on the back, one by one until the backing was freed from the edges. She extricated the print and took a look at it. 'I still don't get it. But I get it.'

She rolled up the print, with the color facing inward. She sat down again just to look at the blue rectangle a little bit longer. She wouldn't be coming back here and needed to be finished with these feelings. For a while. There was a lot to do. She wished she could just take that blue with her, keep it and see it without seeing the destruction around it, but she knew that would make it meaningless.

Everything she had was gone, she had nothing. It wasn't just that she'd lost her home, Iris had almost no one in her life. Aunt Connie was a bitch. No family or real friends to help her or even to have fun with; no exciting parties. No adventures and no good surprises. She had no home to go to, but it was time to go.

She felt in her pockets for her phone and house keys, not that she needed them. She found a hair band in her pocket and slipped it over the rolled-up print. As she did this, she remembered watching *Mister Rogers' Neighborhood* with her dad, and sometimes Mister Rogers would look at the Land of Make Believe through a telescope, or a toilet paper tube.

Iris lifted the poster and looked through it. She didn't see King Friday the 13th or Purple Panda. The walls of the tube were just black shadows, fading into red further along where there was light, with a perfect blue circle at the end. She smiled at that perfect little circle. If only things were so simple. But… the colors started to change. Some kind of optical illusion she imagined. But no, the red part of the tube started to stretch back towards her and away from her as if it was lengthening. She kept her left eye shut even more tightly, unable to look away.

She found herself floating in a tunnel. There was a distant pinpoint of blue light, but surrounding her was red, and yellow energy crackled in thunderbolts as she sped along. She looked around herself in terror as the tunnel swirled and spun. As if separate from her alarm, she also calmly realized this must have been what it was like for the Flash and Iris to travel through time… a blur of red and yellow.

The psychedelic tunnel morphed from circular, to ovoid, and then roughly rectangular and the colors inverted. The tunnel had now become blue, the color of a fancy bottle. The end of the tunnel was a red rectangle. She thought of the Rothko painting, but that's not what she was seeing. There were several rectangles, most red, some black… and a crackle of yellow… yellow numbers flashing too quickly to see.

The voice of an older woman echoed in her head. 'There are many possibilities. If you want something new, something more, it's there for you, Iris. Do you understand?' The spinning yellow numbers were slowing, possibilities were narrowing. Iris didn't respond but she understood. She understood and she wanted something more.

She wanted to feel. She wanted not to be numb. She wanted to be like that other Iris from the universe of vibrating color dots.

'If you go… there's no turning back. Do you understand?' Iris watched the numbers slow even more. 'Do you understand, luvvie? You need to say yes.'

'Yes.'

'Then you need to say goodbye.'

'Goodbye? To who?'

The rapidly-moving yellow numbers stopped in place. The choice was made from infinite possibilities.

Number 22.

Iris opened her eyes.

She was staring at a blank canvas in an alien gallery. A tear streamed down her cheek. Iris looked down at her lemon-colored pumps, her turquoise leggings and burgundy dress. 'What… Oi! What did you do to me just then? What was that?'

'So, you were touched by it? I'm so gratified!'

She turned and looked into the face of a tall, impossibly thin orange alien. She remembered he was an artist. His name was Bandeen. She frantically swatted the alien about his head and shoulders with her purse for a solid fifteen seconds.

She ran out of energy and stopped. 'That was... That… WAIT. Was… Was that...'

The alien kept his face covered with several limbs, but lowered a few. 'That was *Untitled No. 22*. And… you're asking… *Was that real*?'

'Yes. Is that who I was? A girl? A human girl? Who wished to become the fabulous person that I am now?'

'Complete with a glamorous new future *and* history? A new timeline in both directions?' The artist sounded pleased.

Iris seemed calm and yet flabbergasted. Excitedly, she stepped closer to Bandeen to whisper conspiratorially. 'Yes… *Is it true*? Or was what I experienced just a fiction? *A dream*?'

'You might be asking if they're both real? And both true? You may ask yourself… Have you become a part of a *triumphant-space-time-event-as-art*?'

Iris moved in even closer and asked in hushed tones: 'Is that what it was, chuck?'

The artist softened, lowered his remaining limbs. 'That's not for me to decide, you as the viewer—'

Iris resumed pummeling the alien with her handbag. He completely retreated within his exoskeleton, but Iris continued until she was exhausted. She sat, breathing heavily. She could hear him in his shell, checking his hypermail, waiting her out.

She considered poking her parasol up in there to get a reaction but decided her dignity had suffered enough. She stormed out of the gallery and was halfway back to the bus before she realized she had the rolled-up print in her hands. The hairband was around it. It was the Rothko.

Iris took a pneumatic tube back to the vicinity of the bus. The party out of bounds was still going on.

'OUT! OUT! Party's over! Everyone out! Kate, Fred, you… with the mole—Shove off!' A sparkling disco ball with three cobras sprouting out of it hovered near. Iris shouted this being's real, unpronounceable name, surprising him for the first time in eons. 'You're drunk, get out. EVERYONE OFF MY BUS.'

The strange group of misfits from a dozen different time zones found themselves turned out on the street. Liza begged Iris to explain what was happening.

'I'm sorry, but things have to change. And they have to change *now*, this minute, or they'll never change.'

Cindy and Ricky pushed their way to the front. Cindy put the cap back on her bottle of 7UP. 'Iris, you're the First Lady of Infinity. What's the hurry?'

From Liza's shoulder, a sentient tomato called Tomato piped up, 'Let's sit, darling. Talk to us! We can help.'

'No… you *can't*! Don't you *get* it? You're all… *amazing and wonderful*! I lose myself in you and our adventures. I need… I need to break away for a while. I need to change.'

A bald man stepped between Cindy and Ricky and held out a deck of cards. 'Perhaps an oblique strategy…'

'OH CRAM IT ENO!' And with that, Iris Wildthyme slammed the bus doors and tore off into time and space.

The stranded group stood around on the futuristic street looking at each other for ten or fifteen seconds before the bickering began.

Iris opened her eye.

A new start, that's what she'd told herself. The white room was just as it had been when she closed her eyes. White looked different now, with ultraviolet and infrared added to the mix. Momentarily, she steadied herself, getting used to her new normal. 'Not sure I've ever done it standing up before...' She turned around to see if anyone heard her joke. There was no one there, but she wasn't sad. She moved on new limbs towards the black rectangular opening and back into the normal, spatially-limited partition of the bus.

She hesitated for just a moment, knowing she wouldn't be able to undo the next thing she was about to do anytime soon, the second event of this variety in as many minutes, then flipped the switch on the device she'd prepared.

Sparks flew, bulbs exploded and components locked. A single spring fell to the floor and rolled to the lowest point on the uneven floor. The gadget that wouldn't let her bus materialize anywhere near anywhere she'd ever been before had done its work.

A single tear pooled at the base of her new eye. The entire history of the Laniakea Supercluster—locked out of the controls. Earth, Mars, Zwen, Studio 54, The Crystal Palace, Buckhorn; South Dakota, Mars, the Solar System, The Milky Way, (including the most common entrances to the Clockworks)—all out of her reach, even if she did have new, long and exotic limbs.

She blinked the moisture out of her heavily-lashed eye as she looked out the windows of her bus. The window expanded as the bus slowly became not-a-bus. Space was disturbingly purple here. Every so often, it rippled like the surface of a lake, which she was pretty sure it wasn't supposed to do. She made note of something glowing curiously green in the distance, and punched instructions into the controls, setting the bus in motion. She squinted. 'Hmm. Farsighted now. I'll just trust I did that right.'

A red light was flashing but she couldn't read the display. She'd have to find some glasses in the wardrobe. She lurched upright. 'Hang on a tick!' She realized she'd need a whole new wardrobe! Nothing she had would be appropriate.

Iris laughed. 'I will need to find somewhere new to shop.' She laughed, but she was frightened, and that was okay.

It wasn't so scary. She knew she could go back… eventually… to the places and people she'd always loved and *maybe* even to being who she had been. She wasn't sure she'd want to after this. She smiled, excited about the promise of the unknown.

She wasn't sure she'd ever be who she once was.